The Shinto Treasure

A Constance Talant Mystery

By Marcelline Acosta Jenny

Front cover art: Shutterstock/GccDesigns Photography
Back cover art: Shutterstock/ririe

Published by Piscataqua Press
An imprint of RiverRun Bookstore, Inc.
142 Fleet Street | Portsmouth, NH | 03801
www.riverrunbookstore.com
www.piscataquapress.com

ISBN: 978-1-944393-23-6
Printed in the United States of America

THE SHINTO TREASURE

A Constance Talant Mystery

By Marcelline Acosta Jenny

Many, many thanks to Bonnie Kerrick.
Without her urging, editing, and persistence, this book would never
have made it to print.

Prologue

Mayor William E. Marvin scowled and snapped at his assistant, "Whose idea was it?"

"Sir, Mr. Roosevelt's Secretary of State..."

"That bastard Peirce! He's always hated me. Jealousy. That's all it is. Jealous since we were kids. That's what. Yes.... Of course it was Peirce's idea. No doubt about that. Well, if he thinks Portsmouth is going to roll out the red carpet for him, he's got another think coming." Marvin sat back in his creaky desk chair. His pale baby face was pursed in thought for several seconds. Finally, he opened his eyes and said, "Send a wire to Mr. Roosevelt. Tell him that Portsmouth is delighted to host the treaty negotiations for him, but the city is grossly over-budget as it is. It's the destitute immigrants that's draining us. That's what it is. Everyone in the whole world wants to live in New Hampshire. He makes us take 'em all in. If anything happens it'll be all his fault! Tell him that.... Jesu! He brings out the devil in me!"

The mayor jumped to his feet and paced his large office as he continued his complaint. "Roosevelt's a big show off! He wants Russia and Japan to admire the power and wealth of the United States. So, of course he chose New Hampshire to host the treaty. Send the President a wire. Tell him that we are anxious to roll out our finest red carpet for his foreigners, but we just can't afford it. And say that we do not wish to embarrass him by treating the guests shabbily, but unless we get some assistance from the Federal government... Oh, you know what to write. Just do it."

"Yes, Sir."

"Hold on. The President came here to attend a cousin's wedding reception last year," the mayor continued. "He and his party took over entire wings of the Wentworth and Rockingham Hotels. He told us how impressed he is with our fair city, the hotels... oh, and lovely New Castle. He found New Castle enchanting. Who wouldn't?... It's too bad we can't welcome Mr. Roosevelt again. Why can't he come? What excuse did he give?

"Because of some prior commitment? Is that what his office said?" The mayor continued. "And he's sending Peirce? That bastard will try to lord it over us.... Don't put that in the wire. I don't want my animosity against Peirce to be made public. That jackass has become popular with Mr. Roosevelt. I certainly don't know why. Do you?" His assistant shook his head.

"Let's get this over with. Close the wire with an expression of our delight to act as host to the treaty and tell the President that we will, of course, show the Japanese and Russian delegates the best hospitality that it is possible for us to offer, given our budget restrictions. And, close with this: if the Federal government could help finance, etcetera, etcetera, etcetera.... Oh, request Federal Marshals, too," Marvin ended.

"Our Governor McLane will surely send extra state police," said Marvin's assistant.

"Not that old cheap-skate. Jocko will only send enough men to protect himself. That's the way he is! Tell the President that as he well knows, there's bound to be crazies coming to the treaty ceremony. He must know that. Those assassins will come just to see their names spread in the newspapers of the world!

"Our little city's police force is overwhelmed as it is. Ask Roosevelt to send at least a half dozen Federal Marshals, well-armed. I refuse to have any assassinations in Portsmouth! Even if the target is the bastard Peirce. Don't put that in the wire either. Send it off right away. Let's get on to more important matters."

The assistant closed his notebook, turned, and walked slowly out of the mayor's office. "The boss needs a few days vacation," was his thought as he placed his notebook in his pocket.

PART I

Edo, Japan

February 1905

Chapter 1

Twenty-Seven smiled as he studied his image in the full-length mirror. "Am I not as regal in appearance as an Emperor should aspire to be?" he asked Eleven, who had just finished brushing the leader's hair until it appeared to be a wide, shining black ribbon extending down the leader's back to just below his shoulders.

"Most honorable sir, you are more regal in appearance than any Emperor who ever lived. Our present Emperor is as a callow boy compared to your manliness and majesty. And, you are the most intelligent of all men, too. We are fortunate to have your honorable self as our leader," Eleven answered, with the most ingratiating smile she could muster to hide her nervousness and fear.

"A top knot. Put it in a top knot, not hanging down my back like some common dance girl," growled Twenty-Seven as he swiped at her hands. "Give me that," he pointed at a large hand mirror on the table. As soon as she handed it to him, he held the mirror in front of his face, pushed aside his hair, and examined his slightly blood-shot eyes. Then he shook his head violently so that strands of his coarse black hair flew around his head in every direction. Twenty-Seven once again pushed aside the strands hanging over his eyes, gazed hard into the mirror, and suppressed his alarm by growling. "Look at them! Those blasted gray hairs popped out overnight. Pull them out. All of them," he ordered, "then finish. Hurry up !" He closed his eyes, then pressed his fingers against the puffy bags under his eyes. Finally he dipped the tips of his fingers into a moisturizing cream and then gently dotted the cream onto the crow's feet radiating toward his temples.

Eleven's fingers travelled quickly over her leader's head and stopped now and then to pull out a grey hair. When she'd pulled out all of them, she gently gathered the leader's thick hank of black hair and twisted it slowly at the crown of his head. Some moments later Twenty-Seven's black hair was knotted on top of his head to his satisfaction. He pushed the mirror into Eleven's hand, and said, "Give me the grey hairs. All of them. Why'd you throw them on the floor for my enemies to find? Give them to me," he repeated. "And put my mirror away in the drawer." Eleven quickly gathered up the grey hairs and placed them in her leader's hand. Twenty-Seven twisted the grey hairs into one strand and added it to the collection he kept in the small locked drawer of his side table. "Who have you told about my grey hairs?"

Eleven grabbed her stomach that had suddenly cramped up with his last words. "No one, Your Greatness," she answered. "You know that you are my one master. I tell no one of what I do here. They all think that I come to you so that you may enjoy my womanhood. I let them think what they wish. It makes them jealous."

Twenty-Seven smiled, then scowled again and rubbed his arms. "You've let it get cold in here. Stoke up the fire. Throw more ladles of water on it. I want steam. Much steam. Do it. Then go attend to the assassination room. I will be using it soon. I want it warm. Make sure the stove in there is going full blast.

"Wait," he raised a hand. "Find Twenty-Six. Tell him I want to see him. Now…. Wait. Give me the Beretta. Make sure it's loaded." Eleven removed the weapon from the gun case next to the leader's chair. She checked that the magazine was full, and handed it to Twenty Seven. He slipped it into the pocket of his robe. "Okay," he said, "Tell Twenty-Six to come now. Close the door tight. Tight. Why must I always repeat myself?"

Eleven hid the urge to blurt out that the leader's repeated orders were just his annoying habit that was never necessary. All the Numbers knew exactly how Twenty-Seven wanted things done.

Still shivering from the chill of the morning air, Twenty-Seven dragged his stool closer to the stove and pulled on a fine white woolen jacket over his kimono. He was tying the jacket closed when Twenty-Six entered the hot, humid room. "What took you so long?" Twenty-Seven growled. "And close the door tight behind you. Tight. Why must I constantly remind you?" Eleven slipped quickly out of the hot room before Twenty-Six slammed the door.

Twenty-Six turned and stood near the closed door and as far away from the hot stove as he could position himself. "Ultimate Leader, I have good news," he said, and then continued without permission. "Akira Yoshi has just been named first assistant to the Prime Minister." Twenty-Six wiped at the sweat that was already running down his face.

"It's disgusting to have to watch you sweat. Your blood is too hot, Twenty-Six. Sit in the food freezer when I'm done with you," Twenty-Seven said, "And don't waste my time with your so-called 'good news.' The only good news will be when I have the Treasures in my hands... all three of them." Twenty-Seven used to rub his forehead. "Who is this Akira Yoshi?" he asked.

Twenty-Six turned his head to hide his scorn from the aging leader, a scorn mixed with pleasure that had been mounting in him for the past several months. He had preparations to make and a speech to write. He'd decided he'd honor his father by using the old man's sword in his Ascension Ceremony, the samurai sword that his father always kept polished and sharp.

For several weeks Twenty-Six had been practicing his Ascension Oration. *I will say that the Ultimate Leader had become dangerous to our ETA. I did my duty and eradicated him. The murder... No.... The eradication gave me no pleasure. To then move up a level to become the new Ultimate Leader... Why would anyone in his right mind wish that? It is a heavy and dangerous responsibility that brings no joy. Yet, it must be done. And it must be done by me. Tradition is all.*

He knew the others would celebrate the death. The present Twenty-Seven had not been a popular Ultimate Leader since his own Ascension more than four years earlier.

Twenty-Six had carried out his duties to the leader's disgruntled satisfaction. Now he had to prepare himself for his most important and dangerous duty. He was most worried about his own fear.

In the almost two-hundred-year history of the ETA Cabal, the primary duty of Twenty-Six was to serve as the Ultimate Leader's right-hand-man; and, when the time came, to assassinate the Ultimate Leader to prepare for his own Ascension. According to the Cabal's constitution, a strong leadership was more important than any one man's life.

Only twice were the ultimate Ascensions troublesome. In 1967, the Twenty-Six was himself killed by the Ultimate Leader whom he had erroneously judged as being too old and incompetent to defend himself. In 1991, another Twenty-Six informed his girlfriend of his plans for the assassination, in spite of the fact that it was forbidden to share Ascension plans with any other members of the Cabal. The next evening she was his executioner by common consent of the ETA membership. She used a stiletto to kill him—only men were allowed to use a traditional Samurai Sword.

The present Twenty-Six was proud to say he had a philosophic frame of mind. After having spent hours thinking about the group's 'Ascension by Assassination' tradition and history, he had come to the conclusion that the tradition needed to be restructured along the lines of his own ideas. He was a gifted speaker, and was confident he could persuade the membership to his way of thinking.

He'd rehearsed his speech while he paraded back and forth in front of a mirrored wall: *An aura of suspicion and distrust has, to no one's surprise, become traditional among the Twenty-Seven leaders of our glorious organization, particularly those of us who have risen to Twenty-Six and Twenty-Seven. Each of the two top men—and we are always men—spend too much time and energy worrying when the other will attack him. For this reason alone, the lower numbers are in no hurry to be advanced.*

Although the traditions sharpen the senses and hone the martial abilities of the two top men to a super human degree, the beloved traditions are not good for the morale of the lower numbered members or, in the long run, for the ETA itself. We need to rethink this tradition. After all, we are a modern, vibrant organization. It is vital to keep up with the times.

But note well: worthy traditions are never too old. On the other hand, we must be careful not to get mired down in traditions that no longer work. I've been giving this matter much thought. Consider my suggestion: if the ascending Twenty-Six balks at assassination, we might consider life imprisonment for an aging Ultimate Leader.

Another related issue is this: Should we bring more women into the Cabal? It's true that women do not possess a logician's abilities. I cannot name one woman, alive or dead, who could be called the equal of Euclid, Thales, or Archimedes. Not one.... Also, we all know that women do not follow orders as well as men, and therefore, they quite correctly ascend much more slowly, if they're allowed to ascend at all.... Would a female Twenty-Six be able to do her duty and assassinate the Ultimate Leader? I think not. Should a woman ever be the Ultimate Leader? No. Definitely not. Women do not possess Samurai Swords, and must never be allowed to use their father's.

So far, we have been successful in preventing women from rising above Thirteen. It is best that way. No. Do not think of me as a misogynist. I only know what history and logic has taught us about the difference between the sexes. Yes, we must rely on logic. That is what this organization is all about. Twenty-Six ended his ruminations with a smile. *Yes, it is a very good speech,* he assured himself.

In the present generation of leaders, the Ultimate Leadership situation had not yet become of immediate concern. Twenty-Seven was still arrogantly comfortable that all his faculties were as sharp as when he was in his early twenties. He was confident that the day when he would have to watch his back was still far in the future. *After all,* he reasoned, *I am not yet forty-seven years old. Am I not at the height of my manhood and powers?* Nonetheless, since he found his first grey hairs, he kept himself always alert and well armed. And he never put himself in a position in which Twenty-Six could stand behind him. Getting a sound night's sleep was a traditional problem of the Cabal's leadership.

For his part, the present Twenty-Six was extra watchful and secretly pleased at what he considered the leader's growing self-delusion about his ability to continue his role. The day when leadership had to change was fast approaching. Twenty-Seven seemed determined to ignore it. Twenty-Six was anxious for the arrival of his Day of Ascension.

This day, Twenty-Six suppressed a smile of satisfaction at the thought of soon stepping into the older man's shoes. He said to the Ultimate Leader, "Akira is not a memorable man. That's why he was chosen. At the leader's puzzled glance, Twenty-Six said, "Akira is Nineteen." He didn't add: "Have you already forgotten who our high numbers are?"

The Ultimate Leader knew what the second in command really wanted to say aloud. Twenty-Seven's first impulse was to strike out at

Twenty-Six, but he thought that a more measured reaction would accomplish the same end and be less troublesome for him. Besides, he didn't welcome Twenty-Five's ascension. If anything, Twenty-Five was more ambitious and sly than Twenty-Six. Well, he would soon teach them both a lesson about the Ultimate Ascension. Twenty-Seven said, "Oh, Nineteen. Yes, not a memorable man. I don't care a fig about him. Tell me about the 'good news.'"

"Ultimate Leader, we are doing everything possible to bring the *Yata no Kagami*, that is to say, the Sacred Mirror, to you. The *Yata no Kagami* is so well-guarded, only the Emperor himself and the High Priestess have ever been close enough to see it. Only they have ever had the privilege to touch it. Day and night the shrine is surrounded by Imperial Guards. Moreover, the High Protector himself, the *Daiguji,* spends day and night in front of the niche that houses the treasure. No one would dare to try to get at him. He sits directly behind the *Saio.* When the *Daiguji* must leave his post to relieve his kidneys, bathe, or take a short nap, the *High Priestess* guards it alone. Yes, the *Saio* is small and appears to be fragile, but she is as skilled a warrior as the *Daiguji*. She has even beaten the *Daiguji* in some of their war games. I, myself, have witnessed her prowess. In comparison to him, what she lacks in size and strength, she makes up in slyness, dexterity, and intelligence. The Japanese public does not know about her physical prowess. They only fear the large size and strength of the *Daiguji*.

'The *Saio* and the *Daiguji* do not allow anyone the privilege to get close enough to see into the treasure niche. One cannot even get a glance at the Sacred Mirror. It is very difficult to get our hands on it, Most Honored One."

"Why are you telling me what I know?" Twenty-Seven asked with a growl of irritation in his soft voice. "And what about the other two treasures? I must have all three of the *Sanshu no Jingi*, not just the *Yata no Kagami*."

13

"Honorable One, you will soon have all three. We have made our plans carefully. The mirror will be taken first, and delivered to you tomorrow. The sword and jewel will be yours soon after."

"I wanted the *Kusanagi no Tsurugi* first. "

"Twenty-Seven, at the moment it is almost impossible to get within hundreds of yards of the sacred sword. The Emperor and his family are presently residing at their castle in Nagoya. Imperial Guards are everywhere in the city, especially near the home of the sword, the Atsuta Jingu. The Emperor spends many hours in attendance at the shrine. It is not possible for outsiders to even approach the outskirts of the city before Imperial Guards surround them with their questions and demands. The weakest defense of the three treasure sites is now Ise. Of course, this is also because people fear the Sacred Mirror's magical power. They stay far back from the Ise Jingu shrine. Still, the Ise Jingu is well-guarded. And there is always the occasional crazy person who will try anything. Well, we have a way with Akira's assistance... Honorable Leader, *you* will soon possess the Sacred Mirror."

"I ordered that all three treasures be taken at the same time. If only one were taken, the government would increase the guards at the other two shrines. All three should be taken at the same time. Have I not said so repeatedly?"

"With you I heartily agree. However, it is sad to say, Honorable Leader, that we do not have enough men with the essential expertise to carry out your program all at one time. You said..."

"I know what I said. Make sure the *Yata no Kagami* is in my hands the minute it arrives here. And come up with a feasible plan to take the other two treasures. My plan only works if I take all three treasures away from the Japanese people, not just one. You'd better not fail me. It would be easy enough for me to demote you." *Or better yet, kill you.* Twenty-Seven was thinking.

14

Chapter 2

In Japan's outer ministerial offices, Ambassador Komura Jutaro read quickly through the list of demands from the Russians that Prime Minister Katsura Taro had written down for the Ambassador. Komura glanced up at Prime Minister Katsura's assistant, Akira Yoshi, and said, "In the war we won all the Russians' lands in China and destroyed the heart of the Czar's naval fleet in Asia. Believe me, the Russians will not..."

"Yes, Yes, Katsura-san knows the Russians will balk at the extent of our demands," said Assistant Akira with a haughty air that resembled that of his boss, Prime Minister Katsura. "You should know," he continued in the same lofty tones and stealing a glance at the Prime Minister. As usual, Kamura craved his boss's approval, "Russia is a huge country of great untapped wealth. The Czar is stubborn. He is quite regal in appearance, but unfortunately for his country, his mind is very slow. He is not a great statesman. The Prime Minister happens to know that the Russian Czar is being pressured to make friends with the United States. The Czar will listen to what the American leader tells him to do. Even so, there is no guarantee that he will, in the end, follow the President's advice. The Czar is not an intellectual. On the other hand, he is not so stupid and arrogant that he does not know he should keep the Americans' approval.   The Russian ambassadors, particularly the honorable Sergei Witte, are seasoned diplomats and very shrewd. I should be embarrassed that I admire him, but Witte is an accomplished diplomat. And the Americans are attracted to his effusive nature. I was surprised that the Czar was wise enough to send Witte to the negotiations. It may be difficult for us to out-talk him. This is exactly why we must work hard to ensure the President Roosevelt's full support. Our Prime Minister's orders are very clear. It is your responsibility to persuade the American President that our indemnity demands are not unreasonable and that they warrant his support.

"The President is our friend. We must feed his suspicions of the Russians. He is wary of their expansionist moves in Alaska. He also understands our demands that the Russians must pay dearly for the insolence of invading our lands in China. Russia must be taught a lesson. The entire world has learned that the small island nation of Japan is the burgeoning great power in what they insultingly refer to as 'the East'. As if the rest of the world is measured from Europe's position on the globe. Hah!

"Russia should turn its attention to Western Europe and stay out of Asia's waters. We have taught the Russian bear a military lesson; let us now teach him a political lesson.

"Have you any questions? If not, you should go now. Katsura-san has ordered you to find a gift worthy to present to the American president, has he not?"

Komura mumbled an answer, shoved the papers into his briefcase, and turned to leave. "Wait, please, Honorable Ambassador," Assistant Akira whispered as Komura approached the door. "I have an idea for you. Will you please allow me to speak to you?" Komura stopped walking and Akira drew nearer to the Ambassador and lowered his voice to a whisper. "Honorable Ambassador Komura, what would be more fitting than a gift that represents the very soul of Japan?" The two men stepped into the hallway and closed the door behind them.

"What is it?" asked Komura. "Never mind. Akira, I have no more time for you. I refuse to be late for another meeting. It would be especially unwise to keep the Ambassador from Germany waiting for me. Germany must believe we are their good friends. Where is Guard Yoshiro Kenishi? Does he not realize I am the Emperor's important ambassador? I must be guarded and attended to at all times. Where is he? Yoshiro!" he called. A young man hurried through the door and shuffled quickly over to bow before Komura. "There you are. Where were you? Every time I raise my eyes, I want to see you looking at me. You know what will happen to you and your career aspirations if something unpleasant happens to me. Oh, never mind. See what else this man Akira has to say. I have no time for his chatter," said Komura and he hurried out the door.

Guard Yoshiro Kenishi stared with some annoyance and disdain at Akira. "Well?" he said.

"Yoshiro-san," said Akira, "the Minister and Ambassador need to find an appropriate gift for the President of the United States. I have an idea for a gift that only you can acquire for him."

Chapter 3

"Are you completely mad, Akira?" cried Yoshiro. "Only the Emperor and the guardians have ever had the privilege to touch the treasures. Nobody else is even allowed to cast their eyes on them. How do you propose that I get close enough to the *Yata no Kagami* to describe it to a bronze craftsman? No. The Emperor wouldn't stand for it. We would we arrested, even executed, if we attempted to have it copied. And its power is frightening! No one but the *Saio* has ever dared to touch it for fear of its magic.

"No," the guard shook his head, and continued, "Akira, your idea is a bad one. Besides, the American President would not appreciate such a gift. He expects something of great value, not just a copy of our precious treasure. He would not understand what the Mirror means to us."

"You do not understand what I am suggesting," said Akira. "You do not have to actually see it. You could have a mirror made to whatever specifications you desire. I will help you. Our combined powers would come up with a most magnificent bronze mirror. Who would know but us? The Emperor and the *Saio* will never see the design we come up with, and no one else has any idea of what it looks like, not even the *Daiguji*," Akira answered.

"It is said the magic of the Mirror can..."

"Oh, don't be another superstitious moron. Much has been spent on your education. Use it. Listen and think. The Mirror is simply a shiny piece of bronze. Nothing more. It doesn't have any magic. Only the superstitious think of it as magical. And we don't have to make an exact replica. Who would know?

"No, the gift doesn't have to look exactly like the real Mirror. You may use your imagination. Dream up a beautiful design. No one but us will know it is not the real thing. And Sir, if the Prime Minister carefully describes the great awe and reverence that we Japanese feel for our treasured Mirror, the American President cannot help but be honored to receive such a gift. The President is a cultured man. I'm sure he knows that the great and wealthy United States doesn't need to add yet another meaningless bauble to its collection of gifts from friendly nations. He will appreciate the thought that went into our gift to him."

"The Emperor and the *Saio* are not stupid," said Yoshiro, after a few moments of thought. "When they learn that we have tried to reproduce the Sacred Mirror," he continued, "they will be furious. We will be severely punished. And you are proposing that Japan give the United States President a piece of cheap bronze with the claim that it is a copy of one of our most valuable possessions. Ridiculous!"

"Ah, you are right," Akira said, stroking his well-razored chin, "that is a bad idea. But perhaps you have thought of something better?" Akira asked, hiding his sly smile behind his sleeve.

What Yoshiro was not saying was his worse fear. The Mirror's magical power could destroy them if they should try to use the mirror for their own selfish ends.

Chapter 4

Twenty-Seven wrapped his kimono carefully around his slim body to avoid causing wrinkles in the heavy silk as he slid onto the western-style hard wooden chair. "Bring him in," he said in a voice that was hardly more than a whisper. The old man standing by the door of the small room nodded his head slowly and backed out of the door. In a few seconds the old man returned followed by Akira Yoshi. In his wrinkled western suit, shirt, and necktie, the overweight, middle-aged man was immediately heavily perspiring in the extreme heat and humidity of Twenty-Seven's rooms. Akira's eyes were cast down, as if he were frightened to even look at Twenty-Seven. "Sit over there. Under the spotlight," Twenty-Seven said with a movement of his hand to indicate a brightly-lit wooden chair across the room from him. After a few moments of silence, Twenty-Seven said, "You requested this meeting. Speak now."

Akira wiped the sweat from his face, cleared his throat, and said, "Honorable Sir, I have news of the peace delegation preparations that will interest you."

Twenty-Seven continued to stare at Akira who had fallen into nervous jittering on the hard wooden chair. Akira's eyes were raised as if he were looking for words on the ceiling to begin his explanation. Twenty-Seven finally snapped, "Well, go ahead, Nineteen. Don't waste my time. Speak."

"Honorable Sir, I believe I know how you can realize your aspirations," Akira said in a voice that trembled with both excitement and fear. "But Sir, I have many expenses. If you could assist me with a half-million yen, it would help me meet my obligations."

Twenty-Seven narrowed his eyes as he stared at Akira. "So you would betray your Emperor for money," he hissed. "You fool. Why should I not think you would betray me for more money?" He nodded at his two heavily armed guards at the door, and the men strode quickly toward Akira whose terror muted the scream in his throat.

"First, make him tell you what he knows," said Twenty-Seven softly.

Chapter 5

For the past several months, Ambassador Komura Jutaro, had been lecturing his family about what was foremost in his mind: the new world in which he believed Japan must participate in a leadership role. This day, Komura held his only grandson, Isamu, on his lap as he stroked the boy's head and pontificated on the same subject. "Our little child is not yet five years old, but he understands what I am saying," Komura insisted. "Our little Isamu will grow up to be a leader in the Japan that will be a world power," he said to his daughter and son-in-law, Yoshiro Kenishi. "Our traditions are dear to us, but Japan must move forward in time. You are young and inexperienced," he nodded at the parents of the child in his lap. "You have not seen the large world as I have. If we are to survive, we must not just keep up, but surpass all the others in the world as we have in Asia. It is the only way for us to survive the monster countries of this world that will consume us at their first opportunity.

"Russia threatened us, and we have taught that giant a hard lesson, haven't we?" He tickled Isamu's chin, and the toddler giggled. "You see," Komura smiled, "even a young child knows the truth. Except for the Germans, who are our friends, we need not consider the small countries of Europe. They are so busy squabbling with each other, they are no danger to us.

"China dare not threaten us, but the day will come when that peasant country will test its growing strength. Its size alone is daunting. Our sons and grandsons must be prepared to take on China.

"And last, there is the United States. It is a giant that still only looks inward. But it also must have hidden empirical ambitions. That giant needs to be carefully watched. We must be strong and ready to take them all on."

"What are you saying?" Yoshiro Kenishi asked. "Honorable Sir, these are dangerous words. These are the words of the criminal ETA Cabal, are they not?" he whispered.

Komura pushed Isamu into his daughter's arms. He jumped to his feet. "How dare you! Are you labeling me a criminal? Are you questioning my loyalty to the Emperor?" Komura's eyes blazed. "Get out!" he ordered his daughter. "And take the children with you." The tearful woman hugged the baby Isamu, and gathered her two older toddlers to her. She hustled them out the door with her. Komura turned back to Yoshiro. "Well, answer me, you fool. Are you questioning my loyalty to our divine Emperor and to Japan?"

"No, no, Honorable Father-in-Law. Never, never would I doubt your loyalty. I am just so confused. Everything is changing so rapidly. Some say this and some say that. They all say something different. And they all claim to love Japan. Some say we must flaunt our new powerful position. Some say our traditions identify us and define who we are. Therefore, we must guard our traditions with our lives. Others, like the criminal Cabal, say we must throw aside our past and become like westerners if we are to achieve our destiny. Please Sir, I feel like a child who needs your instruction. Please teach me. Please tell me what to think."

But Yoshiro Kenishi was so fired up and afraid of his father-in-law, he couldn't wait for Komura to answer. His words kept pouring out. "The detestable ETA says that now that we have conquered the great

Russian empire with our new store of western armaments and the use of western military strategies, we have learned a great lesson. But I, myself, do not listen to the leaders of that detestable cult. They hide behind these words to modernize our great country when their only interest is to grab control of our government for themselves. They hate and fear our most illustrious Emperor. They are despicable and their organization must be eliminated.

"The Germans are our friends. They have no designs on us. They respect us. We did well to send our most capable military men to train in Germany. We have learned the ways of the European powers and have turned that knowledge against the Russians. Our most illustrious Emperor agreed that we must learn from the Germans. He is wiser than a room full of his advisors."

Yoshiro Kenishi's heart was pounding and sweat was forming on his face, but his mind couldn't stop racing. He couldn't stop talking. "Our precious traditions cannot keep us alive in this new world. Our traditions should be preserved to honor our ancestors, but we must face facts. Our traditions will not protect us in today's evil world. Not even the magic of the Mirror can help us." He didn't stop for Komura's comments, but raced on.

"Our German teachers say that in their calendar it is a new century, the Twentieth Century, that demands new ways of thinking. They are right when they say we must find modern ways to endure in the world in which this Twentieth Century has begun. And they say we must become as expert in the new ways of warfare as we are with our swords.

"They are right. We can no longer rely on our Samurai Swords to defend us. They are powerless against western cannons. We need cannons. We need rifles and firearms and bullets. That's what the German teachers say. They are right. Look what we were able to accomplish against the Russians.

"We must not be left behind. We must not be swallowed up by the larger and more powerfully armed countries of this world." Yoshiro's words kept tumbling out until Komura put up his hands to silence him.

Komura was alarmed by his son-in-law's words. He had been struggling with the same thoughts for months, but he had been in government long enough not to put traitorous thoughts into spoken words. "You fool!" He said silently in his mind to Yoshiro. To himself, he said, *Is it possible to maintain and strengthen our traditions and at the same time adopt western methods of warfare?* He nodded his head imperceptibly. *Yes. We must make it possible. We must do both.... But is it possible?... It must be possible. It is the self-confident path to staying alive. Some, like the ETA, want world power. We, who truly love our country, want the continued respect of the rest of the world. The first step is to protect ourselves and our power. There is no immediate reason to go to war for expansion purposes. We have controlled our growth. But the day will come when we will need to go to war to feed our people. In the past, our Samurai were willing to die for the Emperor. Now we must train them to be willing to die for Japan.*

Komura was equally troubled by more immediate matters that threatened him and his family. *Is my son-in-law a secret member of the ETA Cabal? He calls it 'despicable,' and yet his words echo theirs. The Cabal's pamphlets are pasted all over the walls of the major cities of our country. It hides behind its claim to be a society of great mathematical logicians that can lead Japan into world-wide greatness without war. Who were these great logicians? Except for academicians, has anyone ever heard of them? No!*

Yet, their message is seductive to the young men of Japan, and has created doubts in the young men's minds about the Emperor and Japan's traditions. A great evil. I have pledged that my government will destroy the ETA Cabal, before it destroys Japan. Yes, some say, the message of the Cabal is seductive, but the wisest men in Japan know that

Asia has always possessed great mathematical logicians of its own. Such expertise was not just a western phenomenon. Yes, we Japanese know true greatness and wisdom. The arrogance of western modernization is false, and if we adopt western ways, it will destroy Japan. We will proceed in our own way. But what of my daughter and Yoshiro Kenishi? Do I have a member of the dangerous ETA in my own family? Ambassador Komura knew the answers to his questions. He fought the great fear that felt like a heavy stone in his chest.

Chapter 6

Prime Minister Katsura Taro hated the ravings of the ETA Cabal and had labeled the group seditious, so that it had been forced underground months earlier. He warned his staff and others in the government to be watchful. "The traitors are everywhere," he told them. When he appointed Komura Jutaro to the treaty delegation, he ordered him to investigate each member of his staff very carefully. "Only men who prize our traditions above all else may go to the United States of America with you. None of those so-called modernists may go," he'd said. Dossiers of the staff members were to be sent to the Prime Minister himself so that his own assistants, too, could investigate every member of the treaty party who would go to the United States. The Imperial Guard, Yoshiro Kenishi, was ordered to conduct a final check.

Ambassador Komura had ambitions of his own. He kept himself alert to everything his followers did and said in public, and investigated as much of their private lives as possible. He was determined not to sabotage his future by harboring a Cabal member in his own party. True, Prime Minister Katsura had allowed him to take the Guard Yoshiro to America because he was Komura's son-in-law. Nonetheless, Komura would not have named Yoshiro if he had even the slightest suspicion that the young man had been seduced by the ideas of the ETA. Komura would have found a plausible reason to choose another malleable young man, even at the risk of enduring the displeasure of his daughter and the Prime Minister, himself.

Now Komura was worried. He said to himself, *I must watch Yoshiro Kenishi very carefully. What a nuisance. I should be focusing on my duties to force our demands on the Russian bear, not babysitting Yoshiro. I cannot replace him in the delegation. Not at this late date. The Prime Minister would be offended and also suspicious. No, it is better if Kenishi is with me so that I may keep an eye on him. What did I do to deserve this? I urged Nikko not to marry him. I should have forbidden it. That would be our traditional way, not the stupid modern way of allowing our children to have a say in such an important family matter. It is my own fault. I speak too much of modernization. Kenishi's hot-headed, but he's also too much of a thinker. These qualities should not be in the same man. I fear for my new grandson, I shall keep little Isamu under my wing, and away from his father as much as possible. What a way for a family to have to live!*

Chapter 7
Yoshiro Kenishi

Yoshiro Kenishi had been raised by a father who had instilled his own ambitions in his son. The senior Yoshiro had made plans ever since his boy was born, even negotiating the young Kenishi's marriage to Katsura's daughter. "It wouldn't hurt to have the Prime Minister in the family," he'd said to Kenishi. "And no, she is not a great beauty, but no one would call her ugly. They'd better not!"

By the age of twenty-six, Kenishi had worked himself up to the position of head of the Imperial Guards of Ise Jingu, the most sacred shrine in Japan, and home of the *Yata no Kagami*. He'd been allowed to see the Sacred Mirror, but not allowed to touch it.

Kenishi believed he had risen high without the sponsorship of his famous father or father-in-law. This is what he haughtily claimed to all those who congratulated him and mentioned the two older men in the same breath. *Yes, everyone says that I could not have risen so high without my father dropping a word in the right places. I have worked hard to be the leader of the Imperial Guards of Ise. I have earned it. Yes, my new position is an important one, but not as great as the larger ambitions my family has wished for me since I was a young child. I still have much further to climb.*

The elder Yoshiro had sent Kenishi to study in Germany and then to England for further education. Kenishi had returned anxious for the future of the Japan he knew and loved. He had experienced first-hand the might and power of western armaments. *Japan is still using ancient models of European armaments brought by the Jesuit priests centuries earlier. Those ancient weapons should be in museums*, he said to himself, but dared not say it to others. *They are no match against the new powerful firearms of the other countries. We are the children of the Rising Sun. We must prepare ourselves for our glorious future.*

Kenishi returned home afraid that Japan's beloved traditions would destroy his country. Yet he, himself, loved the traditions. "What else are we, if we are not our traditions? But they will kill us," he'd cried to his father who had the habit of not listening to his children. But these words had raised a red flag in his father's brain. "Be careful," he warned his son. "You cannot express such views outside of this house without fear of being labeled a traitor. It would be the ruin of this family. Leave such thoughts alone. Leave thinking to the scholars. You have only to do your duty. That is what it means to be a good man and a Samurai. Don't think. Our leaders have done your thinking for you. Just do your duty."

Yet, the young Kenishi couldn't drive the dangerous thoughts from his mind. He'd mulled over his leadership ambitions again and again. He felt his duty was to save his country, yet what could one man do? Then one day, when he had opened the *London Times* that he continued to subscribe to at his home in Ise, the answer came to him. *People know only the famous; they admire the famous. I must become famous and gain the confidence of my people. It is my destiny to lead a powerful Japan into the new century.*

Yoshiro Kenishi had learned the importance of journalists and the press when he was in England, but he hadn't thought much about the power of the press in Japan. He thought about it now, when he suddenly understood that celebrity was his short-cut to power. Yet, how was he to gain fame? He searched his brain to find a way to become a national hero. He needed to be celebrated in the new and powerful Japanese media that was becoming more and more ravenous, like that of the west. He'd start by buying an important newspaper. He would see to it that his name came up often on the front pages.

Chapter 8

Yoshiro Kenishi was not as afraid of the ETA Cabal as his father-in-law and other government officials. He had a feeling that haunted him with increasing frequency. He didn't know how or why, but he was certain his future was somehow tied in with the powerful Cabal. Yoshiro was a thoughtful man. *How can I detest it and yet use it to further my ambitions,* he wondered. *By destroying the Cabal and executing all of its leaders,* he said to himself, answering his own question.

Fear and loathing of the ETA was on everyone's lips lately since it had been accused of the assassination attempt on Katsura Taro's life. Yoshiro joined in condemning the Cabal. His condemnation of the Cabal for its attempt to kill the Prime Minister was genuine. He admired Katsura Taro. But Yoshiro's mind was tortured with conflicting feelings. He had seen the world. He secretly agreed with the Cabal that old-fashioned superstitions were killing Japan. Yet, he loved the gods and the Shinto tradition. Some days he was afraid he was going mad with such conflicting feelings. He fought to stay cogent and rationally analytical.

Lately, Yoshiro realized he knew something else about the Cabal that was most important. He well knew that the ETA's sole purpose was to take over the government and to rule Japan. To do that, they had to assassinate the Emperor and destroy the people and the legends supporting him. Yoshiro was having difficulty getting his mind around that. He felt that he wasn't, by nature, a violent man.

The political climate became explosive when Prime Minister Katsura Taro's limousine was attacked by a robed man with a hood covering his head. He'd had a modern weapon that he'd used to shoot at Katsura's limousine as it pulled up to the parliamentary building. Katsura Taro's chauffeur and bodyguard had been killed, but the Prime Minister had received nothing worse than a scratch on his head. The assassin escaped.

The Prime Minister accused the ETA and vowed again to destroy the organization that he had driven completely underground. Still, Imperial Guard Yoshiro Kenishi hungered to know more about a Cabal with such audacity. He cajoled his father-in-law into telling him everything he knew. To allay suspicion that he harbored even the slightest sympathy toward the criminal organization, Kenishi said, "To fight them it is necessary to know the smallest details. Please instruct me," he implored his father-in-law.

His father-in-law's weakness was in fancying himself the 'Great Teacher of the Ignorant Masses', as his own father often teased him. Komura took Kenishi at his word because it gave him another opportunity to flaunt his intimate knowledge of the Cabal. "It calls itself the ETA Cabal because it has named itself after Euclid, Thales, and Archimedes, three of the greatest mathematicians and logicians of all times. Its leaders are numbered from one to twenty-seven, because twenty-seven is derived from the perfect numbers. The most powerful member is Twenty-Seven. Each numbered leader has a cell of members. No one, not even Twenty-Seven himself, knows exactly how many members there are altogether. Some say there are only the twenty-seven with a few hangers-on. Some say many tens. Some say hundreds. Others say thousands. We just do not know, but we will infiltrate the Cabal. I have sworn that we will do it."

Kumaro didn't mention what everyone suspected but didn't say: the ETA had numbered members in the top echelon of the government. Yoshiro Kenishi suspected the infiltration because the Cabal operated as if it were immune to anything the government threw at it. Yoshiro thought that if he could expose any of the twenty-seven leaders who held a high government position, it would be a fast track to celebrity. But it could also make him dangerous enemies.

Everyone also suspected that numbered members of the secret Cabal leadership in Japan were among the most influential men outside of the government. Yoshiro Kenishi wasn't sure he was ready to risk their animosity. He had his ambitions to consider. Then, just last week, his father-in-law had given him an important appointment: a place in the Japanese peace delegation to the United States. Yoshiro Kenishi's name would be known throughout Japan. His prominent future was beginning.

One of the first duties Ambassador Komura gave Yoshiro Kenishi was to choose an appropriate gift for the American President. At first, Yoshiro was silently resentful. *What kind of responsibility is that to give to someone like me? I am not a mere female servant who must run around to the shops to buy gifts for the Americans. What do I know about Americans? I am not a scholar or a historian. How could a fellow like me know what the President of America would want as a gift? Komura-San said to find something that was a symbol of Japan. 'It must be something that will delight Mr. Roosevelt. Something that he will proudly raise above his head and shout, "This is from my good friends of the Land of the Rising Sun." See to it, Kenishi. Use your imagination. Those were Komura-San's instructions. But how could an Imperial Guard like me...*

Then, he remembered the idea of Akira, the Prime Minister's assistant. *Would I dare? Could I get away with it? I fear the gods'*

*displeasure more than that of people. Will Komura approve of my idea?
No. But he need not know it is an exact replica. No one but I myself will
know.*

*Akira is right. It's simple really. What do we Japanese value more
than anything else? The Sacred Mirror, that's what. To bring the
American President a replica of our most precious treasure is showing
him the highest honor. Komura must explain our traditions, and make
the value of our gift clear to the President. Komura is a talented speaker.
By the time he's finished talking, the American President will believe he
has been given a gift of inestimable value.*

*But what if the gods disapprove?... No. I cannot do it. It is impossible.
I, myself, the Captain of the Ise Guards have never even seen it. How can
I have it replicated? We must have the Emperor's approval. No. He will
not allow it. But... No. It's too dangerous.* he warned himself. *This fear
is natural. I should not be afraid. Fear can be a gift. And why should I
be afraid of the Shinto gods? They have reasons beyond our
understanding of them. Has there been a time in recent memory when
the gods made known their approval or disapproval? For example, why
have the gods allowed the ETA Cabal to exist for many decades? There
must be a reason. Why would the gods allow people who want to erase
Shinto from memory to continue to exist? Why have the gods not
eradicated the Cabal? Yes, there must be a reason. Unless the Christian
missionaries are right when they teach that the Shinto gods are
powerless. I believe the Christians are right. There is nothing to fear
from the old Shinto gods.*

*The world is moving fast, but my country, through the soul and
efforts of our people, must move faster. We must occupy a place of power
in the new Twentieth Century. I denounce the gods who encourage us to
stew in our old superstitions. They are powerless in the new world. But
Japan has endured and is becoming stronger. We will be a power in the
new world. It is our destiny; and it is my duty to be in the vanguard,*

even if I must sacrifice my life.

I must convince Komuro-San that a copy of the mirror would be the perfect gift for this President of America. The Saio will not listen to me, but she will not be able to refuse the Ambassador.

Chapter 9
Ise, Japan
April 1905

"I am the *Saio*. I do not take instructions from the Prime Minister. And who is Komura Jutaro? I have never heard of him. Go away, Yoshiro Kenishi. Our personal guard, the *Daiguji*, should not have allowed this audience with me. It is very distressing."

Imperial Guard Yoshiro Kenishi remained kneeling in front of the delicately embroidered screen that hid the Supreme Priestess from his view. He well knew she could see him clearly because she'd referred to the new ribbon on his blue-grey uniform. It was said she missed nothing that went on at the Ise Jingu. It was her job to miss nothing. "Most Honorable One," Yoshiro persisted, "it is not just Prime Minister Katsura who has made this request. It is the Emperor, himself, who desires it."

There was a moment of silence, before the *Saio* asked, "And where is the written request? Unless it is signed and sealed by the Meiji Emperor himself, I will not honor it."

"Honorable One, I am sure you realize that the divine Emperor would never place such a request in writing. It is beneath his dignity. I am sure you understand that."

A few more moments of silence followed before the old woman

said, "Then the Emperor must come to Ise and make the request himself."

Yoshiro covered his shock at the old woman's audacity by coughing. Then he said, "Honorable One, that is not possible."

"Only your request is impossible. Tell the Most Glorious Emperor Matsuhito that he must come and make the request himself. Go now. I am weary of this and of you."

The guard rose slowly to his feet. *To be put in such a position is beyond my ability to comprehend and to cope*, he complained to himself. *What am I to do? I have sworn fealty and obedience to the Saio and to the Emperor. They are both powerful beyond measure. To disobey either of them would be disastrous to me and to my family. This is not my fault. I am following orders. Perhaps the Shinto gods are displeased and intend to punish us. Perhaps they do not wish that we replicate the Sacred Mirror, our most precious treasure. No, I must modernize my thinking. My German teachers are right. To believe in the gods is old-fashioned and superstitious nonsense.*

Komura-San is right, Yoshiro continued to think as he strode out of the inner shrine. *The Americans will not value a replica of Japan's most precious treasure. Even if the Prime Minister explains its significance to the Japanese people, the Americans will not value it. Yet it is the advice of Katsura Taro's assistant. Can his opinion be wrong?*

Perhaps the gods are telling us not to do this. They will punish me. No, I must not think such thoughts. Superstition must be destroyed. It weakens us. My mind keeps going in dizzying circles. What am I to do?

The Germans are right. The world respects armed might and power. Not foolish superstitions. Oh, what am I to do? What else could we bring to America that would be of equal value? What am I to do? He slowed down and walked through the rooms of the shrine, then stopped. He pulled a small wooden statue of Kannon from his pocket. He knelt and placed the statue on the mat in front of him. He hesitated, because he feared that worshipping a Buddhist deity in the sacred Shinto temple might be a sacrilege. Finally, he bowed before the statue, while his mind raced. *The Germans worship a God-man named Jesus Christ. I must learn more about this Jesus. I think He must be a God of War. They say in this new century the small will prevail over the large. Well, they are right. No country is smaller than Nippon, and we have beaten one of the world's giants. I believe all of the gods are on our side.* Yoshiro stared into the eyes of the small statue and sought for a glimmer of compassion in the Bodhisattva's gaze. "Goddess of Kindness and Compassion, the Shinto gods are busy elsewhere. I've clapped and clapped, but they do not come. Please, please help me. Tell me what to do." He sat back on his heels and waited. But the immediate release from his agony didn't come. Finally, he wrung his hands in despair, slipped the statue back in his pocket, and walked slowly out of the room to an inner courtyard.

For some moments he watched the gardener raking the sea of white pebbles on the temple's grounds. He was fashioning the stones into undulating patterns resembling soft ocean waves. Yoshiro made an effort to ease his anxiety by focusing on the waves, but his thoughts continually wandered to his growing family. After having borne two daughters who were now young women, his beloved wife had given birth to a son. They named him Isamu. He was the son Yoshiro wanted more than anything in the world. Yoshiro and his wife had lavished their money on Isamu's training and education. He had made them proud.

And now Isamu had a son of his own. Hirobumi. *Above all,* said Kenishi to himself, *I shall ensure my son and grandson's future. One does what one must. All will be well. All must be well.*

Chapter 10

The old man groveled at the feet of Yoshiro Kenishi, who had just been publicly named the principle guard of the Japanese delegation to the peace treaty negotiations in America. "My sincerest congratulations, Yoshiro-san. You honor me with your presence in my humble studio. To have had this further honor bestowed upon an unworthy old man like me," whispered the craftsman, "my ancient fingers cannot help but tremble."

"This was beyond your ability? Let me see it."

"Sir," the old man bowed his head to the ground, then peered slyly up into the guard's face, "I am still the master of the art. I have labored day and night, but it does me proud. No one has yet surpassed me. You will not be displeased. Look at it. Here it is. Is it not of inexpressible beauty?" The old man pulled his weary body up to a kneeling position and removed a small, round plate-like shining disc from its padded silk wrapping in his kimono sleeve. He offered the disc with both hands to the official. "Sir, to think that I have had the privilege... It is too great an honor for a simple craftsman like me... Sir, to think that the *Saio*, herself, described it to you... I have no words. No, there are no words."

Yoshiro took the disc and turned it over in his hands. He had told the old man a lie. Just a little lie. "I believe it will do," he said, as if the disc were worthless. "Whom have you told of this work you have made?" He asked, and removed a small monocle from his breast pocket to examine the disc more closely.

"No one, Sir. You ordered me to tell no one."

"Are you sure you told no one? If you are lying, I will know."

"I swear it again," said the old man, putting his heavily veined, gnarled hand on a statue of the Buddha sitting on his scarred worktable. "I told no one. Look outside, Sir. The rocky coast and the turbulent sea are our only neighbors. No road passes by. I have told no one, Sir. Not even my wife."

"You're sure you got the bronze right?"

"Sir, I can only guess that it is the same proportions of copper and iron as the original. But look at the color, Sir. I believe the color is right. And look at the finish of the mirror, Sir. That was my greatest challenge. I polished it by hand instead of using our modern machinery and fine polishing talcs that are now being used by craftsmen. I believe you will be pleased."

Yoshiro took the disc over to a window and studied it in the sunlight. Yoshiro turned the disc over and over in his hands. One side of the lozenge-shaped disc was dominated by an etched sun symbol. Other ancient symbols, that only the scholarly few in Japan would recognize, were also etched into the metal and appeared to be floating around the sun. "Bring me the sketches and your working drawings," he said.

The old man brought over a sheaf of papers and laid them out one by one on the trestle table in the sun. Yoshiro looked from the disc to the papers and back again. Finally, he nodded and said, "Very good."

The other side of the bronze disc was polished into a mirror in which Yoshiro could see even the small mole on his cheek. He smiled at the craftsman, and said, "Very fine indeed. If this is not an exact replica of our *Yata no Kagami*, it indeed recreates the glory of the

greatest of our national treasures. A very fine achievement, old man."
He beamed at the old craftsman whose head was bent further as if the
praise was too much for him to bear. Yoshiro placed the disc back in
its padded silk cover and slid it into the vast pocket of his kimono.
Then he called his adjutant into the small hut and nodded at him. Only
a few seconds later, the old craftsman's body lay headless on the straw
mat floor of his workroom. The adjutant knelt at Yoshiro's feet. "You
have been with him day and night?" Yoshiro asked.

"Yes, Sir."

"With whom has he spoken?"

"No one, Sir."

"Has he written to anyone?"

"No, Sir."

"He has spoken to no one? Not even the wife? I want your entire
report."

"She has brought his meals, his bathing water, and fresh clothing to
him. They have exchanged no words. He worked, ate, and slept in this
room. He took no exercise." Yoshiro stared at his adjutant, until the
man continued his report. "I have minutely inspected every item that
has entered and left this workroom, Excellency—even the old man's
night soil pot. He has complained about the isolation, but I swear he
has communicated with no one but me since Your Honor and I first
came to this place." Fear suddenly contorted the adjutant's face, as he
suddenly realized that, except for Yoshiro, he, alone, was privy to what
the craftsman had made.

"Have you dispatched his wife?"

The man's voice shook as he said, "Her body lies in the kitchen, Sir.
I scattered pieces of burning charcoal. The room was deep in smoke
when I left."

Yoshiro nodded his satisfaction, and withdrew a long enamel box
from his kimono pocket. He opened it and showed the gleaming

stiletto to his adjutant. As soon as he saw the knife, perspiration broke out on the younger man's face. He nodded. His fears had been realized.

Yoshiro said, "For your service to the Emperor and Japan, you are given the great honor to die like a true Samurai. Your family will remain under my family's protection for four generations. I swear that to you on my honor. Rice lands have been placed in your sons' names that they might someday be wealthy men. This morning your daughter is betrothed to the Baron Nogano's son. And a shrine to honor you is being built in Edo as we speak."

"I swear on my daughter's life that I will never utter a word about this place. I swear it." But the adjutant could see his words meant nothing to Yoshiro. The adjutant tried to draw in a steady breath through his trembling lips. Finally, he said, "It is an honor beyond my dreams to commit *hari-kiri* for my Emperor," the adjutant whispered, although his lips were trembling so much he couldn't keep the saliva from flowing out of his mouth. Tears streamed from his eyes. He tried to wipe the saliva and tears from his face, but the flow wouldn't stop.

"No, do not use that low, common term. We will use the honored word, *seppuku*, to describe your proud Samurai death," said Yoshiro smoothly.

"Come now. It is time." Yoshiro said gently, and handed the stiletto to the man. Then he removed white silk cloths from a small enamel box that he also pulled from his kimono. He handed the silk cloths to the adjutant whose own kimono had become damp with his sweat. "I am honored to be the Second to my country's newest hero," said Yoshiro. "Did you hear me? You are no longer a lowly guard. You are a hero who is to die as a great Samurai. I honor you. Your family will honor you. Japan will honor you forever. Be proud. Be strong." Yoshiro turned away to give the man a few moments of privacy to prepare himself.

As he had seen in a *seppuku* ceremony he had once been privileged to witness, the adjutant spread the larger white silk sheet on the straw mat floor as straight as he could manage. He took off his kimono, folded it neatly beside him, and knelt on the silk sheet. With trembling fingers, he placed the stiletto in front of him on the sheet. Then he sat back slightly on his heels, his head still bent, but now in deep meditation. For some moments he knelt absolutely still. Yoshiro stood unmoving and remained turned away from his adjutant.

Slowly, the young man opened his eyes and gazed at the stiletto. His hands shook slightly as he labored to pull his loin cloth down to fully expose his abdomen and stomach. He knelt with his head bent and labored to keep himself from swaying and toppling over. Meanwhile, Yoshiro, hearing the faint sounds of the man's preparations, had unsheathed his sword. He turned and bent his legs into an attack stance. He raised his sword over the man's bent neck. The adjutant picked up a smaller white silk cloth and the stiletto. He wrapped the handle of the sharp double-edged stiletto to keep the blade steady in his wet hands. Then, he exhaled deeply and without another sound, plunged the sharp knife into his body with both hands. He grunted with exertion as he drew the blade deeply and horizontally across his stomach. With another grunt of pain he turned the knife in his abdomen and inhaled. Then, with all the strength he had left in him, he plunged the dagger deeper and made the vertical cut. Yoshiro grunted and brought his sword swiftly down on the man's neck. When the head dropped onto the silk cloth, Yoshiro murmured a small prayer and turned away. He wiped the blood from his sword with the young adjutant's kimono. Then he walked over to the trestle table by the window. He rolled up the papers, brought them over to the small stove, and pushed them into the fire. He waited for the papers to turn into white ashes on top of the coals.

The last thing Yoshiro Kenishi did was to kick over the craftsman's small furnace. He stayed long enough to watch the straw floor mats catch fire, and then strode out to his horse. From the saddle, he waited until the craftsman's entire compound was enveloped in flames before he dug his heels into the horse's flank and rode away. The ship to America was to leave in two days. He had packing to finish.

Chapter 11
Portsmouth & New Castle, New Hampshire
September 5, 1905

Komura Jutaro looked up from his uneaten breakfast. "Well?" he asked his assistant who had tiptoed into the delegate's private hotel dining room.

"Yoshiro is here, Sir." His assistant stepped aside, and Komura stared at the muscular Yoshiro Kenishi whose darting eyes seemed to seek an escape route.

"Do you have it?" asked Komura.

Yoshiro shook his head. He tried to blink away the stinging sweat running into his eyes, and in a dry, husky whisper said, "It has been stolen, Excellency."

Komura sat at the window and watched the small whitecaps riffling the grey water of the Piscataqua River, and then he searched the sky, looking for signs of rain to bring relief from the stifling heat that had descended on Portsmouth two days earlier. "Open the window. Break it if you must. Then fan us," he said to the servant who was standing by waiting for a command. The servant ran to the window and with all his strength pushed it open. No breeze entered the room. The servant rushed back and fanned the two men.

After some minutes, Komura turned to Yoshiro, "Your father and I

46

served the Emperor together in Edo," he said, using the traditional name for Tokyo. Komura ran his fork through the uneaten scrambled eggs and sausage rounds. "We ate many good meals at the same table, not animal food like this." Komura pushed his breakfast plate away. "Bring me salt fish congee," he said to another servant who had been kneeling waiting for a command. "And make sure it is hot this time," Komura added. Then he looked at Yoshiro and said, "I have been carefully watching you since the day you started your formal training. Because I have sung your praises, even the Emperor considered you the penultimate Imperial Guard and posted you to Ise Jingu, the most prestigious position of any in the Guard. I rejoiced when you married my daughter. I know you as well as I know my own son, perhaps better." Komura looked up and gave the same disgusted look at Yoshiro as he had given the eggs and pork sausage.

"You do me a great honor that I do not deserve, Sir."

"No, you do not deserve my honor or respect. Such a breach of responsibility demands a punishment." Yoshiro looked up quickly, than lowered his eyes again and said, "Yes, Sir."

"I trusted you. You are my responsibility. You failed me, and as a consequence, I have failed the delegation, but even worse, I have failed the Emperor. We have both failed the Emperor. Down." Komura ordered, and Yoshiro fell to his knees. He sat back on his heels, and touched his forehead to the carpeted floor. He raised his body slightly, stretched out his neck and spread out his arms, waiting for the sword's blow. But Komura didn't behead him, as Yoshiro had expected. Instead, Komura whispered, "Do you love the Emperor?"

Yoshiro raised his head to peer at Komura. "He is my God, Sir."

"Would you do anything for the Emperor? Even die for him?"

Yoshiro's lips trembled slightly, but he nodded vigorously. "Yes, Sir."

"Now that the negotiations are finished, and we have signed the peace treaty, we must prepare to return home. I have doubts about your abilities and your intelligence now, but I cannot divulge this theft to any other in the delegation. We have no gift for the American President. The disgrace will be unbearable. If you do not find it, whatever punishment is decided for me, I will pass the same on to you. Do you understand?" "Yes, Sir."

"Even if it is *seppuku*?"

"Yes, Sir. I would willingly sacrifice this worthless body at your command."

"Yes, that may well be our fate. My poor daughter and grandchildren. You have destroyed my family. Tell me now. What have you done so far to find it?"

"Sir, the Wentworth Hotel manager was told our own servants would take care of us. The American hotel staff was not needed. I heard the manager order his hotel staff not to enter our rooms unless they were specifically asked to do so. I believe it could not have been a hotel employee..."

"Nobody in our party would dare steal the gift."

"Sir, that was the first question I asked myself. Would any of us commit such a terrible crime? Then I thought of the ETA Cabal. The men of the accursed Cabal are everywhere. My sources have told me they have enlisted Americans and pay them well. But I have not yet verified that assertion."

Komura turned his back on Yoshiro who took it to mean that he should stop talking. The ambassador stared into the dark water of the river. He knew his enemies were accusing him of being too soft on the Cabal. For that reason he chose the men he brought with him to the United States even more carefully than usual. He pictured each man in the delegation. His mind raced. *Is it possible that one of the detestable Cabal wormed his way into the treaty delegation? No. I handpicked each and every one of them. They each were allowed to bring with them only one old family retainer to serve them. All of their papers were scrutinized again and again. No, not one in our delegation would have stolen the mirror. Yet... who else? But, no. The pearls were also stolen. None of us, not even one of the ETA, would have stolen the pearls. It could not have been one of us. Maybe the dirty Russians. They would dare to do such a thing. But the doors between our wings in the hotel are double bolted and guarded. Still...*

Komura turned back to Yoshiro to ask him about the Russians. But Yoshiro was already blurting out, "I believe I know who the thief is, Sir. It was one of the Americans who service the Wentworth. When I was thoroughly searching the sitting room once again late last night, in the large fireplace I found an entrance to a secret passage. I stayed up watching all night thinking the thief might return. He did not. This morning, while it was still dark, I entered the passage. It led to the hotel staff quarters."

"And?"

"Sir, I waited until they had all arisen and gone off to their work, and then I searched their rooms and dormitories. I found the pearl necklace." Yoshiro reached into his kimono sleeve and drew out a circle of white pearls that glowed even in the dim morning light.

"That thing can be replaced," Komura said with a dismissive wave of his hand. "What about the Mirror?"

"No sir, I am still searching for it. I now know who the thief is. I shall retrieve it today."

"Do not fail. You are very fortunate that the President Roosevelt was detained in Washington and could not attend the negotiations. If he were here, and we had no token of Japan's esteem to give to him, the shame would be unbearable. I have already written a panegyric about the Mirror for the President Roosevelt to explain its inestimable value to the Japanese people. He cannot help but feel a great honor to receive a beautiful replica of our most sacred treasure. Hah! The gods must be laughing at our arrogance."

"Most Honorable One, we all have faith in you to inform the President of the Mirror's great value to the Japanese people."

"That was my plan. I intended to present the gifts at dinner tomorrow evening, when both we and the Russians are invited to Secretary of State Peirce's summer home. The envy in the Russians' eyes will be very satisfying.

"This is most distressing," he continued. "Go now. Find the Mirror and punish the thief. Do anything necessary to rescue our treasure. But if you must kill him, leave no trace of evidence that would lead the American authorities to this delegation and its mission. No evidence at all. Do you understand? If we are implicated in any way, the Emperor will also be implicated and you will bring unbearable shame to our country. You, my dear daughter, and my beloved grandchildren will pay the price of such carelessness on your part. My wife, my other two daughters, and all their families will also be punished. I am trusting you. Do not fail. Do you understand? Bring the Mirror here before the end of the day. Our lives depend on it."

"Yes, Sir."

"I do not wish to see you again until you have the Mirror... or until you are dead. But you better not die before you find the Mirror. Understand?"

"Yes, Sir. Anything, Sir."

Chapter 12
Newington, New Hampshire
August 31, 1905

Jeremiah Hartz stared out the open window and listened. He batted at a horse fly buzzing around his head and frowned deeper. His son, Russell, was in the vegetable garden shoveling dirt into a tin can with a broken spoon. The boy had been sent out to dig up potatoes for supper, and, as usual, he was playing in the dirt instead of working. "Potatoes!" Jeremiah screamed at the boy, and Russell dropped the old spoon and plunged his hands into the dirt.

His wife, Rebecca, ran among the squawking hens to choose the fattest. "We will eat well tonight," he had told her. "No supper of only boiled potatoes with curds and salt tonight. Soon," he'd added, "we'll be living in a fine house in Portsmouth and dining on meat every day. Hurry." He had playfully swatted her bony behind. "Cook us a feast."

When Hartz was sure he'd be alone in the house for a few more minutes, he took the black round enamel box out from under his shirt. His face reddened. *I shouldn'a took it. But he shoulda hid it better. What'd he expect? They won't call the sheriff. That ain't their way. How'm I gonna sell it? Wonder if it's real gold. He treated it like it was real gold. But it don't look like no gold I ever seen. Real gold is yella, ain't it? I'll melt it down if it's real, and make nuggets. This thing's gotta be*

51

real gold. The Japs ain't gonna give Mista Roosevelt fake gold. I could spend nuggets in Boston. I gotta make them small nuggets. Not here. They'd give me the eye an' ask where I got 'em. Even if they're small. I can't spend them here. But what happened to them pearls? They was slippry. Prob'ly fell outa my pocket, they did. Someone found 'em on the street and stoled 'em. That's the way most people is. Dirty thiefs. It's disgustin'. He moved away from the window and studied the round disc. And then shook his head.

Might as well bring this thing back. Whose gonna buy it? Even in Boston, what good is it? Ain't nobody gonna wanta buy it. Ain't doin' me no good. Thought I could sell it in Boston. No. Who would buy this thing? Might as well bring it back. No, ain't no way I can bring it back. What'm I gonna do with this hunk a tin? "Yeah, comin' Becca," Jeremiah yelled. *What she want now?* He asked himself. Through the window he saw Rebecca wring the neck of a hapless chicken, all the while she was yelling out his name. *What she screamin' 'bout? Her and her big mouth. She never leaves me be. I never have no peace with her. I gotta go see Ada. She knows how to keep her mouth shut.* Jeremiah placed the disc back into the silk-lined box. He shoved the enamel box in his gunnysack as he ran to find out what his wife wanted this time.

Chapter 13

Ada Johnson sat on the top step of her small porch and watched the tree branches swaying in the growing breeze. *Fall's comin' early this year,* she said to herself. Her fingers were busy sewing the ripped hem of her Sunday dress. *I gotta earn some dollars and make me a new Sunday dress. This pretty thing is falling apart inch by inch.* She looked up at the squeaking sound of someone coming through her rusty-hinged gate.

"You oughta ask me to oil that gate of yers," said Jeremiah Hartz. "I could do a good oil job on you, too, Nubi."

"Don't call me Nubi. What do ya want here, Jeremiah?"

"Same as I always want."

"You're still out of luck. I'm not interested."

"Yer pretty uppity, ain't ya, Nubi? What other white fella would want yer black ass?"

"Go home, Jeremiah, and leave me be."

"Gotta present for ya."

"I don't want nothin' from you. Just go away."

"It's from Egyptland. Everybody there's got black skin just like you. Egyptland is where yer was born."

"It's not."

"Then yer grandma. Ya wanta see my treasure?"

53

"No. Whatever it is, I don't want it. And I don't want you, neither."
Suddenly they heard a child's voice. "Pa," it said.

"Oh, now what?" Jeremiah yelled. "Whatchu want? Go 'way. Go
back to your momma."

"Momma sent me to get ya, "Pa," said Russell.

"That bitch don't ever give me a minute's peace. Here, Ada, you
keep this for me." He threw his gunny sack on the steps of her porch.
"Hide it. Don't show it to nobody else. Hear?" Jeremiah turned and
loped off toward his house. Russell ran off to follow him.

Ada picked up the gunny sack and peeked inside. She gasped, then
called out, "Russell, you come back here for a minute, boy."

Chapter 14

Later that afternoon, Jeremiah pushed his son Russell in front of him onto the trail. "Whadaya fuckin' whinin' about now? Yer Ma wants wood for cookin'. It's past time you learned to make splits for her. I'm a busy man. I can't be doin' kitchen work. Come on. Get moving," he screamed, giving the boy another hard kick on his bony rump. Russell cried out. The kick had left him sprawling on the dusty ox path. His father grabbed the whimpering boy by his dirty neck and pulled him back up to his feet. He looked down at the boy's thick shirt. "What you carryin' under your shirt? You put the splits in there? You want muscles in them arms, you gotta carry wood in 'em, not stuff 'em in your shirt. Just look at you. Been feedin' you too much. You gettin' a gut on you, too. An' why you wearin' that thick shirt? It ain't winter, you idjit," he said, pushing the boy along in front of him.

When they reached the spot where a low cutting stump dominated a large clearing, Hartz searched around the clearing and fell into a furious growl. "Some bastard stole some'a my logs. It's yer fault. You walk too slow," he said to the boy. "Now I gotta go an' cut more. Probly Dan'l. I'll kill that lazy thievin' bastard. Stop starin' at me," he yelled at Russell. "And pick up them wood pieces over there and put em in yer sack. Take the goddam sack outa your shirt and put the firewood in it. The dry ones, you stupid donkey, not the new ones.

Hurry up." Jeremiah glared at the young boy. *All I ever do is work for Becca and this brat of hers I don't never have no fun. Gotta go back and see Ada. She must be hankerin' for me by now. What if that fuckin' dish ain't gold? I ain't never been lucky. It probly ain't. Ada'll throw it at me .What'm I supposed to do with it? I'll throw it in the ocean. That's what. It'll sink all the way to the bottom. What were the Jappies doin' with a Egypt dish anyways? Maybe the fishies will roll it all the way back to Japanland. Fishies are smart. They do things under the ocean we don't know nothin' about. They'll roll that thing all the way back to Egyptland where it belongs. Then some whale'll grab it up and swallow it to make the fishies mad.* He giggled.

His son, thinking that his father had come up with another way to hurt him, scurried off the ox trail and into the woods. "Russell, you get yer lazy ass back over here afore I give ya a beatin' you won't never forget. Pick up some more and bring them firewoods right along to yer Ma," Jeremiah yelled. "Yer sack can hold more'n two. Be a man. Don't know why she needs so much wood. She don't cook that good no more. She's one big pain in the ass, yer ma is. Good thing I hauled the cart out here. You get them splits right to yer ma. Right now. You come back and fill up this cart. Then you help me push it back home. You want muscles? That'll give you muscles." Jeremiah laughed. The child picked up two more split pieces of log and scampered off back to the trail.

The sun was almost overhead when Jeremiah had finished sawing off low tree limbs to split into firewood. He bent over to pick up the last log he was going to split that day. *Don't know why I'm botherin' anymore today. Can't use no green wood for the fire.* He bent further over the chopping stump to plane off chips with his axe. *Now what's this?* He asked himself when he saw a man's sandaled feet step next to the stump. He looked up. A thick coating of white covered the man's face and neck, a fountain of fake red hair flowed out from under the man's dark leather helmet and onto his black kimono. Cruel black eyes and a malicious red grin were painted on the white face. A scream stuck in Jeremiah's throat. He managed to gargle, "Who're you? You a Jappie? You lost? What'da ya want here? Wentworth Hotel's that way," he pointed with his axe. "What'da ya want here? You a Jappie?" he repeated.

"Give it to me."

"What'da ya talkin' about? What do I got a yours? I ain't got nothin' a yours. That's what." Jeremiah held up his arms. "Look. I ain't got nothin'."

The man raised his sword over his head. "First your wife, now you, then your son. Give me the Mirror. She said you have it."

"Whata you carryin' on about? She's a liah. I ain't got no mirra." Jeremiah insisted, and swung his axe at the man. He gasped when the man's sword arced through the still air. Jeremiah's hand fell onto the dusty forest floor. The hand, leaning against the stump, slowly released the axe from its grip. Jeremiah's gaze fixed on his severed hand and then at his wrist that was spurting blood over the chopping stump.

"The Mirror," whispered his attacker.

"Look at what you done!" Jeremiah cried. "I tol' you, I ain't got no mirra. Please don't hurt me no more. I ain't got no mirra." He brought his arm up to wipe his face. He wailed when he realized the stump of his arm was rubbing spurts of blood onto his forehead. Now Jeremiah's tears and saliva dripped onto the chopping stump, too. Another swish of the sword, and Jeremiah's entire arm fell onto the stump and then rolled to the ground next to his hand. Jeremiah screamed, and collapsed on top of his severed arm.

"Where is the Mirror?" his attacker asked again while he raised his sword again.

"I give it to Ada," Jeremiah screamed just before the sword split open his head.

Russell thought his mother would be in the yard. She didn't like to feather and bleed a hen in her kitchen, unless he was there to clean up. She wasn't outside. Russell dropped the firewood at the back door and yelled to his mother he'd be right back with more, and then he ran swiftly back toward the clearing before his father came hollering after him as usual. "The firewood's here," he yelled to Rebecca toward the kitchen window. Then he looked down. "You wanna come? No. You best stay here," Russell yelled to his dog, Sparky, who was cowering in her usual hiding place under the house steps. "What you 'fraid of now? Some watchdog you are! You stay here." Russell scurried off into the woods.

Getting closer to the clearing, Russell heard his father's yelling in the silent woods, but he was still too far away to see him. When he heard his father's first agonized cry, Russell halted and spun quickly around looking for a hiding place. If it was a bear, the boy knew it was too late to run away. *Bears run fast. I can't climb a tree to get away from it. Pa already cut off all the low branches. I'll hide in my log cabin. Even if the bear sniffs me, my log cabin is too strong for him to crack open. I think it is. If he ate , he's too fat to crawl in after me An' he won't be hungry no more. But I best stay in my log cabin.* "Come here with me, Sparky," he whispered.

Russell just wanted to run home. The shortest route was closer to the clearing, but he didn't dare. His house was too far. Russell was trembling, but with Sparky in his arms he tiptoed as quietly and quickly as he could toward the hollow log. He reached it and dove into the black hole when he heard his father's screams. He hugged Sparky, closed his eyes, and covered his ears. He had to move his hands down to his mouth and nose to stifle the cries that were moving up to his throat. Tears streamed over his hands as he held his mouth tightly shut. "Hush, now," he said to Sparky who was whining.

Russell had crawled into the log on his side, but the enamel box Ada had given him earlier cut into his skin. He pulled it out and pushed it deeper into the detritus of dead leaves and tree bark with his other treasures at the far end of his log cabin. His fingers touched the nautilus shell he'd found on the beach more than two weeks ago. He pulled it out of the dead leaves and held the shell against his neck. And then against Sparky's ear. She stopped whimpering. Russell listened and waited. His father wasn't crying any more, but now he could hear the bear. It was trudging over the forest floor toward them. Russell loosened his tight grip around Sparky to stop her from noisily wriggling. He pressed the nautilus shell tight against his ear. He tried to hear the ocean in the seashell, but he couldn't. All he could hear was Sparky's panting and the bear trudging toward them.

Then he realized it wasn't a bear crashing through the underbrush. It was a man. Russell heard a man's mumbling. *That ain't no bear. It don't sound like Papa eitha. Who is that? What's he sayin'?* Russell heard the man's heavy breathing and felt the log move slightly. He thought the man had sat down on his log or maybe kicked it. *That don't sound like . Who is that? Where's my Pa? If it's Pa, he'll beat the tar outa me for hidin'.* Russell used both hands to cover his mouth as tight as he could in the damp blackness of the log. Sparky lay silently in his arms.

All Russell knew about God was that you prayed to Him when you needed something. Russell didn't know how to pray. He closed his eyes and whispered silently into his wet hands, *Please God, don't let that man find me. Please God, if it's Pa, don't let him find me here. Don't let him know 'bout my log cabin. An' if it ain't Pa , please God, bring Pa here with his axe to save me.* But Russell knew in his heart that if it weren't his father sitting on the log, dead or alive, his father wouldn't be coming to help him. Russell slowly inched his knees up to his chest. Sparky seemed to share the boy's fear and remained quiet. Russell was afraid to move, but he needed to make himself smaller. He waited. After what seemed hours to Russell, he heard the man groan and trudge heavily away from

Russell's log cabin. Russell could hear the man still puffing out air and muttering.

When he could no longer hear anything but small skittering sounds of wood creatures, Russell crawled out from the log. Sparky trotted out after him.

When he reached the clearing, Russell turned and looked all around him. Blood covered the cutting stump, but his father wasn't there. *He must have got away.* Russell smiled. *Yeah, Pa got away. He ain't a real big guy, but he's smarta'n everbody. And meaner, too. Yeah, he beat up the other guy real good with his axe. That's what. All that blood. Yeah, that's what. But where'd Pa go? Musta got home the other way. But why he gone home that way? It's longer. Well, that man probly knows just one way to get out here. Yeah, that's it. Pa didn't want to meet up with him again, so he took another way home.*

Energized by this thought, Russell ran back toward his house. "C'mon Sparks!" he whispered. When they reached the ox trail, Russell stopped. *Smells like Pa's fire-clearing that stand of brush over near the river like he said he was gonna do.*

Suddenly Sparky started howling, and Russell saw the smoke and cinders rising in the air. He knew he was wrong about the brush fire. The smoke wasn't coming from the river. He raced toward his house, but couldn't get closer to it than the road. Sparky ran with him. Russell bent down, grabbed the little dog, and hugged her. Then he and his dog sat in the dirt among the clucking hens and watched as the flaming roof fell into their little house.

Chapter 15

"Now what we gonna do, Sparks?" Russell asked. "Where we gonna live? Where's Ma and Pa? They run away without me? I'm starvin' hungry. How 'bout you? Let's go dig up some budayduhs and roast 'em in the cinders. Then we're gonna make plans. If Ma and Pa don't come get us, we're gonna sleep in the log cabin tonight. They maybe went to Ada's. She's a wicked old thing. Don't like children or dogs. That's what Ma says. Well, just 'tween me and you, Ada's okay. You ain't fraid of old Ada, Sparks. Right? I ain't neither... . but we'll wait for mornin'. We got things to do. What you think, old girl? Why'd Ma and Pa go to Ada's without me?... Tell you what we'll do, Sparks. We'll eat our budayduhs, then go bring that round thing to the Wentworth. It's bad luck. That's what it is. What do you think?" The dog stared up into the little boy's face for a moment, and then lay down again in the dirt.

"What does that mean? I don't know what else to do with it and that's where Pa stole it out of. That's what he said. Well, he didn' say he stole it. He said he 'come by it 'over there at the Wentworth. Come on, old girl, let's go get it. I left it safe in the log cabin. After we get back, then we'll go over to Miss Ada's."

Chapter 16
New Castle, New Hampshire
September 1905

Yoshiro Kenishi sat at the small desk in his room and put the writing brush down on the ink stone. Then he rolled up the paper he'd just finished inking and tied the roll with a strip of fabric he cut from his obi. He looked around his room once more. All was in order. His clothing was folded neatly and piled carefully in his suitcase. He placed his grooming kit on top of the clothes and, finally, with a sigh and great effort he grabbed his topknot and sliced it off his head. Tears streamed down his face as he placed the knot of hair on top of the kit. He laid his knife and sword on a robe he had placed on the floor next to his bed. *Seppuku is too honorable a death for one such as I,* he said to himself as he picked up the roll of paper and walked quickly out of his bedroom at the Wentworth. The halls were empty. The Russians and other Japanese were at the Naval Shipyard in Portsmouth, and the hotel workers had finished their jobs for the day and gone home.

Yoshiro slipped out a back entrance and strode quickly toward the water's edge. He wedged the roll of paper in the small fissure on a large boulder next to the water. He didn't notice the little boy and dog standing in the bushes watching him. In his agony, he wasn't seeing anything. Yoshiro took off his obi and used it to tie his kimono tightly around his body and legs. Then he sighed and stepped into the water of the bay.

"What's he doin'?" Russell asked Sparky from their hiding place in the bushes when he saw Yoshiro walk into the calm water of the bay. "He ain't swimmin'. He's just walkin'. Maybe that's what those Jap people do. That's why they look diff'rent. Cuz they do things diff'rent. Maybe he's walkin' back to Japanland. What d'ya think, Sparky?"

When the top of Yoshiro's head disappeared in the water, Russell said, "I wonder if they can breathe under water like fishies. They prob'ly can. That's why they look so diff'rent. We'll wait and see when he comes walkin' back out." Some moments later, Russell said, "Nope. He ain't comin' back out. He must be halfway to Japanland by now. Let's go see what he put on that rock there. Whatever it is, he don't want it no more. Come on. We'll go get it and put it with the treasure."

Russell looked down at the roll of paper. "What we gonna do with the treasure and this thing? What is this thing that he put in the split of the rock? It looks like a bunch of papers tied up. What're we gonna do with those? It's dirty in the log cabin. We can't put no papers in there, now, can we? Gotta pertect them. Let's go see if Miss Ada's got any wax paper."

Chapter 17

"Miss Ada," Russell said softly as he knocked on her door. "Miss Ada," he repeated.

"What do you want, boy?" Ada Johnson asked as soon as she opened her door. "What's Sparky doing over by my turnip patch? She better not be digging anything up. That dog's a... what are you crying about boy?"

Russell had to stop sobbing before he sputtered, "Ma and Pa are gone. I thought they was here. My house is burnt up. The Japan man is walkin' to Japanland. An' Sparky and me is hungry. We ain't had nothin' but one budayduh all day. Do you got any wax paper? We need wax paper."

"You take yourself and your dog down to the creek and wash up. What's that all over you? Have you been rolling in that log of yours again? Don't give me that look. Everybody but your Ma and Pa knows about you and your dirty log. Look at you. You've got worms and such all over you. You go down to the creek and get cleaned up. Your filthy clothes, too. And those things you call shoes. Take that mutt of yours, too. It looks like she hasn't had a bath yet this year. Here's soap." Ada handed Russell a large bar of brown soap. "Don't you waste it, none. Don't leave it in the water, neither. You keep it on a dry stone, and you pull some weed to scrub yourselves with. Oh, and take this pail. We'll need drinking and cooking water. And fill the pail before you take a bath. Then you get back here. I'll give you some food. What do you need with wax paper?"

Russell and Sparky ran across to the cow pasture, and Ada Johnson walked to the wall phone. "Mrs. Seaver," she yelled into the phone. "I've got an emergency here. Would you get off for a minute? I understand that, Mrs. Seaver. I agree that party lines are no darn good. But I've got an emergency. Please hang up. ... No, there's no time for me to be discussin' it with you. Come back on in a minute or two and you'll learn what the emergency is." Ada waited, turned the crank, and waited again, "Mary," she said, "please get me the sheriff."

He didn't use much soap, but after dunking himself in the creek a half dozen times, Russell was feeling better. Even Sparky was hopping along beside him back to Ada Johnson's house.

"That's better," said Ada when she opened her door to Russell. "But you're sopping wet. You can't come in.... You either," she pushed Sparky away with one foot. "Boy, what you doin' here? Why'd you come to me? And what do you know about me anyways?" Ada asked.

"Ma says yer mean and godless."

Ada grinned and said, "Your Ma is half right. Now you listen to me. I taught children your age all my young life. There's nothing you can do or say that surprises me or scares me. You understand?" Russell nodded. "Okay. Over here on this top step is a plate of food for you. I put scraps on the ground for Sparky. You come eat. Are you thirsty?" She held out the pail of water to Russell. "No. I don't suppose you are, after your rollicking good time in the creek. Eat up. Then we'll talk."

Chapter 18

Russell was just finishing his buttered potatoes when the police cart drove up. Sparky growled, but crawled onto Russell's lap and watched Ada come out to talk to the policeman. After a few minutes, they both walked over to the boy.

"Boy, this is Officer Richmond. Shake hands like a gentleman," said Ada.

Russell stood up, wiped his hand on his shirt, and held it out, and the policeman shook it. Richmond said, "Russell, it looks like you've got a passel of trouble."

"Yes, sir."

"You don't know where your parents went?"

"No, sir."

"How'd your house burn down?"

"I don't know, sir."

"Where were you when your house burned down?"

"In the woods."

"With your dog?"

"Yes, sir. She ain't allowed away from the house. But Sparky carries on so when I go into the woods. But I made good and sure Sparky stayed right with me all the time. Ma's afraid she'll get babies in her tummy if she wanders off."

66

"What were you doin' alone in the woods. Don't you know there's bears in the woods?"

"Yes, sir."

"Well?"

"I was gettin' splits for Ma's cookin'."

Richmond turned to look at Ada, "Yeah," he said, "I saw a sack of fire wood out there on the ground outside the house."

The policeman turned back to Russell. "Where'd your Ma and Pa go?"

"I don't know, sir. I thought they was here with Miz Johnson."

"Ada says she ain't see them. She says your Mama don't like her."

"Ma say's Ada's a mean one." Russell turned to Ada, and said, "I'm sorry, M'am, but that's what Ma says."

"I know, boy. She took pleasure in calling me Ada, and not Miss Johnson. Like it was disrespectful. I once taught your Ma in school and more than once I gave it to her on the palms of her hands with my ruler. Not hard and not a lot. I don't take pleasure in giving a child pain. But even the sight of a raised ruler can sure put the fear of God into a bad child. Right, officer?"

He reddened and nodded sheepishly, but said to Russell, "Where did you say your parents went?"

"I told you, sir. I don't know, sir."

"He doesn't know Officer Richmond. Isn't that what he already said?" Ada snapped at the same time Russell answered the policeman.

"Well, if either of you hear from them, you let the police know. I'll see what I can find out. I'm sending Services out here to talk to the boy. Where's he gonna live? You takin' him in, Miss Johnson? You go off now and play, Russell," the policeman said. "If his Ma and Pa were in their house, they're burnt to a crisp now," Richmond said as he strolled back to his cart.

"Do you want to stay with me 'til your parents get back?" Ada asked Russell.

"Can Sparky stay with me?"

"Well, the way she shadows you, I don't know how I'd stop her. But I've got rules! You've got to help out around here, like getting water from the creek. And Sparky better follow my rules too, or she'll be tied up out here all day and night. Got it, Sparky?" The little dog wagged her tail and jumped up and down as if she understood Ada. "And you bark loud if boy dogs come round. I don't want any pregnant dog around here. You understand, Sparky?" The dog wagged her tail as Ada untied her. Sparky ran for her food scraps.

"Now listen," said Russell to Sparky, "you can't like it too much here at Miss Ada's. This ain't our own house. We can't stay here. The Services won't allow it. I don't know why. The Services lady says there's a family out on Appledore that wants a boy like me to be their boy's friend and help with the chores. Why do you suppose they need to bring somebody in to be their boy's friend? He's prob'ly a bad boy. Or maybe he's feeble-minded and crippled, and can't do no chores. I'll be like their slave. Like Miss Ada says they do in Egypt. When I'm growed up, you and me is goin' to Egypt. Miss Ada says you're my white Anubis. She says that's your real name. Anubis. You like that name? I wonder where Ma and Pa got to? Well, they'll be back for me. I'm sure. They won't leave me behind. When she's feelin' good, Mama says I'm their little bundle a joy. They'll be back for us. Don't you think so, Sparky?

"I don't wanna go out to the Isles, do you? I heard tell that Appledore is the best of them. But I don't want to live on no island. Appledore is where all them people were murdered... No, it were Smuttynose. But Appledore is right next to Smuttynose. I don't wanta go. What'll happen when there's a hurricane? We ain't got no boat. And I can't swim so good. You can, but not me. You're gonna have to save me. I don't wanna go live on no island.

"Miss Ada says we gotta go, though. It's the law. I don't know why we can't stay here. Miss Ada don't have no children to help with the chores and things. And she ain't 'zactly mean like Ma says. She don't yell at us. I don't think she hates us. I stood right up to her, and I said 'I ain't goin' nowhere without Sparky!' and Miss Ada she said, 'Well, I don't want no dog here. You just take her with ya to the Isles. And ya better hope they don't make her into stew.' That's what she said. No, Sparky, you don't gotta be scared. Nobody's makin' you stew over my dead body. So don't you worry. We are gonna like it out in the Isles of Shoals, cuz we gotta. An' we gonna go on a boat. You, too. You been around them a lot. Me, too. But you ain't never been on no boat before. Me neither. Not out on the ocean. I hope we don't get sick. Mama would never get on no boat cuz she said she got sick. I hope I won't get sick cuz I can't swim. That would be real embrassin'. No call for you to look scared. You know how to swim."

PART II
One Hundred Years Later

Chapter 1
Portsmouth, New Hampshire

Sister Anne Farrell made up her mind and sealed the DSL envelope. A deep frown turned her blue eyes into long dark slits. It wasn't that she doubted she was doing the right thing. The same thoughts had gone around in her brain since the funeral. *There's no doubt in my mind at all. It's my duty. I have to let the Japanese know what I discovered. I have to do that. It's the right thing to do. The question is how to tell them, and, more important, who to tell first.*

She closed her eyes and said another prayer to Saint Anne de Beaupre. She kept her eyes closed as she finished her prayer and thought about her problem again. *I can't go directly to just anyone in the government. That would be unwise. Not everyone in the Japanese government is honest, trustworthy, and efficient. That's true of any government, not just Japan. They're just people. There's good and bad everywhere. Oh, why am I carrying on like this?... Anyway, the fewer who know about this matter, the better. I'm sure of that.*

I can trust Seiji. That's something I'm also sure about. On the other hand, I could be putting my old friend in danger. It's best to warn him. He's an old man now. He would understand the danger, and he would not go out looking for trouble. Age must have mellowed his machismo by now. I pray I'm right.

Good old Yoshiro Seiji! I used to know him even better than anyone here in America. Now, I've got to trust that Seiji won't act on his first impulses. He's old now. He would think about it carefully and then would decide what to do about this situation. He couldn't be the firebrand he used to be. He must have learned to be wary and circumspect. Oh, I hope he's not too old-thinking.

He wouldn't come to Portsmouth himself; well, anyway, not alone. And he wouldn't expect me to be armed and ready to move. We're both too old to be of any use in the field. Our reflexes aren't what they once were. And we mustn't endanger the others. When they find out I've got it, there's gonna be trouble. But Seiji and I can handle trouble. Well, at one time we could. I don't know what I can do anymore. Besides I'm a nun now. Those early days are gone forever. For both of us. He would realize that, wouldn't he? We can't do it alone. I've got to get us help. Yes, he's not stupid. He'll agree that we need younger warriors.

Sister Anne let her mind wander for a few moments through the roster of people she'd known in her life. Then she smiled. *Well, Connie and Sharon. You would come if I ask it of you, won't you?* She gazed at the blank wall for some moments before she added, *Yes, I believe they would. Seiji and I need strong allies. ETA Cabalists will be coming. The worst of them will be those who are willing to kill to prevent any others from finding the treasure. What could we alone do to stop them? Even the Japanese government has never been able to destroy the Cabal. Defending against those killers would require...* Sister Anne stopped thinking, and walked to the telephone.

The line was picked up on the second ring. "Talant Searches," said a woman's voice.

"Connie," said Sister Anne. "I need your help. Can you come?"

"Of course. When? Right now?"

"Connie, it's a really bad situation. I'm going to call Sharon and ask her to join us." She waited for the young woman's reaction.

"Auntie Anne, it must be really bad if you need to call her. What's going on? Are you absolutely sure we need her?"

"Yes. But if you feel you can't work with her..."

"I know you like and trust her. I don't think she gets much of that.... Well, as long as we can trust her to work with us, I'm okay with it. She wouldn't do anything to hurt you. I don't think she'd want to harm either of us. But we should still watch our backs. I don't completely trust her. She's unpredictable; and she never lets anybody get close enough to really know her. You understand that. Right?"

"Sharon is often able to overcome the terrible things she suffered in her youth," the nun answered. "There is a part of her that responds in kind to people who love and respect her. You two have gotten along in the past. I see no reason why that can't continue."

"Sister Anne, I confess it. I actually like her. But you've got to know that inviting Sharon here right now isn't the best idea you ever had. Google her. She's wanted by practically every law enforcement agency in the world... which isn't an exaggeration. How will you get in touch with her? The cops must be listening in on calls to her cell phones and watching for her emails. Are you sure she'll come?" Connie didn't wait for an answer, but continued, "And, what's going on that you need us? How worried should I be? Are you in trouble? In danger? It must be really bad if you need both of us."

Sister Anne could hear the worry in her niece's voice. She thought a moment before she said, "Sharon and I have a conduit that can still be privately and safely used. I'm going to try to reach her as soon as I get off the phone with you. It's best that I speak to both of you at the same time. I'll call you back when I get in touch with her. I hope that the two of you can come as soon as possible. We could have our initial meeting here in the convent where we're sure to have privacy. I don't trust the phone."

Chapter 2
Ise, Japan

Yoshiro Seiji tore open the DSL envelope. *What could my good old friend be sending me? Must be something that's too important to wait until Hirobumi goes to the United States next week,* he thought as he emptied the large envelope onto his desk. He glanced at the top page of the papers held by a large manuscript clip, and went pale as he recognized his father's calligraphy. As he read, his knees gave out and he grabbed for his chair. His hands trembled as he continued reading, and his dark eyes welled up in tears that rolled down his cheeks.

"Grandfather!" cried Hirobumi, who had just entered the study. "What is it? Let me help you," the young man ran over to Seiji, took his arm, and helped him to sit in his desk chair. His grandfather rubbed at his eyes, but pulled the papers over and continued reading. As he finished reading each sheet, he slid it over to Hirobumi. Soon, Hirobumi, too, was leaning on the desk for support. He fought back tears.

"This cannot be true. Is it written in Yoshiro Kenishi's hand? Are you sure? Do you recognize the calligraphy? Are you sure it is his calligraphy? Could it be true, Grandfather?"

"The shame of it... the pain... it is too much to bear," the older man answered, now sobbing into his wrinkled hands. Hirobumi wiped angrily at the tears that coursed down his own cheeks.

"What's that noise? What's going on here?" cried Hirobumi's mother as she ran into the small study. She pushed past Hirobumi and hurried to her father-in-law. Hirobumi started sobbing himself when he saw his strong grandfather lay his head on his mother's shoulder and continue weeping. She patted the old man's shoulder. "Hush now, Father-in-law," she whispered. "Tell me what is distressing you." She reached out to her son. "Come here, Hirobumi. Let me comfort you, too. Tell me what has happened. Come. Don't hold back. A man is never too old for his mother's comfort."

Hirobumi ran to her open arms and pointed with his chin to the top of his grandfather's desk. "These old papers are causing my men to weep? What are they?" She pushed her son and father-in-law gently away and grabbed the papers. "I don't care what they are. They are yellow with age, and don't matter any more," she growled. "All I see is that they are causing you pain. They are evil. They should be burned." She gathered the papers in her arms and hurried over to the small coal stove which was empty and cold in the summer. "I shall set these evil papers afire," she said as she grabbed the large box of matches sitting on a nearby shelf. At this, both men stared at the woman and both yelled, "No!"

Chapter 3
Tokyo, Japan
(formerly Edo)

In his Armani business suit and tie, Twenty-Seven could pass for any of the other business people out for lunch at Chateau Restaurant Joel Robuchon in the heart of Tokyo. In fact he preferred Japanese food to the French delicacies on the menu of this, the most expensive restaurant in Japan. But Akira Yoshi was an enthusiastic Francophile who had been educated in Europe and England. Plying Akira with excellent French food and wine was an easy way to gain the man's confidence and cooperation. If he balked later, Twenty-Seven was prepared to simply eliminate him.

"Honorable Leader," said Akira, "I understand what it is you want from me, but I don't know how I can do it. I'm not good at artifice, and I have no physical skills. I'm just a bookkeeper, a very good bookkeeper, but just a bookkeeper. Nothing more.

"Akira," said Twenty-Seven as he refilled the man's Sake glass, "the part we're asking you to play is very small, minimal actually. You swear you love your country. This is your way of proving it. Don't you trust us?"

"Yes, Sir... But, Sir, the treasures..."

"Think no more about it. We will handle everything. Your part is relatively small." Akira's lips were trembling. He opened his mouth to speak when Twenty-Seven, smiling, tapped him on the shoulder. "All has been carefully planned, and all will go well. Akira, just think about it. You will go down in modern Japanese history as a great hero."

Chapter 4
Kyoto, Japan

Hirobumi Yoshiro slipped off his clothes and shoes in the dressing room and pulled the white seamless garment over his head. A pair of paper sandals waited for him outside the dressing room curtain. He slipped into the sandals and shuffled toward the scanner. After the lights glowed green, a young man stepped out of the scanner room. He bowed to Yoshiro, and said, "This way, Honorable Sir." He pointed to an intersecting hallway a few yards down and led Yoshiro toward it. After turning into the smaller hallway, they walked through a series of rooms and more small hallways. Yoshiro was soon disoriented. He knew the purpose of the long, convoluted walk was to do just that. He admired the minds that created this clever deceit.

The men walked for another few minutes until the guide pushed open a metal door and said, "The files will be sent to you, Honorable Sir. Please sit. This door will remain locked at all times. When you are ready to leave, simply rise from your chair."

Yoshiro entered a small room in which floors, walls, and furniture all seemed formed from a single piece of grey metal. The one metal chair arose from the floor, and the long table in front of the chair cantilevered off the wall. Yoshiro fought a sudden feeling of claustrophobia and looked around him. He examined the room and wasn't surprised to see cameras trained on him from every corner of the ceiling. *There's nothing to do, but sit,* he decided. As soon as he sat, a small metal door in the wall at the far end of the table yawned open, and a metal box slid onto the table. Yoshiro reached over and pulled the box toward him as the small door snapped shut. The metal box was marked "Ise Shrine. 1900 - 1924." He unlatched the lid. Inside the box, stacks of paper were neatly piled and tied together. A fast look at the stacks told him the papers were fastened together by subject and date. He went through each stack and put aside those marked: "1905." He sighed, put on his reading glasses, and untied two sheaves of papers marked, "Reports" and "Duty Rosters."

Chapter 5
Ise

Chieko Shimizu placed the bowl of rice on the tray. "Take this away," she said, pointing to her dinner tray. "It would not be a good idea to eat tonight. You should know that. My body must be clean and pure for tomorrow. Please bring me two bottles of water. Not too cold."

"Princess, the *Saio's* condition has deteriorated very badly. We fear she will not live through the night," said the servant.

"I must speak to her before she dies. I will go to her immediately. Make the arrangements for my transportation. Tell the *Daigugi* to expect me. I will speak to the *Saio* privately. No guards, servants, nurses, or doctors are to be in attendance. See to it. Bring my white kimono. I will wear it. You will help me change my clothes. Quickly. And you will accompany me to the shrine. Instruct the Imperial Guard Yoshiro to ride in the car with us. Bring my bottles of water.... Let me see... Have I forgotten anything?"

"Honorable Princess, you never forget anything."

"No. I do not. I dare not forget anything ever, not ever. It is my responsibility to remember everything.... I shall be making my way to the car as soon as I have my weapons. You know the two I prefer. Bring along a box of ammunition for both. Hurry, and prepare for my departure. I must talk to the *Saio* before she dies."

Chapter 6
Kyoto

Later that evening, Hirobumi Yoshiro travelled to his family house in Kyoto. He regretted that he'd left his wife and children in their home in Ise. He missed them, and particularly wanted his wife at his side to help him face the next few minutes.

The nurse was surprised to see Yoshiro enter the door to the small house. She bowed to him. "Honorable Sir, we did not expect you," she said, bowing yet lower.

"How is she?"

"Honorable Sir, her condition is the same. I have just fed her a little congee, and I am about to prepare her for sleep."

"I need to talk to her first. Please bring me a pot of *genmaicha*." Yoshiro walked quickly to the back of the house where, many years ago, his grandparents had built a bedroom overlooking the garden. The shades were drawn over the large picture windows. In the dim light he found his grandmother sitting up in her recliner chair by the fireplace. The old woman wore headphones over the white cap that covered her bald head as she watched a large television screen on the opposite wall. Yoshiro stood silently and waited for her to notice him. As soon as she saw him, his grandmother picked up the remote control from the chair-side table, clicked off the television, and then pulled off her headphones. She stared at Yoshiro through her thick eyeglasses for a few moments before she said, "What has happened, Hirobumi?"

"Honorable Grandmother, I must speak to you." Yoshiro pulled a hassock over to her chair and sat. He didn't start speaking until the nurse entered the room and put a tea tray on a table beside him. "Shall I pour?" she asked.

"No, thank you. I'll take care of it," Yoshiro said. The nurse nodded and walked quickly back out of the room. Yoshiro rose, closed the bedroom door, and returned to his seat next to the recliner. "Can you hear me, Grandmother?" He asked in a soft trembling voice.

She fumbled putting on her hearing aid and finally asked, "What did you say?"

"I need your help, Grandmother."

"I'm too old to help you or anybody. You can see that."

"Grandmother, first, please understand. I love my country and the Emperor more than my own life."

The ancient woman slowly raised one hand and pushed at the air between them. "You Yoshiro men are all the same," she whispered. 'What of the wives and daughters? Have we no value? I hoped you would be different. You were the most intelligent of our grandchildren. The others did without new clothes and toys that children from other families enjoyed so that we could save money for your training. We remained in this cramped house and ate nothing but rice and pickles so that we would have the money to send you to England and Germany for your education. But your thinking is still like your father's and grandfather's. That thinking plunged us into a terrible war. I love my Emperor and my country, too; but I love my family more. You should do the same," Nikko's voice had risen and echoed in the large room.

"Grandmother, please. I swear I love my family above all else, but I must do my duty. Please, Grandmother, tell me about Grandfather and

84

the *Yata no Kagami*. I know that you know what he did. He told you everything, because he could never keep anything from you. Whatever he didn't tell you, you dug and found out for yourself. Please tell me what you know."

Chapter 7
Portsmouth, New Hampshire

As she arranged the flowers for the altar of St. Peter's Chapel, Sister Anne Farrell fingered the stem of a pink carnation. She remembered that she had taken one just like it from the altar before the funeral. Ever since she had pulled it away from the other flowers, her conscience had dogged her. *It can't have been all that wrong. It was for a good cause. Russell would've appreciated it,* she thought as she contemplated the funeral.

It's very quiet here this morning. Where are the birds? Russell would've liked bird music, I was thinking as I walked toward the gravesite. It was kind of Jerry to give me a ride to the cemetery. He and Ashley could have gone in the funeral parlor's limo. After all, they're family. But I'm glad Jerry decided to drive here himself. He's not by nature a kind man. I'm surprised he offered me a ride. And he sprang for the funeral, too. Will wonders never cease! Well, I guess I'm here because he didn't want only Ashley and himself standing at the graveside.

I shouldn't be thinking about that today, I should be thinking about poor Russell. Oh, the carnation is starting to wilt in this heat. It needs water. Well, yes actually I was stealing, even if nobody will miss one little flower from the altar. I had to do it. Where else was I going to get a flower this morning?

Well, Russell would've danced a jig at my stealing a flower for him.

The nun couldn't help but break into a big smile. She looked up and saw Jerry and Ashley staring at her. Ashley was stifling a giggle, and Jerry scowled. Sister Anne stopped ruminating. At the side of the grave, the minister had his eyes closed as he continued to pray, and she closed her eyes, too. At the minister's "Amen," Sister Anne opened her eyes. She tossed the flower onto the casket as it slowly descended into the open grave.

The casket reached the bottom. Ashley and Jerry picked up and tossed handfuls of dirt onto the cheap coffin which startled the nun: the casket sounded empty.

For an instant sister Anne wondered if Russell was even in the coffin. She shook off the thought as she followed Jerry and Ashley back to Jerry's silver Cadillac. *Well, at the end he was nothing but skin and bones. He's not taking up much room in there*, she decided.

"Sister Anne," said Jerry as he turned onto Middle Street, "I have a trunk load of plastic garbage bags I took from Uncle's room."

"'Trunkload!' scoffed Ashley. "It's only two black garbage bags."

Jerry ignored her comment, and continued, "They're full of old notebooks and scraps of paper. Looks like he kept a kind of diary.

"The paper's not dirty or nothin'. God only knows why he was writin' about his life. He never did nothin', did he? No. All he done was walk around talkin' to himself. That's all he done.

"I looked at some of them scraps. He just wrote about what he had to eat and who he talked to. Boring stuff like that. I don't want them papers, and Ashley can't read. Can you, Dopey?" He punched lightly at Ashley's bony arm. Ashley gave him a side-ways scowl and squirmed closer to the passenger door.

"I can too. I don't want none of his dirty old junk anyways," said Ashley.

"So if you want 'em..." Jerry was saying to Sister Anne at the same time.

"Yes," said the nun. "I had no idea he kept a journal. I'd like to know how his mind worked. You know, he was quite intelligent."

"Pop-pop intelligent? Are you kiddin' me?" Ashley chimed in. "All he knew how to do was dribble, and talk about some stupid bogass treasure. He didn't never have a treasure. Anyway, where would someone like him get one? He ain't never had one. Answer me this: if he had a treasure, how come he didn't have nothing?"

"Well, I didn't know him as well as his family did," said Sister Anne. "I enjoyed the conversations he and I had every now and then, though."

"It's just hard for me to believe the old guy could carry on a conversation," Jerry continued. "All he ever did was walk around mumblin' to himself. That's all. Nobody paid no attention to him. Just you . "So you gonna take his junk... er, papers, or what? "

"Yes, I'd be pleased to have Russell's papers," Sister Anne had said. "I didn't know he could write. His parents neglected him so. They never cared if he went to school."

Well, I cared about Russell, and I hope I've done the right thing, thought Sister Anne, as she later pondered what she had discovered among the scraps of paper in the garbage bags Jerry had given her. Most of Russell's papers had to do with the Japanese treasure that had been his obsession since he was still a child, and the obsession had only increased over time. He wrote about finding a safe hiding place for it, but he moved it more than once. She was attempting to bring order to his papers, so she could discover the last hiding place of the treasure. She'd decided it should be returned to its owner. Nonetheless, she promised herself to put together his autobiography, too, even if it centered on the treasure. Or, she thought guiltily, *because it's centered on the treasure.*

At the bottom of the plastic bag she'd found a roll of papers tied with a hemp cord. When she untied the roll, she was surprised to see that the papers were written in a different language. She couldn't read it, but she recognized the characters. It was Japanese. She knew who to send it to in Japan to have the rice papers translated. She'd sent the package by DSL to Japan days ago.

Chapter 8
Ise Jingu Shrine

"You've known all along," Chieko said to the dying woman. Chieko's eyes blazed with anger and accusation.

"Come closer," the old lady whispered.

The young Chieko Shimizu crept over on her knees to where the old lady lay on her mat. The incense burners had been covered early in the morning, but the old lady's feverish body radiated spicy aromas from her deathbed. Chieko bent low so that her ear was only a few inches from the old woman's mouth. The smell of sandalwood was overwhelming. Even the old *Saio*'s breath smelled of ginger when she whispered, "I am dying now. I have been useless for too long. You must do what I should have done."

"No, Aunt, don't die yet. First, tell me everything," cried Chieko, the next *Saio*.

The old woman pulled at her niece's robe to draw her even closer. "I have so little time left to me. Just listen." Then the old woman whispered with the urgency that her imminent death demanded. What the old woman whispered to her left the young woman as breathless as the Saio. She grabbed at the scarf around her neck to loosen it. She forbade herself from sinking onto the tatami mat flooring as she bent over to hear the final words of her predecessor.

"Forgive me. Forgive me," the old lady whispered, then she seemed to sink deeper into the thin mattress as her mouth and eyes sprang open. Only a slight gagging sound came from her throat. A few moments later, Chieko placed the back of her hand on her aunt's forehead. It seemed to her it was already cooling, although the old woman was not yet dead. She could see a very faint pulse slowly beating in the old woman's neck.

Chieko moaned softly. The temple priest—who also served as the *Daiguji guard*—had been observing the scene from the far corner of the inner shrineroom, and silently ran over. The old lady's eyes and mouth were gaping open as if in terror. Chieko Shimizu was slowly slipping onto the floor. The priest resisted the temptation to grab Chieko before she fell over. No man was allowed to touch the women, even in dire circumstances. He threw a scarf over his sleeve and held out his arm. Chieko only hesitated for an instant before she grabbed onto it. He rose to his feet and pulled her gradually to a standing position. After a few moments she had composed herself and was standing firmly on her feet. Chieko nodded her thanks to the priest. Then, she clapped her hands three times. The rice paper door slid open, and a woman servant came shuffling on her knees into the death room. The servant glanced at the old lady, and leaned over to touch her forehead to the floor in front of the next *Saio*.

Chieko slid down on her knees again. Her attention was focused on the old *Saio*. "I cannot forgive you", Chieko whispered silently as she leaned over and stared at the dying woman. "I will never forgive you or your predecessor. You were both unworthy. You failed in your duty to guard the treasure. You are unworthy of my admiration. I do not honor you."

Chieko rose to her feet and said to the servant at the doorway, "Call Atsuko to come to prepare my aunt for her death. I am going to my quarters. Draw my bath, please. Tell my sister to come to me immediately. Then call the Imperial Guard Yoshiro to my presence in the Ise Geku in one hour." She turned to the *Daiguji*. "Thank you for coming to my assistance. It is time for you to go and prepare the temple for the funeral ritual and my investment ceremony." The *Daiguji* bowed deeply to the next Supreme Priestess and backed out of the door.

A new servant had come in to pull a heavily embroidered silk white cloth over the old woman so that she could be undressed and washed. Chieko said, "The *Saio* is still with us. I will send for you when her spirit leaves. Your duties must wait. Leave now. I must make a telephone call." As soon as the servant left, and slid the door closed behind her, Chieko turned away from the door and drew her small cell phone from her sleeve.

The call was answered after only one ring. "Yes, Princess," a man's voice said.

"Saito-San, I need to see you immediately in the Ise Geku."

"I shall leave at this moment."

"Good," she said, and closed the phone

Chapter 9
Portsmouth

'Hi, Sharon," said the young woman dressed in black as soon as she entered the convent's small visitor's parlor. "You may not remember me; it's been a while. My name's Constance Talant... Connie..." Connie held out her hand to the strikingly beautiful blond woman sitting in the wingback chair facing the doorway. "I guess Sister Anne called you, too. Hmm, you're all in white and I'm all in black. Female Yin-Yang, one might say."

The blond woman held out her hand. "How do you do, Constance." Sharon Meadows spoke softly and politely, but she wasn't smiling.

"Nice to see you again," Connie said, and was about to continue talking, but was interrupted by the opening door and the heavy-set older woman who stood beaming at the two young women. "Look at you! You're my Yin and Yang, right Connie?" said Sister Anne, who then walked quickly forward and grabbed the two women's hands. But you've become reacquainted already," she ended, as she joined the younger women's hands. "I'm so glad to see you both! Sharon, you're looking very well. You're so fair that one wouldn't think that white would look so good on you, but it does. Connie, do you have any clothes that aren't black?"

"Only a naughty red mini night gown," Connie answered.

"But you two are not here to discuss clothing. I've left the teakettle on to boil, so let's get down to it. I've made up folders for both of you," she said, handing each of them a file folder. "Read what's in them first; then we'll discuss why you're here and whether you each want to take on this job. And if so, how much money I'll have to raise in order to pay you. I'll be right back with some tea for us," she said from the doorway.

Some minutes later Sister Anne pushed a loaded tea cart through the door. Both women acknowledged her arrival with a fast glance, but went right back to reading the papers in their file folders. Sister Anne wordlessly poured two cups of tea and set them on the side tables next to the women's chairs. She poured a cup for herself, sat down on the hard settee, and waited.

Sharon was the first to break the silence in the room after she put aside her folder. "First, Sister Anne, you don't have to raise money to pay me. I'll see if I can get a percentage of what the Japanese government pays for the retrieval of their treasure. We can talk about that later. Second, you're to stay here. You can't go on the search. I'm assuming a nun won't or can't use a firearm. And I won't have time to babysit, so you'd be more hindrance than help. In other words, you don't have any further role in this hunt."

Sharon turned to Constance Talant. "Connie, I've been described as a 'hired gun.' A little dramatic, but that's close enough as to what I can do and who I am. How are you in difficult situations? Are you willing to kill if you have to? If not, it's time for you to bow out of this job, too. I can handle it alone."

"Target practice with my Walther handgun is my favorite pastime. I'll shoot to mame, but not to kill. And I was a licensed tai kwan do instructor. I can take care of myself."

"Playing is far from the real thing, isn't it? The real question is: are you any good in the field with a weapon or in martial arts?"

"Expert in both."

"You better be. I'll have your back and expect you to have mine."

"Others will be joining you," said Sister Anne.

"What others?" both Connie and Sharon asked. Sharon added, "We don't need others."

Chapter 10

"This year the Portsmouth town government, with the aid of the Japan Society, has decided to celebrate the hundredth anniversary of the signing of the Russo-Japanese Treaty," said Helen Hudson, the eighty-three-year-old President of the Society. "We were able to find some of the descendants of the Treaty signers, but they're unable to accept an invitation to the celebration," she continued. "However, the town was finally able to contact a descendant of the Imperial Guard to the original delegation. The man's name is Hirobumi Yoshiro. He has agreed to come and will be arriving from Japan in a few weeks.

"It was not easy to find the Yoshiro man. We had sent an invitation to Yoshiro Seiji, the son of Yoshiro Kenishi, the treaty guard of 1905, to come to Portsmouth to celebrate the anniversary. Kenishi is, of course, deceased. But the almost ninety-year-old Seiji declined the invitation because of his ill health and advanced age. Seiji's son, Yoshiro Isamu, is occupied with important business matters, and can't participate just now. The family finally decided to send the youngest man of the Yoshiro family, Hirobumi, Kenishi's great-grandson. We are delighted that he is coming."

Sister Anne, one of the original members of the Japan Society, sat quietly with the others in the Levenson Room of the Portsmouth Library. She remembered little Hirobumi. Well, he wasn't little anymore. By her reckoning he was in his late twenties, maybe early thirties. She was so looking forward to seeing the boy again. *He probably doesn't even remember me. He was so young. I was only a teenager myself. Well, almost twenty, and my hair was brown, and not grey, and I was quite a few pounds thinner, too. I'll bet he could have translated Russell's papers, if I showed them to him.* In the next instant she wondered if it was wise to show the papers to anyone other than the one Japanese man she knew personally and trusted.

A month ago she'd sent copies of Russell's papers to Hirobumi's grandfather, her old friend, Yoshiro Seiji. She hoped he would know what they were. She had a strong feeling they were written by Seiji's father, Yoshiro Kenishi, when he was in Portsmouth for the signing of the treaty in 1905. The papers Russell found were discolored and brittle. In some places, the copies were barely readable. Anne had taken the time to examine them closely. And she was confident that the papers had belonged to Yoshiro Kenishi. He had written mostly in Japanese. But every now and then she could make out in faded ink an August or September date or a word written in English. Her old friend, Seiji, was in his nineties and almost blind, but she was hopeful he could still see a little since they continued to write little notes on their Christmas cards to each other every year. She was anxious to discuss the papers with him.

She'd gone to the Athenaeum and public library to learn about the treaty and make copies of the papers. After some minutes of research, she learned that the Japanese ambassadors to the treaty negotiations in 1905 were men named Komura Jutaro and Togoro Takahira. She didn't think Russell had found their papers. Those ministers were too important. All of their papers would have been saved in a Japanese archive somewhere. After plowing through them, she was certain that Russell's papers had belonged to Yoshiro Kenishi. He had just been a guard, not a delegate. His papers wouldn't have had any historical significance to the delegation at that time. She thought that maybe the papers were pages from his journal or at least his notes while he was in Portsmouth.

Poor man. She'd read in the old newspapers that Kenishi had drowned after he went swimming in the Piscataqua River on August 30, 1905, after both sides had agreed to the treaty terms. His body had washed up down river from the Wentworth Hotel. Portsmouth authorities insisted it was necessary to conduct an investigation into the death. But the Japanese authorities politely refused it, saying that they would conduct their own investigation. Japanese servants had quickly taken Yoshiro's body back to their ship that was sailing for Japan that same evening. *A sad ending,* the nun thought. *If these were Kenishi's papers, I should give them to Hirobumi. He would be interested to have something of his forefather's.* Then, she thought further. *Because Kenishi was an eye-witness to the historic event, his papers might be valuable today. Yes. They would. I'm sure of it. I'll ask Hirobumi to donate them to the Portsmouth Historical Society. Well, not if they're a suicide letter. And if that's the case, I don't want to cause the young man any pain, either.*

Chapter 11
Ise Jengu

Chieko Shimizu stared up at the opening door and jumped to her feet. When she saw the guard's haggard face, she gasped and whispered, "What has happened, Hirobumi? What can I do to help you?"

"My legs do not wish to support me. May I sit, please?" the Imperial Guard asked. He dropped to his knees onto the tatami mat. Slowly sitting back on his heels as if he were an old man, he reached inside his guard's uniform and pulled out a roll of papers. His hands fell to his lap as if the papers were too heavy for one man to hold. "I cannot talk. Here. Read," he said, thrusting out the roll to the young woman.

"Hirobumi, you are frightening me. No." She pushed the papers away from her. "How can you be so cruel to your oldest friend? If these have brought you to such a state, why do you wish to inflict the same pain on me? No," she said again. She grabbed the papers from his still outstretched hand and threw the roll high against the wall of the large reception room. The roll came undone on impact, and sheets of papers fluttered to the floor. Hirobumi struggled to his feet and walked slowly over. He bent down to pick up the papers. Then he knelt once more and shuffled them into order. He turned back to Chieko and held the papers out to her. "Here. You must read. Please. It is your duty." He turned away so she wouldn't see the tears that continued to roll down his face.

Chieko took the handfuls of paper and stared down at them. "The writing is faded on these copies. Before I read, tell me what these are and where you found them."

The young man sighed deeply and, turning away from Chieko, wiped away the tears on his face. "They are..." he whispered, and couldn't go on.

"What, Hiro? They are what?" The young woman demanded, pushing the papers into his hand.

"They are copies of the journal of my forefather, Yoshiro Kenishi," he finally whispered so softly that she had to strain to hear him.

"Yoshiro Kenishi? The Imperial Guard who died in America? Give them to me," she said, grabbing back the papers.

Chapter 12
Portsmouth

"Sister Anne," Connie Talant said to the old woman, "all this is hard to believe." Connie pushed the file folder across her office desk to the nun. "But, of course, because it's you, I want to believe it. So what do you need from me? Everything in here is about something that may have happened a hundred years ago. I say 'may have happened' because you took the word of a dirty old bum who died—what did you say?—about three months ago? Did you actually see the treasure he wrote about? And what's the urgency now?"

"Constance, to me, Russell Hartz was not a dirty old bum. He was a man who, I believe, was as much sinned against, as sinned. He lived a long time. A very long time to suffer. He was over a hundred and ten years old when he died. That's what he claimed to be, but nobody ever cared enough to check. It would have been easy enough, because he was born right here in Portsmouth. But nobody bothered to look up his birth records. I do not accuse only others of neglect. I, myself, never looked to find his exact date of birth. Well, it seemed intrusive and not really relevant to his life.

"In one of our many long conversations, he confessed he was a congenital liar, but he said he would try hard to tell me the truth. I don't know why exactly, but I believed him. I guess it's because I had known him practically all my life."

"You couldn't have been childhood friends," Connie said. "He was more than a generation older than you."

"You're right. We weren't childhood friends. I met him when he used to hang around the boats. I was always at the boatyard when I was a kid—well, when Mama allowed it. Papa had a fishing boat he named after my favorite literary character. He called it Maid Marian. Do you remember your grandfather's fishing boat? Probably not. It was little more than driftwood by the time you were born."

Sister Anne thought for a moment, before she said, "I don't know what Russell was doing at the boats. I don't think he had anyplace else to go. And the boatyard was always bustling with activity. Maybe he liked that. When he was little, he liked to be in the middle of all the action. And the boatmen didn't mind him hanging around. People said you could see it on his face, how much he loved being there.

"I don't know what happened to him in later life that made him so afraid of people. When he was young, he said the boatmen all liked having him around. He was built small. The men all teased him about being a tiny shrimp that should have been thrown back. Russell loved it when they made a fuss over him, even if it was for their own amusement.

"A couple of times I saw him sneaking out of a boat that its owner had covered up tight for the season. I think maybe he spent the night on those boats. Or maybe he just crawled into one of them to get away from the world for a little while. I don't know. And I never told on him. That seemed the wrong thing to do.

"When he was a kid, every now and then somebody would throw him a little job at the boatyard. He was like a fixture that was always there. Nobody paid much attention to him. They let him have the run of the place. They only noticed when he wasn't around. You'd hear: 'Where's Russell? Anyone see Russell today? That scamp.' They liked having him around. I don't know how to explain it. He was like their mascot. No. He was like a mirror to them. When they talked to him, it was like they were talking to themselves. Golly, I haven't thought about those days for a very long time. This must be boring for you."

"Not at all," Constance said, "It never occurred to me that nuns had a childhood." They both laughed. "Go on. Tell me more about Russell."

"Good ol' Russell. I don't know if I liked him or not. I didn't *not* like him. I guess, like the men, he was just like a fixture that was always there. But I tried to always talk to him, directly to him. As you said, I was much younger than he was.

"Russell seemed ageless to me. He wasn't dirty. And he wasn't stupid. He was uneducated, but very intelligent. I found him interesting, especially when he talked about his treasure. Sometimes tears would run down his face. He told me the treasure had cost too many lives. I don't know what he meant by that. I asked him, but he would only look away and cry harder.

"We were kind of like friends, even though we were much different in ages. Now that I think of it, Russell was like a pet to the boatmen. I'm sure they knew he slept on their boats. But Russell was very clean about himself. I wouldn't be surprised if he left his 'bedrooms' cleaner than when he found them. I often wondered about his treasure and where it was. Did he hide it on one of the fishermen's boats? If so, it must have been quite small, whatever it was. Boatmen treat their boats like babies. They take care of every inch of them. If he hid it on a boat, it would have been found by now. That's for sure.

"Listen to me prattling on and on about him."

"He made a lasting impression on you, I guess."

"You'd never think it to look at him, but I think he did. I know he'd like that idea. As I said, nobody paid him much attention when he was alive. Even the cops. He was like a street lamp that won't light. They didn't notice him unless he wasn't there."

The nun pulled her rosary beads from her pocket and was silent until Connie said "I guess you two were closer than you imagined."

"Maybe so. Isn't that often the case? Dead people seem to occupy the mind. Maybe it's their spirits prompting you to remember them. Oh, never mind that. That's old lady talk. When he fell sick, I think he knew he wasn't going to make it. He wrote me a note and asked me to come to visit him. It's sad to think he had no one closer to him he wanted to ask. Then, I thought maybe because I'm a nun, he felt he should get some religion now that the end was near. That's what I hoped. Russell didn't go to any church that I know of. It's a subject we never talked about, even though I tried to bring it up several times.

"No. He didn't want to see me at the end because of my vocation. I learned that fast enough. He didn't mention God at all. I guess he was an atheist, not even an agnostic. That's another reason why my heart went out to him. I think atheists must be very sad people. Well, we don't have to discuss that now either, do we?" she asked rhetorically.

"I went to see him when I got his note asking me to come. His room was filled with shopping bags stuffed with anything you could think of. His room only had a bed in it. He used the shopping bags as bureau drawers and closets. But his living arrangements were not dirty or smelly. No, Russell was bad at shaving, but he kept himself and his room neat and clean. He didn't own very much so his room was easy to keep tidy. I guess because his clothes were so raggedy, people also thought they were dirty. But they weren't. Russell was basically a clean man. Even his shopping bags were carefully lined up against the wall of his room.

"Well, when I went to see him after I got his note, he asked me to take all this." She pointed to the shopping bags brimming over with papers. Jerry Jenkins gave them to me after the funeral.

"Russell said the papers were the only valuable things he owned, and he wanted me to have them. He said if I would read them all, I'd learn a surprise. "

"And did you?" asked Connie.

"Yes. I learned Russell had hidden something he called his 'treasure.' He mentions it throughout the papers. And he moved it from place to place."

"What was his treasure?"

Sister Anne chuckled. "I don't know. When I brought them back to the convent I shoved the bags in an old coal bin and mostly forgot about them. Just recently I've thought about them and decided to go through them. It's time I put them in the trash. I've sorted and read about half of these scraps of paper. I read them carefully. I still don't know what his treasure was or where he finally hid it. Look at these two bags. They practically take up half of my tiny study. I would be glad to cart them over to your office. I just can't find more time to look through them. I'm ashamed to say I've neglected some of my duties because of them. Oh, not the duties other people depend on. I wouldn't do that. But... well, I must put all of Russell's papers aside now. I hate to do it. But I have responsibilities that need tending to. I believe he wanted them read. I feel guilty that I'm not acting according to his wishes."

"I'll help read them," said Connie. "I'm fascinated to think the papers could lead to a genuine treasure. Let's take them over to my office."

As they were walking to Connie's office, Sister Anne continued her almost obsessive dialogue about Russell. Both Connie and Sharon listened attentively while navigating the worn brick sidewalks.

"One has to be suspicious of anything Russell said, and no doubt, wrote. And, I think Russell's idea of a treasure and yours or mine would be completely different. But, thank you, I don't think he'd mind if you read his papers. I've had time to sort through only some of his grocery bags. I was determined not to rush through them. Not so much because of his so-called treasure. Heaven only knows what that could be.

"Well, I just assume what he wrote meant something to him. I've made up files according to what he was writing about: people, his health, even the weather. He put the date, day, and time on every sheet. But, he didn't use years, just months and days. Although, I must say his life was uneventful. Mostly he wrote about what he saw, did, and felt. I'm putting together a kind of psycho-biography of Russell Hartz. Not by date. You can't trust his dates.

"I like to think that when Russell died, God let him into Heaven to make up for his miserable life. But my good sense tells me that couldn't be true. Russell was coarse, dishonest, and unkind. And those might have been his best characteristics. But that's what his life taught him to be. Well, I'm not being completely fair. He returned in kind. If a person was good to him, he tried to be the same. If he just couldn't bring himself to be polite, he learned to keep his mouth shut. Oh, enough of this. You want to know about his treasure.

"You will read about Russell's treasure when you go through the files I've put together. Well, not *his* treasure—*a* treasure.... Oh, I just remembered: In a note that he once taped to my bicycle, he asked me to send the treasure back to its owner. But he never told me what it was or what he did with it. I thought that perhaps I would one day search for it, and then return it to its owner.

"On the other hand, I'm not absolutely convinced the treasure actually exists. It might just be a story he amused himself writing. I wouldn't put that past him. Honesty was not something he valued. It would be like him to be up in Heaven or down in Hell now laughing at me and my efforts on his behalf. But I don't care. I'm doing it as much for Portsmouth as for Russell."

"What do you mean?"

"I think people here should get to know a man who spent his whole life in their midst. So far as I can tell, the people of Portsmouth won't be inclined to celebrate his life no matter how well I'm able to write his story. But they will have to acknowledge that he lived among them. Perhaps that's enough."

"I don't understand what good that would do," Sharon observed.

"Perhaps none. But no one should pass through life unnoticed. I believe he had a story to tell. He liked to talk. You couldn't shut him up when he was young. As an old man, he was a mumbler. And then there's his treasure."

"You just said you weren't sure there was a treasure," Sharon reminded her.

"I know. But I think he believed there was one. So, I've never known if it was real or not, and I made a conscious decision not to ask him what the truth was. On the other hand, others may have believed he knew the whereabouts of a treasure. On the third hand, a part of me wants to believe his stories. Sometimes I think I should follow through and search. It's become one of my many 'Someday Projects'. I must stop doing that. I don't have that many 'somedays' left.

"I wouldn't know where to start looking anyway. He was all over the Seacoast and out to the Isles. Instead of wandering around and digging holes to look for his treasure, I'm spending my life in the convent praying and teaching. It's my job. If you don't do your job, then what are you? You know the old German saying: 'A man is what he does.' That goes for women, too. It's an existential concept, isn't it? A nun dedicates her life to God and good works. She doesn't go searching for a treasure. Hmmmm. So much for my thirst for adventure. My, it's hot in here, isn't it?" the nun eyed the casement air conditioner.

"Sorry, it doesn't work, and I can't afford a new one," Connie said.

"The sun's starting to dip. Let's go down to Prescott Park. There must be a breeze out by the water." She reached over and opened the refrigerated box. "I'll just grab a couple of bottles of water. Let's go." The women got up and walked to the door. Connie pulled a small ring of keys out of her backpack. "Don't know why I bother," she said, turning the key in the lock. "Nobody seems to want to walk through this door. And they'd do me a favor if they stole some of my old junk furniture that I rescued from people's sidewalks during cleanup weeks. That sign painter, Joseph Stein, did a good job on the window, though, didn't he?" They turned to admire the black lettering on the door: TALANT SEARCHES.

"Maybe you're not getting work because people think you're a talent scout. There can't be that many people in Portsmouth, New Hampshire who long to be movie, television, or Broadway stars," said the nun.

"I thought of that, and yes, a few stage-type moms who can't spell have dragged their cutesy little kids in. Joe's coming back next week to put 'Private Investigator' in smaller letters under 'Talant Searches.' But someone did come in a week ago to give me a job to follow his wife. That's a crappy way of earning a living, but I need the work. I try to stay away from any of those types of jobs that appear to be too scruffy. But who am I kidding? They're all scruffy. Hopefully better jobs will come in and my business will be up and running. I was doing pretty well in Boston—but then, that's Boston, not wholesome, sleepy, Portsmouth."

"If you'll excuse me," Sharon said, "I need to go check in at the Sheraton. Connie, I'll catch up with you later." Without pause, Sharon stood up and, after touching Sister Anne's shoulder, strode out of the office. The nun and her niece watched Sharon's white-clad figure melt into the bright hot air as she stepped through the open door frame. The nun then turned her attention to personal matters.

"Constance, I believe what you need is a good, steady job in a service industry that helps people, "said Sister Anne without missing a beat. "You are by nature and upbringing generous and intelligent. You could spend your time benefitting mankind, not scraping, looking for bottom feeders. I take it your trust fund hasn't run out yet. I hope not."

"From your mouth to God's ears." Connie grinned. "It isn't much, and I'm working my way through it. But you know me. I don't live high on the hog. I'm good at scrounging meals at my parents', and mom always sends me away with heavy care packages."

"So will you take on my assignment?" Sister Anne asked. "I can afford to pay a little, but you know..."

"You can't think I'd take money from you, Aunt Annie. Get outta here!... I just leafed through that one file you gave me to read. Leave the files with me. Leave those trash bags with me. Sharon and I will sort and organize the papers, as we read. But here's my question. Not everything was written by Hartz, right? There are some sheets written in... what? Japanese? Chinese? They appear to be copies, not the originals. Where did he get those? Do you know what they are?"

Sister Anne hadn't walked out onto the sidewalk yet. She said, "Constance, let's not walk just yet. I have many things to tell you, and I want to show you some of the papers that I know are important. We'll leave your door open and hope cool air and not just dust blows in. How would that be? After that we'll go to the park. Is that okay?"

"Sure, that's okay with me. You want to tell me why? Never mind. We'll just stay comfy here.

"Here's my biggest question," Connie continued. "Why has this become so important to you now? These things happened a hundred years ago. So, why now?" They walked back into the office. Connie picked up the plastic bag, opened it wide, dived in, and brought out sheets of paper. "Here. Look at these. These papers weren't written by Russell Hartz unless he could write Chinese or Japanese." Connie looked at the papers more closely. "It's Japanese. I learned enough in college to know the difference between written Japanese and Chinese. But I can't read either one. What a mountain of work! Do you really think anybody besides you really cares about the scratchings of a nutty old guy, even if he knew how to write Japanese?" Connie lightly slapped down another folder of papers onto her desk.

"As I tried to organize the papers, I read what I could," Sister Anne answered. "Constance, the more I read, the closer I came to believe there really is a treasure hidden somewhere in or near Portsmouth. You see the copies of rolls of rice paper that were written in Japanese? I brought them to the library and made copies. I couldn't read them, but I have a friend who can. I think they hold the key to the treasure.

"I still correspond with friends I met in Japan when I was a missionary there. I sent the copies to one of them. I've heard back from him. He was so excited, he actually called me. I was happy to hear his voice, but not what he said.

"If he's right, Connie, there's a great cause to worry. Let's take that walk now. I think it might be best to be moving,"

"Sister Anne, what are you worried about? You're afraid someone's listening to our conversation? Who? What's going on?" Connie asked. She hesitated a moment, then she unlocked her desk drawer, pulled out her small Smith & Wesson handgun, and slipped it into her back holster. She shrugged on a lightweight jacket to cover it.

"I don't think that's necessary, yet," said the nun. "I'll tell you why this matter has taken on an urgency now. But let's wait until we're outside." Connie pulled her swollen office door tight behind them, and the two women descended the stairs to street level.

"I can't pursue this matter by myself," Sister Anne said as soon as they started walking down Bow Street. "I need help, from you and Sharon. But I don't want to put you in jeopardy. Still, I need someone to follow through on this for me. I would have to get permission from the Mother Superior in Massachusetts to pursue this, and it's not likely I'll get it. I'll ask anyway. I'm risking my order's severe disapproval, but I must do this. And I know I can't do it alone.

"But, you two can't handle this situation alone either," the nun continued after they'd walked toward the water. "You'll need help. According to my Japanese friend—his name is Yoshiro Seiji—these papers are very valuable. It has to do with a situation that could cause a national emergency in Japan. I don't know what he means by that. He also tells me Russell's treasure is the crux of the situation and searching for it could create a good deal of chaos not only in Japan, but also in the United States. Bad trouble. Dangerous trouble. People could be hurt or killed."

"Sister Anne, it sounds like this is not a job for amateurs. Do you remember Jeff Savage? He works at the NSA now. Let's talk to him." Sister Anne nodded her agreement. "Do you think Russell's so-called treasure is here in Portsmouth?" Connie asked. "You said he used to travel the Seacoast quite a bit."

"I think he would keep his treasure close to him. I would. Wouldn't you? So, it's probably in Portsmouth, or near here. I don't know. His papers will tell us. We have to find out what Russell did with the treasure. My friend's grandson, Hirobumi Yoshiro, is coming with others to the United States to help us find it. There'll be three coming to help. Perhaps it's best not to get our government involved in this yet."

"What in heaven's name is the interest in all of this? If there's danger, where's it coming from?" Connie asked.

"Seiji told me a powerful Japanese organization of fanatics and dissidents has found out why Hirobumi is coming to the United States. They know it's about the treasure, and they want it. I don't know how they found out, and I don't know why it's important to them," Sister Anne said. "Perhaps it's worth a lot of money. Seiji tells me the organization is a fanatical cult, and it's sending members here to find Russell's treasure. I don't know how many are coming to Portsmouth. But it seems to me they're coming to find it not just because it's worth a lot of money, but for other reasons. I don't know what the reasons are.

"Read this letter that Seiji faxed me, Constance. He wrote it in English for my sake. It should tell you a great deal about the dangerous people we could be up against."

"We? And how did we get from shopping bags of dirty papers to dangerous outsiders coming from Japan to Portsmouth to make trouble?"

"Yes, 'we.' I am hiring you to help me find the treasure. But you must be aware that the venture is dangerous. You once said you're quite proficient with firearms. You might have to be. It's also good that Sharon has joined us. She is very much a woman warrior. For myself, I firmly believe in the principle of non-violence, but that doesn't mean I can't help in other ways, Constance. Above all, we must prevent the cult from getting the treasure. My understanding is that it belongs to all the Japanese people."

"Sharon is right that you should back out of this," said Connie.

"I can't do that," Sister Anne answered.

Chapter 13
Tokyo, Japan

"What's your name?"

"I don't have to talk to you. I want my lawyer."

The guard laughed and turned to Hirobumi Yoshiro, and said with a large grin, "The kid wants his lawyer. He's been watching too many American movies." He turned back to the young man who could have been any one of the hundreds of university students and others who crowded the Ginza. The guard pulled a black robe from the youth's book bag. "Now what's this?" The guard asked with a grin. "Isn't this what you were looking for?" he asked Yoshiro, throwing the robe to him.

Yoshiro grabbed the robe and said to the young man, "I'm going to the meeting in your place tonight. You'll be released later, and the robe will be returned to you. Right?" he asked the guard, who nodded. "Little man, if I were you I wouldn't tell anyone about this," Yoshiro said. "The Cabal won't like it. They punish members who get careless. You know that. The police launch will be fishing your body out of Tokyo Bay tomorrow morning. If you get what I mean." Yoshiro bundled the robe under his arm, saluted his fellow guard, and ambled out of the station.

Chapter 14

Twenty-Seven stared at the gathering of men who stood in hooded long red robes below him. His was the only face that was uncovered. The others' hoods were pulled down low and except for their eyes, the hoods completely covered the men's faces. Numbers were stenciled on their hoods. Other men stood in the back of the auditorium. They wore long hooded black robes and masks without numbers.

Under his glossy black hair, which was pulled into a tight topknot, Twenty-Seven's handsome face was damp with sweat that highlighted the sharp angles of his cheekbones and jaw. His silver-threaded scarlet kimono picked up points of light. In the soft spot-lights on the raised platform he gleamed like a ghostly apparition.

His apostles stood mesmerized as Twenty-Seven stormed back and forth in front of them, as graceful as a ballet dancer. He thrust his arms into the air. His kimono swirled around his swiftly moving slim body. He glowed in the semi-darkness. Suddenly he stood quivering with his knees slightly bent as if he were about to leap into the assembly of men. Then, quickly straightening up and standing on his toes, he drew his sword from its scabbard, brandished the sword above his head, and screamed, "The people are Japan. The people must take Japan into the modern age. The people are Japan. Say it," he shouted and the men shouted his words back.

"Japan belongs to all the people. Say it."

The men shouted back obediently.

"Japan belongs to all of us. Announce it to the world. A New Japan is proudly marching into the twenty-first century. Imperial Japan is finished. Say it."

His men screamed back: "Imperial Japan is finished."

"You apostles in the back: Imperial Japan is finished. Say it."

The black robed men in the back of the auditorium screamed, "Imperial Japan is finished."

Twenty-Seven then swiftly sheathed his sword. "Listen to me," he exhorted in a voice that was now hardly more than a whisper, so that even the men in the front had to strain to hear him. "The sacred regalia belong to all of us, not just to the Emperor." Twenty-Seven leaned over and stared at one of the young men who stood in the second row gazing up at him. "What did you say, Nine?" He asked the young man who had lowered his eyes when Twenty-Seven singled him out.

"Nothing important, Sir."

"Well, what was it? Tell us all. We all want to hear your words of wisdom."

"Sir, I have no words of wisdom. I am not wise. I only meant to say that the Imperial regalia was given to the first Emperor by the gods," the young man whispered.

Twenty-Seven drew himself up to his full height. "I stand before you as your elected servant," he thundered. "Look at me! Am I not your elected servant? Are we not all your servants?" He pointed at his chest and then at his guards who were also the only men in traditional kimonos. They all wore scarlet headbands that dropped down and covered their faces, and swords hanging from the scabbards around their waists. "Am I not Twenty-Seven? Am I not the personification of your Will and Determination? Am I not your Facilitator?" Everyone in the room nodded vigorously. Even Hirobumi Yoshiro, who perspired in his black robe, nodded.

Twenty-Seven turned back and glared at the terrified Nine whose hood had been torn off his head. Sweat ran off the young man's face and into the collar of his robe. "You are among the chosen, and yet you doubt? You question? You are one of the enemy who wallow in the superstition that's preventing Japan from ruling the world?"

"No," the young man screamed. "No," he screamed again.

Twenty-Seven nodded to two giant-sized men who stood guarding the main door and had been staring at their leader expectantly. In a few moments they stood on either side of the young man and, hands under his armpits, hustled him out of the room. One of the guards pulled Nine's hood back on to the young man's head, and placed his fat hand over the man's mouth to stifle his screams. "We will need to raise another to Nine," the Facilitator said softly to the others.

His voice rose again. "The ETA Cabal has thrived for more than two hundred years because we love Japan and the people love us. Time and again we have saved our Japan from its enemies. Is there any one else in the room who doubts our mission? Does anyone here believe our forefathers in the Cabal were wrong? Does anyone among the brethren believe our hard-working forefathers, the heroes who worked so hard on our behalf, were wrong? Is there any one else among us who loves the Imperial family more than Japan? Is there anyone standing here who doesn't understand the Imperial leaches are killing us? They almost killed us before. Are you going to let them kill us now? I have sworn in your name to destroy that kind of thinking before it destroys our beloved country. We are Japan. We are *Nippon*. We are the Land of the Rising Sun. Not those morons who live in the palace. Is there any one else who loves anything or anyone more than our country?"

All the hooded figures shook their heads and stamped their feet.

One stood tall and said, "Excellent Father, tell us what we must do. We will go home and organize our people, and it will be done as you order.... We are the people of the Rising Sun!" He screamed.

Chapter 15
Ise Jengu

"Sister," said Chieko Shimizu, "you are privileged to be the first of service to the next *Saio*."

Hideko Shimizu knelt before her twin sister and whispered. "However I can serve you, dear sister, is my pleasure."

Chieko leaned closer and spoke in tones so low her sister had to strain to hear her. Some moments later Hideko stared into Chieko's face. "Of course, dear sister, I shall do your bidding, but what can be done?" Hideko asked. "It is impossible. Where are you going? Why? If it is discovered..."

"Only our old family servant, Atsuko, will know. I have ordered the others to stay out of the death chamber. They will not disobey. Atsuko and the Imperial Guards will keep everyone away. I will return as quickly as possible. In the meantime, help the *Saio* to remain alive as long as you can. You must sit at her side day and night in my robes. Keep your face turned away. We look so much alike in our figure, and have the same mannerisms. No one will suspect it is not me in attendance. Atsuko and her daughter will do whatever needs to be done to insure that. Trust no one else. Do you understand? Trust no one else."

Chieko shuffled over to the old woman and whispered, "Do not die, Auntie, until I return. I know you hear me, and I know you will not die until you wish to die. As the new *Saio*, I am ordering you not to die until I return. I am going on a mission to do what was your duty to prevent. Stay alive until I return. It is the least you can do," she said angrily. Chieko stood up and walked quickly to her private door where the old retainer, Atsuko, stood waiting. "You heard?" The old woman nodded. "You understand the situation?" she asked Atsuko. The woman nodded again. "I am counting on you. Send for your daughter. Only you two women and my sister are allowed in this chamber. The guards will be stationed outside the doors. I will order the others to stay out. All of Japan is counting on you and my dear sister. Do not fail," said the next *Saio*.

Chapter 16
Tokyo, Japan

The sword master bowed to Twenty-Seven and said, "Honorable Sir, it is always my pleasure to exercise my skills with you. Of all my pupils, you are the best."

Twenty-Seven said, "These toys are fine for a good leg exercise," he tossed his epee to an assistant, "but I much prefer my sword." He strode across the gym floor and pulled the sword from its housing. He brandished it over his head. "What is a more satisfying weapon than a Samurai sword?" he asked the men who had assembled to watch the experts in their swordplay.

"Nor is there anything more beautiful," agreed the sword master. "Unfortunately," he continued, "these sacred weapons are useless in today's world."

As he spoke, two black-robed men came into the gym. The young woman between them held onto their arms as they dragged her into the warm room. "What have you there?" asked Twenty-Seven.

The older of the men answered, "This woman said it is urgent that she talk to you."

"Come out here," Twenty-Seven said to the woman, as he slid aside a door to the inner courtyard. "Master, you accompany us, but keep your distance." Twenty-Seven used his sword to gently nudge away the servants who were waiting for him. "Get my lunch ready," he said. "And close the door." Then he led the woman across the courtyard to a secluded corner. "Go ahead. Talk."

"Sir," the woman looked boldly, and Twenty-Seven believed seductively, into his eyes, "my name is..."

"We don't have names here. What do you want?"

"Sir, I am one of the tea girls of the *Saio*."

"And?" Twenty-Seven took practice lunges as he waited. "Get to the point," he ordered.

"Sir, the *Yata no Kagami* is missing."

Twenty-Seven stopped in a full lunge position, then slowly drew back his sword and stood up straight. He held the sword down toward the ground. "What does that have to do with me?... Oh, well, go on," he said. He cast his eyes down to the ground, too, so she wouldn't see the gleam of interest.

"Sir, the mirror was stolen. It is in America. Chieko Shimizu, the next *Saio*, is leaving this afternoon to find it and bring it back to *Ise Jingu*.

"Did she send you here to trick me?" He growled.

"No, Sir."

"Did anyone else send you to trick me? Tell the truth, if you know what is good for you."

"No, Sir. No one sent me. I came of my own accord. My cousin is a black-robe. He told me all about you and the brotherhood. I admire you greatly. I am here to ask that you allow me to join. And if you want to help me support my old mother..."

"You just called it a 'brotherhood.' That is exactly what it is. No women are welcome to join us. But you will be rewarded for this valuable information." He turned to the men who had come in with the woman. "Gentlemen, take this lady's arms so that I may give her a reward." The men ran over as Twenty-Seven raised his sword. He brought it swiftly across the air and split the front of the woman's body open. She looked down in disbelief, then horror, before she collapsed onto the ground. "Take it away," he said to the men. To the sword master who had stood silently watching, Twenty-Seven said, "You see, Master, there are still some good uses for the sword." He turned to the servants who had stood aside watching, "Clean up this mess," he said as he wiped the sword with his kimono sleeve. "And get me clean garments. The woman was juicy."

Chapter 17
Ise Jingu

To Commander Hirobumi Yoshiro's surprise, Chieko Shimizu came out from behind her modesty screen. She stared into the guard's eyes. "Yes," she said, "it is as it has always been. I can still see into your soul." Finally, she said, "Come out here with me, my friend." She led him into the peony pavilion from which they had a full view of the garden. No one else was outside enjoying the beauty of the spring day. "No one is to enter or disturb us," Hirobumi had ordered his men before going into the garden.

Chieko sat on a cedar bench. Yoshiro knelt a few feet from her and stared down at the grass. "Hiro," she said in the soft voice he knew so well, "I am appointing Honda Shohei to temporarily replace you as head of the Ise Guard."

Yoshiro's head rose sharply. He stared at her in surprise. "Why? Do you no longer trust me because of what you read in my forefather's papers? Have I displeased you in any way?"

"Quite the contrary. Hiro, my friend, I need you to go with me to retrieve what Yoshiro Kenishi lost. I must myself go and do this now, before the old *Saio* dies. It is my duty. I need you to go with me. In this world too many people still believe a woman is incapable of achieving a warrior goal. I need you along to give me legitimacy in those ignorant people's eyes. And I believe you would desire to go. When I am *Saio* I will be forbidden ever again to leave the sacred temple grounds. You know that. I must leave immediately while I can. There will be danger. The Twenty-Seven Cabal has found out."

"At this moment the honor is too great for me to bear. My only desire is to serve you and bring honor back to my family name. The Twenty-Seven will be dangerous enemies."

"You are willing to fight by my side?"

"Honorable One, your Samurai skills are as finely honed as any man's. I told my honorable father that during our last sword practice, you kept up with me. Your prowess with the sword is as good as mine. Better. You have more patience and do not attack heedlessly. I am only fit to be your servant. Father says you are as good with a firearm as you are with the sword. My only wish is to earn the honor you are bestowing on me. You know, Supreme One, that my life belongs to you. I shall fight to the death beside you with gratitude. Whatever you wish of me shall be done."

Chieko Shimizu rose to her feet and stared at the kneeling guard. "I know that of all men, Hiro, you are my oldest and dearest friend," she said. I also know that you love Japan, and above all others, I can trust you. You are invaluable to me. But even so, I also know the pain you are feeling because of Yoshiro Kenishi's... Never mind, I will not twist the knife in your wound.

"Ah my friend, how well I know you. I am concerned. If you cannot separate out your emotions... Oh, this is very, very difficult." Chieko sank back down on the bench.

Hirobumi made a reflexive move to assist her, but held back. "Highness, you know that I would slit my own throat before I would utter one word about this. It is a matter of great shame to me."

Tears filled her eyes, as Chieko whispered, "And you know that I, Chieko, am your friend. I will always be your friend. However, when I am the new *Saio*, my duty will come before everything, even friendship. You understand that?" Yoshiro nodded.

"I can hardly get the words out of my mouth, but I must." Chieko wiped away the tears that she couldn't stop streaming down her face. "I grieve for my predecessors' failures to do their duty, but I also grieve for your pain."

"I didn't know my evil forefather. I do not wish to know the man who wrote that despicable journal. The friend in America who sent the journal to grandfather was right to send it. It gives us the opportunity to expiate his grave sin. Did the American nun realize the extreme pain this knowledge has caused in us? Would a friend do that? I believe she would. As painful as it feels, she would want us to know the truth so that we might right the great wrong done by Yoshiro Kenishi."

"Yes, Hiro, a true friend would want you always to know the truth."

Hirobumi paced back and forth on the floor in front of Chieko. "My illustrious forefather," he murmured bitterly. "It was good he died while still a young man. Who knows what other evil he would have been capable of. But his seed is in me. As it is in all the Yoshiro men. But not my grandfather. Perhaps the evil stopped with my grandfather. My grandfather was goodness and love combined in one man. I hardly remember him. Only that his touch was gentle, and he always carried a sweet for me to find in his sleeve. I have a volume of his poetry that shows us what a good heart he possessed." Yoshiro's voice trembled. "I cannot tell my father. Everyone in the family says Kenishi was swept away by the current when he tried to take a swim. They say it was one of the hottest summers the Americans had experienced in years. But they have no explanation of why he was fully clothed. Now we know what we've only suspected. *Seppuku* would have been an honorable death, but the way he chose..." Hirobumi couldn't manage to finish his words.

"Listen, Hiro," Chieko was sobbing, but she managed to choke out

125

a whisper that he strained to hear, "My friend, these are the last tears you will ever see me shed. Strength is demanded of me. You must continue to cry until your grief is emptied. Then we must both abandon tears and act.

"We must go and find the mirror. If we are unsuccessful and the Twenty-Seven finds it, it could bring about the ruin of our country." She grabbed at her chest and tried to catch the breath that seemed to have deserted her again, and said, "If I alone could...but no. I cannot do it alone. Today's world would not accept a woman warrior. I need your help. And I understand that you need to take this journey with me. We must do this together.

"Yoshiro-san, listen. I do not know how much more I can bear. Listen. I command you never to repeat what I am about to tell you. Swear to me that you will obey my command. Our lives and our Japan depend on your silence. If you believe your emotions will get the better of you, and you are unable to keep a secret that could destroy our world, you must tell me now, and leave."

"I swear I shall divulge nothing. How could I bring more shame on my family? I could not. Chieko, I shall kill myself before I repeat anything that is said between us in this peony pavilion."

Her mental distress had become physical, and Chieko writhed in discomfort. Finally she said, "I trust you, because I must trust you," she said. "I am sorry to have to put it in such a manner, my friend. No, you are no longer my friend. You are the *Saio*'s most trusted servant. Perhaps this shows you how frightening this is for me. Yes, I must force myself not to think of you as my friend, only my trusted servant. You must also know that if I fear you will repeat our words to anyone, even your wife or your father, I will come after you and kill you. That is the way it must be. And after I kill you, I will kill myself." The guard nodded. She could see he was struggling to keep tears from rolling down his face again.

"Oh, the pain is too much to bear," Chieko moaned. "For both of us. I understand that. Listen, my dear friend Hiro, we have known each other all our lives, have we not? You are as close as a brother to me. If we cannot trust each other, who else is there?" Chieko stared at Yoshiro for some moments while her mind raced.

But can I really trust him? He now knows what his forefather did. Will his emotions get in the way? Oh, I am too young and inexperienced to take on this problem. My predecessors were derelict in their duty. It is shameful. Should I, too, wait for my successor to find it? No, I must do it. I should not trust anybody to help me. But I must have help. Or should I, myself, go alone on the search? I could send Hirobumi alone. He is intelligent and courageous. But I fear that his emotions will win out over his good sense. And, I cannot rely on someone else to do that which is my duty. Yet, I should not leave here. If the Saio should die while I'm away. No. She will not die. I will not allow it. Chieko held her head in her hands as her thoughts spun.

But it is not up to me. There is so little time. As soon as she dies, I will be forbidden to leave the temple. Shinto gods, Buddha, and Jesus Christ, please help me. Oh, my mind is going in circles. Can I really trust Yoshiro? But he must carry the burden with me. Can he complete the mission successfully himself? No, it is my duty. What if it is no longer in Japan? Was it wrong for me to call in Saito? Is my trust in him misplaced as well? Should I send them both away, and go on the search myself. No, if I am up against The Twenty-Seven, I cannot do it alone. And if the Saio dies, I must hurry back here and tell the men to continue. Time. I need more time. It will soon be forbidden for me to leave Ise Jingu. I must not break the tradition. I am the very embodiment of Japanese traditions. I must not destroy one tradition for the sake of another. Yet my duty is to protect the Yata no Kagami. How can I defy tradition and yet do my duty. Oh, it takes a person wiser than me to make these decisions. Buddha, help me!"

Hirobumi Yoshiro saw the agony in Chieko's face. He knew he shouldn't touch or even look directly at his oldest friend. He found it more difficult than he would have imagined. As children he and Chieko had played in the sand together. They'd run through the fields. They'd laughed and sang together. In the surf they splashed each other. Now, he stole a furtive glance at her. The serene girl he knew only a short while ago was transformed into a woman, a priestess. Her womanly face was white and strained with her inner pain. His own face was twisted in the same fear and pain that mirrored Chieko's agony. He wished above all to be able to forget his own agony. To reach out to her, to comfort her and to relieve her pain, and his own pain at the same time. He knew that they each needed the comfort of the other, but it was impossible. *Be strong. Get it out of your head. We each stand alone in our misery. It is the way it must be. Be strong, Hirobumi,* he warned himself.

Hirobumi erased the longing from his eyes and waited for Chieko to speak. He had never touched Chieko. From the time they were toddlers he was forbidden to touch her. How difficult it was when they played together. She had no compunction about playfully punching him, but even she knew from early childhood that her hand should not linger on a boy for even a moment. And a boy should not put even a finger on her.

Over the years they had learned to back away from each other. Now, she would shrink from his sympathetic touch. Perhaps banish him from the shrine, or even kill him. Yes, if she believed it was her duty, she would kill him. He understood that. Hirobumi tore his gaze from her face and stared down at the floor.

Chieko sat with her eyes closed and fought back her fear and panic. *I will soon be the Saio. It is my duty to do all that is necessary.* Then she opened her eyes and stared at the Imperial Guard for a few moments. She was trembling. She felt dizzy. One hand pinched the other to prevent herself from fainting. Finally, she gulped and croaked softly, "Yoshiro-san, listen carefully. I can hardly speak. Can you hear me?" Yoshiro nodded. "Yoshiro-san..." She gulped again and her voice became hardly a whisper. "Hirobumi, it is my duty to find the Sacred Mirror. It is your duty to help me." She felt the strength drain out of her body, and she clung to the edge of the bench to remain sitting upright. Yoshiro's eyes glazed over in shock as he watched her struggling to maintain her composure. "I have not yet told you the worst," she whispered.

Yoshiro couldn't believe anything could be worse. He turned away from her dark eyes and the tears that spilled down Chieko's cheeks. "Hiro, I am sorry. It is so painful for me to tell you that my predecessor believed your grandfather had the worst of all motives. They believe he stole it for political purposes. They believe he was a member of the hateful ETA Cabal. They believe he plotted the assassination of the Emperor and his family." She heard Yoshiro's swift intake of air and watched his breast swell, then deflate as the air seeped out of his trembling mouth. Now she stared deeply into his own tear-filled eyes to look for his strength. She was terrified to see the fear and panic that reflected her own. "Hirobumi, you must store their suspicions in the back of your mind and not let them influence you. I know you are a true patriot. I have looked into your soul more than once and have seen the goodness and honor in you. I have complete faith in you.

"You and I must go and bring the *Yata no Kagami* home to Ise Jingu before the *Saio* dies. Tomio Saito will join us. Yes, I understand the doubt in your eyes. I have thought it over carefully. We are both strong and proud, but we need his strength and his worldly knowledge and resources.

"We have almost no time at all. Someone has betrayed us. The ETA Cabal has found out the mirror is not here. The traitor must have been in the shrine. Later, we must find out who among the *Saio's* servants alerted the Cabal to the missing treasure. But now, our first mission is to find it and bring it home. The Cabal will be racing us to locate it. They will be anxious to stop us by any means necessary. We must be prepared to kill them first."

Chapter 18
Tokyo, Japan

Hirobumi Yoshiro ordered his driver to stop three blocks from Saito's headquarters. His driver was skillful and navigated the streets quickly. More important, his driver could be trusted. Yoshiro was sure no one had succeeded in following his nondescript grey Honda through the heavily trafficked Tokyo streets. And he doubted anyone would believe that the head of Japan's Ise Imperial Guards was going to the headquarters of one of the most powerful Yakuza bosses in Japan. Yoshiro directed his driver to a quiet street parallel to the commercial district and then into a small deserted parking area. When not a car or a pedestrian was nearby, Yoshiro got out of the car, and told the chauffeur he should keep driving. "Keep the dark windows closed and return to this spot at exactly 9:23."

The chauffeur nodded. Then Yoshiro jumped out of the car. He was dressed in jeans and a t-shirt. He appeared to be like all the other young men who crowded the Ginza. He strode quickly down a side street and into a shopping mall. He glanced in the window of the Armani Boutique. He shook his head as he recalled that just last week he had coveted the cashmere sports jacket that the live model tonight casually draped over one shoulder as he slowly paced in the store window. Now, to Yoshiro, the expensive jacket was no more desirable than grey sackcloth.

Outside, at the other end of the stores, and just to the left of the mall, was a heavy metal door marked 'SERVICE.' It swung open as soon as Yoshiro approached it. A strikingly beautiful, tall woman stood with her hand on the door. She grinned at Yoshiro. They knew each other very well. When he was still a cadet with the Tokyo police force, she'd been brought in for questioning more than once. She wasn't as young as she appeared to be from a few feet away, but her face was still lovely and unlined. She was slim and dressed in a form-fitting sheath covered by a gold-threaded cardigan whose pockets slightly bulged with the small pistol and folding knife that she could use with great skill. Yoshiro grinned back. "Are you behaving yourself?" he asked.

"Same as usual," she said. "Excuse me, Honorable Sir. It's my job. Most men enjoy it. This won't take long." She walked over and quickly, but thoroughly, ran her hands over him. He hadn't even felt her remove them, and tried not to look surprised when she handed him his wallet, small notebook, and fountain pen. She held on to his handgun. "I shall return this to you when you leave. This way," she said, walking in front of him and then holding another heavy metal door open for him. Tomio Saito stood at the far end of a long hallway, and beckoned him in. Muscular men, in small rooms along the hallway, turned their faces away from Yoshiro as he walked toward the gang leader.

"You find this catastrophe amusing, Saito?" Yoshiro moved his black Go pebble to a position that he knew would lose the game for him.

"Don't you? At the very least you must find the situation ironic." Saito paused, his finger over his white pebble. Finally he spat out, "I refuse to win when my opponent chooses suicide. Take back that move and make another. Fight like a man."

"This is only a foolish board game. I'm sick of it." Yoshiro yelled back, sweeping all the pebbles off the board with one hand while he pounded the table with his other. "I find nothing amusing or ironic in this catastrophe or in your attitude. Only terror. I would not be here if I were not terrified of what might happen."

"And because the future *Saio* requested it of us."

"Yes, of course," the guard admitted. "I admit I was surprised that she contacted you. If you love Japan and the Emperor as she believes you do, you will also be as terrified as I. I do not have the same confidence in you, but I obey my superiors. And I believe that someone like you will be able to function even in a state of terror."

"As you are functioning."

"No, better than I am able to."

Saito's eyes narrowed. "I do love the Emperor and Japan, but I love Chieko more. She is as dear to me as a daughter. Whatever the girl needs from me, I willingly give.

"And don't try to convince me that you feel helpless, or that you don't know what you must do. You have never cringed from imposing the punishment of death on others. I have seen it. I have also witnessed you in other circumstances as well. You are not afraid of death for yourself."

"I am only afraid of failing," Yoshiro answered. "I believe that together we will not fail. But I am also terrified the news will get out. The press is everywhere. If the news gets out before we find and restore the mirror, we will have failed."

"The only way the news will get out is if you talk. Chieko and I will not," said Saito who settled back in his chair and played with his teacup.

"The Twenty-Seven could leak the news," Yoshiro said.

"They could, but they won't. They don't want to go public with themselves. And it is too large a matter. And they want to be the ones to release the news to the world when they are in possession of the treasure. They want to have physical proof to back up their allegations. They would wish to coerce the *Saio* into admitting it. She cannot be coerced. And the *Saio* is never available to the media. She speaks only to the Emperor and to the gods. She would not lie, and she will be expected to talk to no one."

After hearing a quiet knocking on the closed door, Saito said, "Enter." A young woman came noiselessly into the room with a teapot to refill their cups, but Saito waved her away. "And close the door. Lock it," he said to her retreating figure. Finally Saito said, "Who else knows you have come to me?"

"No one. I was not followed."

Saito was always skeptical, but he believed this guard. He knew that he might have to trust Yoshiro with his life and was comfortable with the idea. "Who else knows about the mirror?" he asked.

"We, three... and the ETA Cabal."

"I was wondering if you would tell me the truth," Saito said, as he placed the Go stones back in their pouches. "How did The Twenty-Seven find out?"

"We don't know. We're afraid one of the *Saio*'s servants overheard us and betrayed us."

"The Twenty-Seven are almost all men. There are very few female members. But the men have wives, sisters, and daughters. Before we do anything else, Chieko and you must find the servant. She must be eliminated. We must destroy Twenty-Seven's conduit. If you can't do it, I will."

"Chieko has decided that matter can wait. The most important thing is to find and retrieve the treasure. Neither Chieko nor I will shirk our duty. I will arrange for the servant to be found and dealt with."

Saito raised his hand to quiet Yoshiro. He pulled a cell phone from his coat pocket and looked at the screen. A few minutes later he said, "A woman's slit opened body was found this morning on the beach.

She was dressed in an ancient style kimono, and her hair was done in an ancient style. I believe Twenty-Seven exacted your revenge on the traitor. My men say he has his own warped sense of honor. I disagree. He knows better than to give sanctuary to a traitor, because she would just as readily turn on him." Saito didn't try to hide the irony in his tone when he continued, "And the thief or thieves. They know, do they not? If my information is correct, the mirror was stolen a century ago. By now they must all be dead." Saito smiled. "To think that the head of the Ise Imperial Guard and the head of the most powerful *Yakuza* in Japan will be working together would be amusing were the situation not so dire."

"It is not I who wanted your assistance. However, if Chieko trusts you, then so do I. Why it was stolen? That is the question that must be answered." Yoshiro folded his arms and pressed them against his stomach as if he were in pain, then added, "I have thought it over again and again. Chieko and I have told you everything. I do not wish to believe Yoshiro Kenishi stole it for political reasons. I don't know how he could have pulled it off. It would have been almost impossible even for him, an Ise guard. One hundred years ago an armed guard watched over it day and night. He must have replaced it with the fake while he was on guard. I don't understand how he got away with it

"And then to find it was later stolen from him... I do not know how we'll find it in America, but Chieko and I are determined to bring it back.

"This will never happen again. Since I have been commander, an Imperial Guard and an electronic alarm system guard it. The alarm code is constantly updated. No one will be able to bypass it. The *Saio* has one-half of the password, and I have the other half. I swear on my honor that I will divulge my half to no one. The new *Saio* was just given the other half. When we bring back the mirror, we will have to put our knowledge of the password to good use. And then we will change it again.

"I do not know how much more Chieko told you, but if we're going to work together, you should know everything I know. It is painful for me to say it, and more painful for me to believe that Yoshiro Kenishi took the mirror from the shrine and left its replica. I would not have believed such a thing, but I have the proof written in his own hand. In America it was stolen from Yoshiro Kenishi. Everyone believes he committed suicide because he failed in his duty to protect it. We know it was more complicated than that.

"I cannot believe a foreign thief would have stolen it for its historical significance. No, its intrinsic value would mean nothing to a foreigner," Yoshiro continued, after some thought. "Although any thief would steal it if he believed he could get money for it. No, I believe the thief must have been Japanese. Japan was changing rapidly even then. At one time no Japanese man would have even dared to look at it. Then there is the ETA Cabal—and other similar dastardly organizations—but none as powerful or far-reaching as The ETA. They are capable of anything that would destroy our Japan. Only they would have dared to steal it. The ETA should have been eliminated more than a century ago. How has it managed to stay alive? Only one way. There are Cabal members in high places protecting it. Are you sympathetic to the goals of the Cabal?"

Saito looked up sharply and stared at Yoshiro. "No," his voice shot back. "If Chieko had the least fear of that, she would never have called me. Listen Yoshiro, we will return to being enemies when this is over. For now we are forced to trust each other if we are to be successful. Let us waste no time sniping at one another. Chieko is worried that time is running out."

The guard thought for a moment before he replied. "Yes, we must act rapidly. In accordance with tradition the present Ise Jingu will be rebuilt again in 2013 when its twentieth anniversary is reached. The *Saio* is to examine and once more vow to the safety of the *Yata no Kagami* before the construction begins. She cannot lie. That would be a sacrilege. And Chieko is incapable of falsehood. There is a serious time constraint. The old priestess will die at any moment. Chieko must assume her religious duties immediately upon the old woman's death. Yes, there is no time to waste."

"Traditions must be treasured and preserved," Saito said in agreement and took a large swallow of his remaining tea.

Chapter 19
Portsmouth, New Hampshire

"Mr. Yoshiro," Constance Talant said after she'd read his card, "I've just moved to Portsmouth. I'm glad you found me."

"Sister Anne advised us how to find you here, rather than the address we had in Boston. You know why we are here in Portsmouth. We are honored to meet you. May I present Mr. Tomio Saito, a well-known businessman in Japan. And may I also present Miss Chieko Shimizu. As you may know, we are in America on her behalf. We know that we are asking for your professional help, and we insist on paying for your time. Shall we talk about that now?"

"No. Let's do that later. But if you can manage it, I'd like a five hundred dollar mobilization fee."

"Yes, of course. That is not a problem." Yoshiro took a large wad of American currency out of his briefcase. He counted off five hundred-dollar bills and handed them to Connie.

"Thanks," she said, and added, "I'm pleased to meet you both. Welcome. I had a pretty good business going in Boston, but I'm excited about having my office here in Portsmouth now" Connie said, realizing she was being as polite and circumspect as the Japanese. She shook her head slightly and said, "Shall we get to it? How can I help you, Miss Shimizu? Do you speak English."

"I speak some English," said Chieko, "but Mr. Yoshiro speaks much better English than I. I wish him to speak for both of us. If there is anything else to be said, I shall say it."

"Okay. That works for me," Connie said.

"May I first say," said Yoshiro, "Miss Shimizu preferred that we hire a woman investigator, if we could find one. I had no objections, of course. It has been my experience that women can be very great warriors. As to business: We will have to arrange money transfers to the bank here. What are your terms?"

"Depends on what happens. Let's leave that for now. You need a *warrior*? Sister Anne said it would involve some danger. Tell me more."

Yoshiro smiled. "Our journey here to America is for reasons that we do not wish to make public."

Connie sat back in her squeaky desk chair, once again thinking she needed to oil it, and said, "That's taken for granted. Talking to me is like you're talking to a lawyer, if you know what I mean. Every word is confidential. One thing you should know is: I won't accept a job that is illegal, unethical, or even immoral. I have a conscience that won't quit. By the way, Miss Shimizu, your English is fine. You speak it with no discernable accent at all," she added.

"My father was in the diplomatic corps. English was our second language. I received my college education at Oxford University. I studied in Munich, too. My grasp of the German language, however, is not as good as my English."

"We did not try to look for a private investigator in a small city in America who speaks Japanese, especially a woman," said Yoshiro. "We believed that would be impossible to find. It seems very few besides we Japanese speak our language. Still, we feel it is vital that we communicate well to each other. The job we want to hire you for concerns a very sensitive matter. There is nothing illegal, unethical, or immoral in what we need of you." Yoshiro assured. "Would it interest you to know that my good wife is Christian, too?"

"Too?"

"Just my assumption as to your religion because of your association with Sister Anne. I know of no great world religion that condones immorality or illegality, much less unethical practices. But I do not think any religion is as vocal against these things as are Islam and Christianity. I am not as familiar with the tenets of Islam, but I know it is difficult to be a perfect Christian. I much admire Christians who attempt to live according to Christianity's dictates. As you might know, generally speaking, the Japanese don't traditionally agree with the idea that one must hold onto only one religious belief. Like many others, my wife is Christian, Buddhist, and Shintoist, all at the same time. It is quite possible to live in such a way. She sees no reason to believe any faith need be exclusive. Although she was educated by Roman Catholic nuns and admires them greatly.

"At any rate, through my wife, I met your Aunt Cecelia, when she was a missionary in Japan. My parents had the good fortune of hosting her when she came to experience the wonders of Kyoto. She was a good woman. I met other American nuns through her. They were all good, honorable ladies. And they were always interesting. We had many conversations. My personal favorite was Sister Anne. We communicate often by mail. She was stationed in Massachusetts, but she was transferred to Portsmouth just this year. I believe the gods are smiling on us to have such friends and allies in the United States."

"Yes, I agree. Although, nuns are never pushovers." At the confused expression on the man's face, Connie said, "I mean nuns are strong in their faith. That makes them also strong in other ways."

"Ah, yes. I understand. Sister Cecelia radiated strength and goodness. I know you were like a daughter to her. She bragged about you constantly. Consequently, I know much about you. What she said very often to me was that you have Samurai blood in your veins because you are courageous, skilled in the arts of war, and possess a very fine-tuned sense of honor. She said that if the time ever arrived that we came to the United States to solve a problem, there would be no one we could trust more than you.

"She and Sister Anne were as natural sisters. Yes, very close. Sister Anne has been to see you. I believe she has given you some of the reason we are here. I am counting on your aunt's assessment of you. And as I mentioned, Miss Shimizu prefers to work with a woman, especially a woman like you."

"Sister Cecelia was my biggest fan, and I hers. I still miss her and think of her almost every day. I always will. You were fortunate to have known her, but I was the luckiest in the world because she was my hero and role model. She was also the soul of discretion and very private. I don't remember her saying she had a Japanese friend. Although she never volunteered information just for the sake of talking."

"Our relationship was not exactly friendship, but she inspired confidence," said Yoshiro. "And she connected us to you. I was pleasantly surprised that you are now here in Portsmouth, the city of interest to us. I am not a man who believes in omens, but it does seem significant to me that you are here."

"You and I have to spend some time together and share our memories," said Connie. The world is a poorer place without her, don't you think? But she would be scolding me if she were with us now. She would be saying, 'Let's stop dancing around.' So Mr. Yoshiro, let's get to business. Tell me what I can do for you."

"Yes, that would indeed be Sister Cecelia speaking. I have first a question. You are familiar with the peace treaty that was negotiated in Portsmouth in 1905?"

"Well, I know that a peace treaty was signed here more than a hundred years ago. I think it was between Japan and... hmm, Russia,

141

right? But I wouldn't have been sure the exact year it was signed. And I don't know why a treaty was signed—something about a dispute in China, if memory serves. But I don't know why they came here to do it," Connie confessed.

"On the one hand, it is good that you have no preconceived ideas. On the other hand, you will have to 're-invent the wheel,' as the saying goes." Connie stared at Yoshiro and waited for him to continue.

"I am looking for something that my forefather lost while he was here with the Japanese peace delegation in the summer of 1905. Well, 'lost' is a euphemism. The item was actually stolen from the delegation. It is an item that is very precious to the Japanese."

"Something precious to the Japanese, but stolen over a hundred years ago. That's a challenge." Connie said and reached down into the stash of bottles of water she usually kept nearby in the summer. She offered bottles to the others. They declined the water. She took a fast swig from her own bottle and said, "It's been unseasonably hot this year."

"Yes, it is quite warm," said Yoshiro, who added, "I am afraid we have a pressing time constraint. It is crucial that Miss Shimizu return to Japan as soon as possible. You will forgive me if I hurry this along."

"You're in the driver's seat. Let me just say this: if this situation is vital to the Japanese, you may be talking to the wrong person. It may be beyond my abilities. Perhaps our governments should be talking." When she saw Yoshiro's frown deepening, she continued, "Well, that's up to you, of course. For now, I'm listening."

"We do not wish to go public with this problem. Only a very few of us know, and for now it's best to keep it that way. Sister Anne trusts you. Therefore, we are trusting you.

"To give you a brief background," Yoshiro continued. "A Yoshiro man has been in the Imperial Guards for more than a century. I am the fourth generation guard in this tradition. I have been raised in the

142

knowledge that the Japanese Emperor, his family, and his goods are precious to the well-being of Japan and must be preserved and guarded at all costs. Tradition is dear to all of us."

"I understand that," Connie said. "And you've come to me because of your Japanese traditions?"

"In a manner of speaking. It has to do with a gift that the Emperor sent to your President Roosevelt, Theodore, not Franklin." For the next several minutes Yoshiro talked about the loss of the mirror.

"And you say your forefather wrote that he killed the thief, but he never found the mirror?" Connie asked.

"Yes. Yoshiro Kenishi was very, how do you say it?—hot-headed. Yes, hot-headed, but he only did what any Japanese at that time would have done to punish the thief. It is considered brutal behavior now. He had to do it. It was a matter of honor."

"Mr. Yoshiro, I think you know that in the United States it would have been considered a brutal murder even a hundred years ago. But that needn't be our concern right now. Did Yoshiro Kenishi cover up the killing somehow?"

"Yes, but, as you say, that is not what is important today. And that is not why we are here in Portsmouth. We are looking for the mirror. It was stolen somewhere here from a place called The Wentworth Hotel. The treaty was signed on September 5th, 1905. Our delegation returned to Japan days later. The mirror is still missing."

"Why the sudden interest now, after more than a hundred years?"

"It is a matter of my family honor." To Connie's skeptical glance at him, Yoshiro added, "We have already spoken of the importance of tradition. My family name is also still very important to the Japanese because of our position in the Imperial Guards. I expect my son to follow in our footsteps. For his sake and his children's sake, our name must not be besmirched by what occurred here more than a century ago. I do not believe that Americans have the same attitude toward their traditions and family names."

"Perhaps not. But you still haven't answered my question. Why now?" Connie said.

"I could have just let the matter rest, but I believe it is because the matter has made my father very ill, that I feel a need to protect my family. This," said Yoshiro, sliding a file folder over the desk to Connie, "is the translation of an investigator's report my grandfather, Yoshiro Seiji, hired this P.I. to find the mirror. There are also photos of drawings of the replica and an exact description of the mirror itself. I believe that the replica is exactly like the original. My grandfather's report is included. The matter also ate at his health. He held nothing back in his report, although it sickened him. I have alluded to my father, Yoshiro Isamu. He spent hours drawing up plans to find the treasure. And as I told you, it also ruined his health. His file is also included."

Connie opened the folder. *He still hasn't answered my question,* she said to herself. Aloud, she said, "Give me a moment to glance at these few sheets. Please enjoy your tea while I read." Connie looked over to Chieko who simply smiled in return. "I guess you want me to read this, too. Right?" Connie asked. Chieko just nodded.

Yoshiro had just drained his cup when Connie shook her head and said, "Not an awful lot to go on, but in any event most of the important facts in this file are over a hundred years old. The trail is very cold by now. Yet, I'm intrigued. One question. More than one replica could have been made, right?" Yoshiro and Chieko nodded. "But you don't know that another was made, do you?"

"No, we do not know. We think not," said Chieko.

Yoshiro added, "The craftsman is dead. I do not know that it would be possible to find out if more than one was made. What are you thinking?"

"I'm wondering why a replica would be so important. Perhaps if only one were made, it might be fairly valuable. And I suppose in historical terms, the replica brought here would have some extrinsic value, but not an awful lot.... I believe there is something you're not telling me. If you want me to work with you, I've got to trust you. And the same goes for you; I don't work with people who don't trust me."

"I have told you everything that is important for you to know except for one thing. There is a very old criminal group in Japan that has plotted the demise of our Imperial traditions for more than a hundred years. It plans to install its leader as the next Emperor. The group is known as the ETA Cabal. There are twenty-seven leaders. We do not know how many actual members there are. As you can imagine, the Cabal has been underground for many years. We have been able to infiltrate it, but not on a continuous basis, and not in the higher leadership echelon. It was not a top priority because in the past we have considered it nothing more than a collection of crackpots.

"The government is always busy with other important matters. Too busy to go after a small group that receives no support from the people. Since the end of the Second World War, the group has grown, but we have not been able to find a good enough reason to shut the movement down. So far as we know, they are committing no crimes. They do not even publish seditious material, only pseudo-religious injunctions and mathematical treatises. Japan has been a democracy since 1945. People are free to say what they wish, so long as they do not engage in seditious behavior. Of course, the Cabal was at the top of our list of suspects in the theft. However, we have received information that the Cabal is now also in search of the mirror. Therefore, we believe it may not have been they who stole it. On the other hand, who knows what happened a hundred years ago?"

"Yeah, 1905 is a long time ago. They could have stolen it and in the interim lost it. The question is: It's been over a hundred years. Why would the Cabal be looking for it now? Because you are?"

145

"Forgive me for saying so, but Japan is a much older civilization than the United States. It does not seem so long ago to us. As I have said, traditions are much more important to us. One hundred years is not a very long time. As to why the Cabal is looking for the mirror, it is quite simple and quite horrendous a reason. The Cabal hopes that if it possesses the mirror, it can show the people that Japan's most precious treasure has no value. That the reverence with which we hold the mirror is nothing more than stupid superstition, which, like the Emperor, should be eradicated. The Cabal plans to destroy the mirror in full view of the people to prove that it is powerless."

"How did the Cabal find out the mirror is missing? You say your search is classified information. Well, somebody leaked it, didn't they?"

Yoshiro and Chieko glanced at each other, before Chieko said, "One of my assistants told Twenty-Seven—the leader. We have been told that she has been punished."

"Hmmmm. Okay. But I'm still wondering if I'm the one you should be talking to. I've never taken on anything like this. I don't want you to think I have more experience than I do. If you want to take the problem to one of our agencies, like the NSA, it might be a better move on your part."

"Please excuse me for being cynical, but government agencies also harbor traitors."

Connie stared out the window for a minute. Finally, she said, "I'm finding this an intriguing mystery that I'd like to solve. And you, yourself, have people who'll join me. To be honest, my calendar is empty, so I'm available. If you still want to hire me, I'm on it."

Yoshiro glanced at the other two and all three nodded. Saito said, "Of course, you may expect our complete cooperation in helping you find the mirror. As for retrieving it, Yoshiro and I have friends who will help. And I have employees, but I'm afraid they are under surveillance." Saito didn't say it was the U. S. Government who was watching his men. "If Twenty-Seven brings the Cabal against us, we will need all the help we can get."

"Okay," Connie said, "Let's talk about finding it first. I don't go out blind. I need to be armed with all the information I can get before I start any job. Here's what I'm thinking. First, I want to know everything there is to know about the treaty. I need files on all the men in the Japanese delegation, from top to bottom, everybody, including servants; and also the same information on the Russian party as well. I'm sure you have that. I also need to know from you what security measures were put in place to protect the gift. Who was directly responsible for its safekeeping? Was it just your grandfather? Third, you must have some suspicions yourself as to the disappearance of the mirror. Do you think the ETA Cabal stole it a hundred years ago? If so, the answer to the mystery might be in Japan, not here. It's important that I be privy to your thoughts.... all of your thoughts.

"I'll also be researching what security measures were taken here by our government to protect the peace delegates and the negotiations.

"And I have to educate myself about the real mirror, the craftsman who made the replica or replicas if he made more than one, the Russo-Japanese War itself, and the treaty. I need to have that background information. You'll have to let me know about the craftsman. I'll get on the Internet to learn about the war and the treaty, but, of course, your first-hand info is invaluable.

"As to the treaty, we have a really good historical society in Portsmouth, and a place called the Athenaeum where many written historical records are housed. I imagine the University of New Hampshire must have something in their archives about the treaty. The Portsmouth Public Library, too. You said the negotiations took place in the naval yard. I wonder what the Portsmouth or Kittery naval yard has in the way of archives? It could be an excellent resource. I suppose you think my preparatory needs are extreme. Well, yes they

are. It's my way of doing things. Oh, don't worry. I don't expect you to
pay for my education.

"Once I actively start looking to find out what eventually happened
to the mirror that went missing in Portsmouth, I'm on the clock. I get
$125 an hour, plus expenses, with a minimum of $500. I will report to
you by phone or email once a day, and at the end, provide you with a
written report, the location of the mirror, if it still exists, or the mirror
itself, if that is possible. You don't have to decide right now whether to
accept my terms. Just get back to me one way or another. Here's my
card with my cell phone number on it." Connie rose from her chair
and bowed. "Goodbye, Miss Shimizu, Mr. Yoshiro, and Mr. Saito. I'll
await your call. In the meantime, I'm going to spend my spare time
learning about the real mirror, the war, and the treaty, just for my own
enlightenment. Starting here." She pointed at her computer. "Oh, just
to satisfy my curiosity—if the official gift to Roosevelt was lost, what
did your people give to the President in its place?"

"My grandfather's ancient and very valuable Samurai sword," said
Yoshiro.

Chapter 20

Sharon Meadows picked up *The International Herald Tribune* out of the heap of discarded newspapers piled on a table at Breaking New Grounds in Market Square. Her eyebrows raised in surprise, and then she frowned when she read the Personal column: *Darling, If only we could relive those halcyon days in Venice. Please contact me. Yours forever, Horace M.*

Sharon asked for another espresso shot, paid for her now fortified cup of strong black coffee, and walked out of the café. Around the corner, she found a free spot where she wouldn't be overheard. She took her cell phone from her handbag. She opened the phone and punched in a number in Vienna. When the connection was finally made, and a man's pleasant voice said, "Hello. With whom would you like to speak?" Sharon smiled.

"I'd like to speak to Horace M., please," she said, and then she took another sip of coffee.

After a few moments, the man said, "The United States. Portsmouth, New Hampshire. Two Japanese men and one woman who arrived this week: The men are Hirobumi Yoshiro and Tomio Saito. The woman's name is Chieko Shimizu. Prenom, then surname, like in the west. None of them are fools, and they are all very capable of taking care of themselves, even the woman."

Sharon had started smiling as soon as he had said 'Portsmouth.' But, she needed more information. "Three?" she asked. "That's a challenge. Who's the client?"

"You know I'm not going to answer that question."

"And you know I don't take on political jobs."

"It's not political."

"If they're not easy targets, I'll have to get all three at the same time. I'm assuming they have ground transportation. Did they rent a car? Or were they picked up by someone? Find out. Hang up. I'll call back in a few minutes," she said. She bent the earpiece half of the phone back until the phone broke apart. She threw it in a nearby trash container and pulled another cell phone from her bag. Soon she was back on the phone, but calling an alternative number in Vienna. "I'll be staying at the Sheraton in Portsmouth starting tonight under the name of Ellen Hunt. FedEx me their dossiers and photos and their ground transportation. How much?"

"Twenty each, plus expenses."

"Forty each, plus expenses."

"Okay."

As she closed the second phone, Sharon realized she could have demanded more money, but shrugged it off. *I may have lots of faults, but greed isn't one of them. Hmm, Portsmouth...too much of a coincidence. Is Sister Anne's problem related to these people? Is it a trap? No, she wouldn't be party to that. But she might be the sacrificial lamb they're using to get to me. Interesting.*

Chapter 21

"Is Mr. Hartz at home?"

"Who're you? What'd ya want?" Connie guessed the woman who came to hang out of the first floor window had heard her ringing the doorbell but was in no hurry to answer the door. The woman was still in a dingy threadbare nightgown that hid nothing. Her greasy blond hair fell in strings onto her grey, bony shoulders.

"Are you Mrs. Hartz?"

"I said, what'd ya want? Who ah you anyways?"

"My name is Constance Talant. I'm a private investigator...and writer. I'm looking for Mr. Russell Hartz."

"A private investigator, huh? You don't look like no private dick. I thought only guys could be private dicks," the woman giggled, and added, "if you know what I mean, honey."

"I'd appreciate it if you could tell me what you know about Russell Hartz," Connie said. She had no interest in playing the woman's dirty little word game.

"He's in the cemetery on South Street. Ain't nobody bought him a stone yet. Never will, most prob'ly. Somebody over there in the office will tell you where he is."

"Are you his daughter?"

"Ah you half-blind? Do I look old enough to be his daughter? He was over a hunnerd when he kicked. His granddaughter is what I am, and I don't take no pride saying it. What'd ya want?"

"Miss Hartz, could I come in and talk to you?" Connie couldn't think of anything she'd like to do less than walk into this woman's apartment on a hot day. "If you'd rather," Connie said, hoping she would," I could meet you around the corner at Café Kilim. I'll buy you an iced tea."

"My name's Ashley Coles. I ain't no 'Miss Hartz.' I want coffee, and I ain't had my breakfast yet."

"OK. Breakfast. Ten minutes?"

"Yeah, whatever."

More than half an hour later, Ashley came sauntering up to the sidewalk bench Connie'd been able to snag outside of Café Kilim. She would have preferred sitting in the air-conditioned café, but she saw it was too small and intimate to keep their conversation private. Ashley had a loud voice and, Connie figured, no sense of what it meant to be discrete.

"Ashley," Connie said when the young woman stopped in front of the bench, "I didn't know what to order for you and it's lunchtime. Here's the menu. Order whatever you'd like. But I only have twenty-dollars on me, so don't go crazy."

"Yeah, whatever. What'da we do, order inside?"

"Haven't you ever eaten here? Kilim's right around the corner from your apartment."

"Yeah, whatever. I wish't they had French fries. I'm so hungry. I'm gonna have dessert, I guess. I'm eatin' for two again." Ashley smiled and patted her bare, slightly stretch-marked white stomach.

"Yeah, whatever," Connie said sarcastically. That made her smile. But she knew better than to let Ashley see it.

After Ashley had eagerly consumed her sticky pastry, Connie turned to her, and asked seriously. "I want to talk about your grandfather, Russell, now."

"Great-grandfather, is what he said he was. But he wasn't great, if ya know what I mean. Ya know that sayin' about the good dyin' young? Well, it's true. That guy was so bad, he shoulda lived to be two hunnert, not a hunnert and fourteen. If that's what he was. That's what he said. But he lied about everythin'. I happen to know he was only a hunnert and a little.

"You think you're getting' stuff out of me jus' cuz you bought me a sandwich and a root beer?" Ashley jabbed at Connie's arm, and added. "I'm jus' messin' with you. Yeah, okay, what the hell. I'll tell you everything you need to know. Here it is. You ready?" Ashley took a deep breath. "Best thing Pop-pop ever done was die. He was a sonofabitch. Any questions?" Ashley grinned at her little joke.

Connie again warned herself that even a slight smile would encourage Ashley to continue trying to make little jokes. Connie set her face into a grave frown. "Would you tell me everything you know about him? Like where did he live? What did he do for money?"

"Pop-pop had a shack over in Newington. He didn't have no steady job. He was on the welfare. He was so freakin' lazy, I had to go with him to get his checks and then go cash them. I kept a little for myself. Why shouldn't I? If it wasn't for me, he wouldna collected at all. He couldn't understan' why the govmint would pay him for doin' nothin'. That's how dumb he was.

"In the old days he used to work on the lobster and fishin' boats when he could find somebody stupid enough to take him on again. When it got cold, he stayed in the Salvation Army shelter, if there was room. More like if they'd let him in. But they got to, don't they? The people in town were used to seein' him rootin' through their garbage cans. Some people even wrapped up good food scraps for him and put them on top of the garbage. They thought he was too proud to beg,"

Ashley said, as if reciting from a prepared script she kept in her head. "Too proud to beg! That's a laugh. He didn't have no pride. He was just too lazy to beg. That's all there is to say about him. To make it short an' sweet, he was a lazy bum."

"But he kept up this shack in Newington?"

"Yeah, he had that shack.... caint say he 'kept it up'. It's more like a dirty pile of ol' wood."

"One more thing," Connie asked. "Did your grandfather ever talk about his father? Was he a fisherman, too?"

Ashley's dull eyes suddenly appeared to have turned sharp and wary. "What'd ya wanna know 'bout him for?" Ashley asked. "You ah bein' a little too arquisitive, ain't ya? Next thing you'll wanna know my bra size."

"No. I'll never want to know that. Well, never mind. Anyway, it's not important," Connie lied. "As a writer, I'm particularly interested in the early maritime history of Portsmouth. I was just hoping... Oh, never mind. From what you tell me, Russell may not have been the kind of man who liked to talk about himself."

"You still ain't told me what you ah doin' here. Why'd you come lookin' for Pop-pop? Not like to talk about himself.... are you kiddin'? That's all he ever did. Listen, I don't have no time to talk to you no more. I gotta go meet a guy."

"I'm trying to find fishermen who remember the old days. Just research for my book."

"Hell, what'd you say your name was again? Did you say 'Constenz'?" Connie nodded anyway. "That's a funny name. Well, hell, Constenz, Pop-pop wouldn't be no help. He wasn't no real fisherman. He didn't have his own boat or nothin'. Hell, by the time he kicked off, he couldn't even remember to stand up and pee." Ashley's voice suddenly turned into a snarl. "And look. I know you are lyin'. I ain't stupid. I don't know what you really want. But you come aroun' here askin' your questions 'bout my family again, and I'll call the cops on you. Got it?" Ashley jumped to her feet and stormed away from the café.

Chapter 22

The bare polished wood floors of the convent house reminded Connie of the floors of her great-aunt's convent in New Jersey. The parlors were similarly simple and functional. A large crucifix hung on one wall of the parlor in which she waited. The facing wall held a picture of Christ pointing to his Sacred Heart. A statue of Mary, mother of Jesus, dressed in the usual blue, stood on a pedestal in the far corner. Connie sat on a hardback sofa and studied the picture of the Sacred Heart. It was the exact same picture in one of her old classrooms. Connie remembered it from the time she was a kid and the nuns were prepping her to make her First Holy Communion. Christ's face was filled with love and compassion. Connie remembered gazing at the kind face in the picture for minutes at a time, while also wondering what His heart was doing on the outside of His body. *Well, I guess cuz he was God, anything's possible.*

Connie felt comfortable here in these surroundings. They felt familiar. She was thinking *I might be ready to start going to church again*, when she heard soft footsteps approaching. She rose to her feet. Sister Anne came rustling into the parlor. "I was wondering how long it would be until you came to see me," she said.

"The days are getting shorter, but the rain's stopped, and the sun's still high. It's a lovely afternoon. Let's take a walk. You tell me what you know first, and then I'll decide what I want to tell you."

As they walked, Sister Anne fingered rosary beads she had pulled from her pocket, the only visible sign that she was perturbed. After Connie had finished telling her what she wanted the nun to know about the mirror, a suddenly pale Sister Anne said, "Let's sit for a moment. That looks dry." She pointed at a covered concrete bench in the pocket park they had just entered. 'I love to look at the world when the sun is horizontal. It's especially beautiful in Indian Summer, isn't it?"

"Sister, are you feeling okay? You're looking a little ragged."

"Yes. You're right. I am trying to avoid telling you what I know. And yes, I am tired. But not afraid. I have been praying so hard. In any event, I cannot continue to do nothing."

"Here's what I'm investigating," Connie declared. " Mr. Hartz's father, Jeremiah, stole an antique Japanese mirror during the peace treaty negotiations in 1905. Did Russell Hartz ever talk about it?"

"A mirror? No, he didn't talk about a mirror,'' Sister Anne replied. "He did say he knew the whereabouts of a treasure; something his father stole when he was working at the Wentworth years and years ago. That must be what you're referring to. He was always muttering about it. As I've said, I doubted if it was really a treasure. If it were worth anything at all, he would have sold it. On the other hand, I thought he might have dreamed up the whole story, just to get attention. That's the kind of man he was. He was a dreamer and he craved attention. I have to admit, after a while, I came to half believe in his treasure because he talked so much about it, and he needed someone to believe in him and trust him.

"I believe that a small part of him genuinely believed he had a treasure. He spoke about it as if it were real, and I started believing in it. But there was something... you know, Constance, I believe he was actually frightened of his treasure. Yes, I believe he was. He used to say he was going to bury it real good because it had *joo-joo* and would kill him. Yes, now it's coming back to me. He said it had *joo-joo*. That's why at one time I even thought it was Haitian.

"Well, to tell the truth, I thought if I sprinkled it with holy water and said a prayer over it, he'd believe the *joo-joo* was gone. The priests and my sister nuns at St. Peter's wouldn't approve of that at all. In any event, I never saw his treasure. He could have hidden his treasure anywhere. He lived all over the Seacoast and in the Isles, too. On Appledore. Or was it Smuttynose? No. There was a terrible murder there at the end of the 19ᵗʰ century. He was afraid to live there.

'When he was an adult, he wandered around all over the place, because he worked on fishing and lobster boats all his adult life. He knew every nook and cranny of the Seacoast area. Yes, it could be anywhere. I've sometimes thought that maybe I should look for it. But one minute I believe it exists, the next minute I don't.

"If Russell had something that was stolen, I should do something about that. I'm ashamed that I avoided the subject. I should have known that anything the Hartzes had of value must have been stolen. I should have helped Russell. I've been praying for guidance. Perhaps God will help you to help me do my duty. I pray it's so.

"And I don't know where Russell's treasure is. But I have an idea...."

"Would you lead me to it?"

"I don't know yet."

Chapter 23
Tokyo, Japan

Twenty-Seven kicked the desk leg and swore again. "Why is there no one I can trust to do anything the way it should be done? Why am I surrounded by idiots?" He kicked the desk leg again, and then reached down and rubbed his sore foot. "You there," he yelled at a muscular young man who stood next to the door and waited to be of service. "Make yourself useful. Go tell my secretary to get me a plane ticket to Portsmouth, New Hampshire, in the United States. Then go pack my bag. I want a flight out tomorrow morning. Do it now, and hurry up about it. Then come back and give me a massage. My back is killing me!"

While he waited to hear that arrangements had been made, Twenty-Seven sat at his desk and opened the middle drawer. He pulled out three photos. He put the photo of Tomio Saito aside. "I don't need to be reminded what you look like," he muttered. The photo of Chieko Shimizu was obviously taken without her being aware of it. The photo was blurred, and a fine gauze scarf obscured what he could see was a beautiful face. He stared at the photo and tried to tear the scarf away. "I see you, Priestess. You can't hide from me." After some minutes, he pushed her photo aside and studied the face of Hirobumi Yoshiro in the last photo. "Ha! You guards believe yourselves to be great warriors.

But you've never dealt with me."

At a soft sound at the door, Twenty-Seven's hand went to his sword. He glanced up to see his secretary staring back at him. "Well?" Twenty-Seven said.

"Honorable Sir, I have made a reservation for you on Japan Airlines, leaving tomorrow morning at 7:14. You must fly to Boston, Massachusetts, and then take a limo to Portsmouth, New Hampshire. The limo has also been arranged. It is about an hour's ride from Boston to Portsmouth. Is there anything else you wish?" the young man asked.

"Where's... no, never mind. Lock the door. Then, come and give me a massage. You know my body better than anyone, *koishii*."

Chapter 24
Newington, New Hampshire

"Hello, my name is Sister Anne. What's your name?" She asked the little girl sitting and rocking her doll.

"I'm not 'lowed to talk to stranjuhs."

"That's a good policy. Where's your Mommy?"

"Hildy!" yelled the girl. "Hildy!" she yelled again. A small dog came scampering out of the woods. "Stop!" yelled the girl before the dog could jump on her lap. "Sit!" the girl ordered, and the dog sat on its rear. Its bushy white tail swept back and forth in the dirt. Hildy stared up at the girl in happy anticipation. "Smell that?" she asked Sister Anne.

"Your dog Hildy has been skunked."

"Yup. He's cute, ain't he? But Mommy says Hildy's more stupid than cute." The girl looked back at the dog. "Hildy, what you chasin' now? Ain't you been 'nuf trouble? No, that were not a invite to jump all over me. You stay there!" She looked up at Sister Anne, "Mommy was mad as a hive a bees being visited by a bear. 'I ain't wasting my money on that stupid dog,' she said. She took my money out of my piggy bank and went into town to buy a bunch a tomato juice to take Hildy's stink away. She'll be right back. You better go way now. Mommy ain't in no mood for visitors, and I ain't to be talking to no strangers."

"Can I talk to your Daddy?"

"I ain't got no Daddy."

"You're not here alone are you?"

"My baby sitter's in the toilet."

"I'll wait and talk to her. What's her name?"

"Bridey. But you'll be waitin' a long time. I locked her in the toilet."

"Why?"

"Cuz she said it was gonna rain. Look. It ain't raining, is it? No, it ain't. She lied. She just want for us to stay in and watch her tv shows. That's the truth of it." She turned and said, "I see you, Hildy. You get back there under that tree and you stay there 'til Mommy comes back." The dog slunk back to the edge of the woods.

"I ain't supposed to be talking to you, but here I am gabbing away like you're my friend. My name's Amber. And that there's my dog, Hildy. He's a boy, but I didn't know that when I got him. He likes his girl name anyhow."

"Well, Amber, I think we should go into your trailer and release Bridey. She must be very sad."

"She ain't sad. She's mad as hell. But she can't do nothing about it cuz Mommy won't pay her if she hits me. Mommy'll beat her up. That's what."

"I feel sad for Bridey. Let's go release her. Then we three can sit and pass the time of day. How about that, Amber?"

"That's what old people do. They pass the time away. No. We ain't goin' to sit and pass the time away. We'll just sit and talk. You stay here. Strangers ain't allowed in the house." Amber ran off to the trailer. She returned a few moments later with a chubby teenager with white streaks of blond hair among the black on her head. Bridey sported piercings in her nose and ears.

Amber hugged her baby sitter. "You get off of me! I'm that mad at you," said Bridey. "Who are you?" she asked Sister Anne.

"Let's sit over there on that boulder. I'll tell you all about why I'm here. And I'll give you each a Tootsie Roll." She pulled the candy from her pocket.

"I ain't supposed to take no candy from a stranger," said Amber.

"I'm here. You can take it cuz I'm here," said Bridey, grabbing a Tootsie Roll from the nun's hand. Bridey tore off the wrapper and stuffed the candy in her mouth.

"I didn't know any old man named Russell," said Amber, stretching her dusty thin legs across the warm rock.

"She's just a baby. She don't know nothing. I remember that old fart. He was ugly as my rump. He tried to touch me once. I hauled off and kicked him right where it hurts. He never tried nothing again, I'll tell you that," said Bridey with a snaggle-toothed smile.

"What was he doing out here?"

"He was all over the place. That's what my Mama says. She said he was harmless enough. He wouldn't know what to do with me, if he caught me. That's what she said. He said he was looking for Miss Johnson's house. The old fool. Miss Johnson was dead before I was even born. They pulled down her cabin just after somebody killed her."

"Do you know where Miss Johnson's house used to be?"

"Sure I do. Where you going Amber?"

"I got to go to the toilet."

"You hurry up then."

"Where was Miss Johnson's house, Bridey?" Sister Anne asked.

"Right about where you standin'. Oh, here comes Miz Morehouse now. Amber, if you know what's good for you," she yelled into the bathroom window of the trailer, "you better not tell her 'bout locking me in the toilet."

Sister Anne walked to the old Chevy as the woman was getting out of it with a bag of groceries. "May I help you, Mrs. Morehouse?" asked the nun.

"It's Miz Anita Morehouse, and I don't need no help. Who are you? What do you want here?" Hildy came running up to Anita, and licked her leg. "You go 'way, you stinking mongrol. What's going on around here? Bridey, you gone crazy? You entertainin' strangers? Where's Amber at?"

"She locked herself in the toilet, Miz Morehouse. She was talking to this stranger lady and even took candy from her."

"Oh, yeah! Who the hell are you?" Anita said, pulling a large can of tomato juice out of the grocery bag, and raising the can over her head as if ready to bash in Sister Anne's head.

The nun put her hand up to protect her head, but didn't back away. "My name is Sister Anne Farrell. I'm a teacher at Saint Peter's in Portsmouth."

Anita lowered the can, but kept it in her hand ready to throw. "What do you mean, 'sister? You one of them church ladies? Where's your long black dress? They all wear them black dresses, right? And cover their hair and stuff. You don't look like no sister. Well, maybe you do. Nobody wears ugly clothes like that no more. So what do you want here?"

"Ms. Morehouse, perhaps you could give me a few minutes of your time after you've seen to your daughter and put the groceries away. I'm in no hurry. I'll wait quietly over there." She pointed to where Hildy sat.

"You're going to stink as bad as him, cuz he'll jump all over you if he thinks you are paying him the least bit attention. No. You go sit on one of them chairs. They're a little rusted out, but they're safe enough to sit. Go on now. Wait. You give the kids that stuff they're chewing? What is it? Candy? You got any more? I'm that hungry. I was going to stop at Gilley's for a burger, but I used up all my money on tomato juice we can't even drink. Rotten dog!"

Chapter 25

"Sure, I remember Miz Johnson. She was a tough teacher, but outside the school she was a nice lady, as I remember her. My ma didn't allow me to talk to her outside school cuz she wasn't white, but she was a nice lady. I was littler then Amber when she got killed. They tore down her house cuz they was going to build a plant of some kind out here. But that never happened. My old boyfriend, Tommy, bought this piece a property for a song just about. He died cuz he crashed his car. That's the kind of driver he was. But he left me the trailer and the property. He loved me. I guess that proves it."

"Was Tommy Amber's father?"

"No, I had her after Tommy was long dead. To tell the truth, I don't know exactly who her daddy is. I'm that surprised she didn't turn out a idiot. Some of the men I... Well, never mind that. I needed money bad in those days. Don't judge me. I didn't know how to apply for the welfare. But my next boyfriend, Jack showed me. Now I finally got a job. It don't pay much, just enough to keep us eating. So far the tax collector for this dump ain't caught up with us. I ain't got no money for taxes anyhows. You can't get money from a stone, you know. I expect they'll be throwing us off the land pretty soon," Anita said, scanning the yard. "You never said what you want here."

"I don't think you can help me. I had a friend. Russell Hartz. He spent some time with Miss Johnson before she died."

"Dirty ol' Russell? He was your friend? You gotta be kidding! I didn't think he had no friends in this world. 'Specially not a nun! He used to come out here all the time."

"You knew him, then?"

"I wouldn't say I knew him exactly. I didn't want to know that dirty old guy. I just saw him all the time 'round here. I heard he buried his dog out here and come out to visit the grave. That's more than a little crazy, wouldn't you say? Who'd go visiting a dog's grave?"

"Where is the grave?"

"Ain't here no more. People started throwing stones at the crazy old guy and told him to stay away from here. One day there was an empty hole where his dog used to be. Can you imagine that? He come in the night and dug up that old dog. That old dog couldn't have been no more than a bunch of bones and dirty hair by then. That Russell was crazy as a loon. That's what he was."

"Maybe so, but he was a man who at least loved his dog. Can you tell me anything more about Russell?"

"No," said Anita, eyeing Hildy. "What you want to know about him for, anyway? Why's he your business. Go away now afore I sic Hildy on ya. She can be like a sick rat when I tell her to."

Chapter 26
Portsmouth, New Hampshire

Sharon Meadows had parked her rented SUV herself, rather than hand its key to the valet at the Sheraton. The cache of weapons hidden in the rear of the SUV could never have been missed by a curious valet. Still, when she returned to her vehicle, she checked that all was intact. Now, she sat in the driver's seat and considered her next move. She swiped her smartphone and searched for Constance Talant's name.

How long since I saw her in Venice? Why'd she move? Why'd she contact me? More important, why did Yoshiro go see her? And why was that other guy, Saito, watching me? How'd he catch on to me? I'd better find out what's going on here. It seems all wrong. Are they here to kill Connie? Why? Or are they here to kill the nun? Where's Chieko Shimizu? I'm supposed to be tracking them, not the other way around. Just what's going on here?

Only minutes later, Sharon pulled in front of an old white frame house on Summer Street. Connie's dark blue Volvo was parked in the driveway, and the interior lights of the house were on. No other car was parked on the street. Sharon walked up the path, climbed the three steps to the porch, and listened for a moment for sounds from the house. Nothing. She took two steps to the front door and pressed the doorbell.

Connie had been thinking about what to have for dinner. She didn't feel like cooking. Besides, there was nothing in her fridge to make for dinner. Seconds after she heard the doorbell, she peeked through the curtain on the door window and broke into a wide smile. She pushed open the door. "I was right. I knew you'd come here. Come in. Come on in. I was just about to heat up a TV dinner. Did you eat? I've got a couple more in the freezer. God, I'm glad you came over!" Connie's words came tumbling out as if they had been bottled up for too long. She pulled Sharon into her house.

In her kitchen Connie took two TV dinners out of her freezer. "Salisbury Steak or Chicken Tahiti? I'd recommend the chicken," she said. Sharon pointed to the chicken. "Good choice," Connie said as she pulled the frozen dinner from its box. "I'm gonna fill you in on the last few years since Venice, while I warm up our dinners. There's the coffee pot. The coffee's in the freezer. You do know how to make coffee, don't you? My mom sent me a box of her homemade molasses cookies yesterday. We'll have them for dessert, after we finish our fine entrées." Connie wrinkled her nose at the boxes. "So, now that we're not in the convent office, tell me what you've been up to? First, you tell me then I'll tell you why I asked you to come."

Sharon seemed to intentionally wait until Connie was ready to put a forkful of chopped beef into her mouth, before she said. "So how's business?"

Her usual warped sense of humor, Connie thought before she said, "In Boston it was the expected array of spouses spying on each other, and every now and then something interesting. It kept food on the table—such as it is," Connie grimaced at her divided plastic plate. "Up here, the job we just got might be the best I'll ever have. Also, the most dangerous... which is why you were called in. Let's have coffee first, and then I'll tell you what else I've discovered."

After Connie poured them each a cup of strong black coffee and placed a plate of cookies on the table, she said, "There. Help yourself."

"So why exactly am I here?" Sharon asked, and bit into a molasses cookie. "I'm supposing it has to do with the Asian folks you're hanging around with."

"Jeez, 'no grass grows under your feet,' as my mom says. So you saw them already. Yeah, that would be like you. They're Japanese and they're good people. Well, Mr. Saito is a *Yakuza* boss, but he's on the good side on this, so I'm all right with him. You're on the good side right now, too. Hope you haven't been doing something you shouldn't. You promised Sister Anne you'd rethink everything. That's why she sent for you. She trusts you. I guess I do, too. At least I'm trying to. The last thing I want to do is have to visit you in jail. And my guess is the last thing you want to do is *be* in jail. Anyway, you and Mr. Saito ought to get to know each other. You've got a lot in common."

"So why am I here?" questioned Sharon.

"Did you know I was living here? Did you..."

Sharon put her hand up to stop Connie from talking. She heard a subtle sound at the doorway and looked up to see an Asian woman staring back at her.

Connie smiled and said, "Sharon, this is Chieko Shimizu. Chieko, this is my friend, Sharon Meadows." The two women nodded to each other. Sharon gave no indication that she had been studying a photo of Chieko only a few hours earlier.

"Come, sit with us, Chieko," Connie said. Chieko walked into the kitchen and sat at the table next to Connie.

"Here's dinner," Connie said to Chieko. Connie reached over Sharon's still-full plate and pushed it toward Chieko. Chieko deftly pushed it back. Connie knew she was beaming like a fool at them. "We're like the Three Musketeers," Connie said. Chieko looked bewildered and Sharon rolled her eyes. "You two need to see each other in action to appreciate what I just said. Well, with any luck we won't have to take any action, but if Mr. Yoshiro is right, we can expect an influx of members of a Japanese secret sect any time now." Chieko nodded.

"Sharon, if you're not going to eat it, put your dinner up on the counter. My neighbor's dog always manages to show up when I've got extra food. He's not as fussy as you. His owner says he gives him plenty of dog food. But the dog prefers people food. I guess this qualifies," she said, looking down at Sharon's congealed dinner. "Let's just enjoy the cookies. And I'll tell you more about the coming war."

Chapter 27

"How many members of the Cabal are we expecting?" Sharon asked.

"We don't know," said Chieko.

"I've been told there are twenty-seven cells, but we don't know how many men are in each cell," Connie said. "Evidently the cells and their leaders are numbered. The highest number is the most lethal."

"Surely, they're not all coming to the U.S.," said Sharon.

"We don't know," Chieko and Connie said at the same time. Then Chieko said, "On our side there's the three of us, Mr. Yoshiro and Mr. Saito. I myself doubt that the whole Cabal is coming from Japan. I have heard that the Cabal has members in the United States, but I do not know that for certain."

"So it'll be five against who knows how many," Sharon noted, but she was thinking, *How interesting. My targets are three enemies of the ETA Cabal. Well, I guess I know who my client is.* She decided she'd have to think more about her assignment, especially if they were Connie's associates. *Complications*, she thought, then she tuned back in to Connie.

"Yes, but we five are probably worth twenty of them," Connie said.

"And if there's twenty-one of them?" Sharon asked. "Anyway, the thing is, I don't get it. What does the Cabal want? You said the mirror is a historic treasure. What good is it to them?"

"Chieko, you tell Sharon about the mirror," Connie said.

"Gladly," said Chieko. "There are different renditions of our creation story. I will tell you my favorite." She took a breath. "In the beginning," she said, "there were two gods: Izinami, the female god and Izinagi, the male god. They begat all the other gods. The two most important were Amaterasu, the sun goddess, and Susuno-o, the storm god. Amaterasu is, as Christians would put it, the patron saint of Japan.

"Susuno-o was very much like his name, very volatile, and unpredictable. One day, in a particularly bad mood, Susuno-o destroyed Amaterasu's rice fields. You probably know that in Asia rice fields are vital to the life of the people. Amaterasu was so angry she ran and hid herself in a cave. The world was plunged into darkness.

"The gods tried everything to persuade her to come out of the cave and bring light back to the world. They even performed lewd and lascivious dances to tempt her out. But she would not.

"Then, the gods had an idea. They made a mirror and they yelled to her: "Amaterasu, you don't have to come out. We have another sun goddess. You are no longer needed."

"Amaterasu couldn't believe her ears. She sulked for a while, but finally, she could not stand it any longer. She had to see the new sun goddess for herself. Amaterasu moved softly to the cave opening, pushed the boulder door a fraction of an inch aside, and peeked out. She gasped with surprise to see a bright light illuminating the earth.

"But, the gods had tricked her. They had placed a mirror in the opening, and Amaterasu saw her own reflection. It was too late for her. The gods pushed the boulder further out of the way, grabbed her, and pulled her back out into the world.

"We Japanese believe the gods gave our first Emperor the mirror that we call *Yata no Kagami*. It is housed in the Ise Jingu, a special shrine in Ise. The High Priestess of Ise, the *Saio*, is charged with protecting the mirror. The present *Saio* is very, very old and will soon die. I will be the next *Saio*. My oldest friend, Hirobumi Yoshiro, has told me that the mirror at Ise is a copy, not our real treasure.

"It was, of course, a great shock. I confronted the present *Saio*. She confessed to me that it is true. I am very, very angry at her and her predecessor. They both knew our treasure was not at the shrine and did nothing about it. So now it is my duty to search for the Yata Mirror and bring it back home."

"The two Saios before you knew about the missing *Yata no Kagami* and did nothing?" asked Sharon.

"Yes. The last words the *Saio* had for me before she fell into a coma confirmed Hirobumi's words. On her death bed my predecessor told me that she and her predecessor knew the mirror was long ago replaced by a copy before it was brought to America. She said they felt powerless and did nothing. It is the *Saio's* duty to protect the *Yata no Kagami*. That is the vow we pledge. My two predecessors failed in their duty. The *Saio* said she and her predecessor were not allowed to leave the shrine. So now I must find the mirror before I become the Saio."

"As I understand it, there was some confusion," Connie added. "An exact replica was made of the mirror about a hundred years ago. Well, the replica's not exactly 'exact.' The replica was caste in a modern bronze. The real treasure is an old, imperfect, bronze and that's the one that's missing."

"And why does the criminal ETA Cabal want the mirror?"

"*Yata no Kagami* is a symbol of the Emperor's authority. If the Cabal can show that Japan has been without its sacred treasure for more than one hundred years, the Imperial family will fall and so will Japan. The Emperor's denial of his deity in 1945 and the adoption of democratic political institutions were not enough for the Cabal. The Cabal's aim is to destroy the Emperor and his family and to set itself up as the legitimate government of Japan. If they can get their hands on it, they'll claim that the mirror was passed to them."

"Well, excuse me for saying so, but that's crazy. I've spent some time in Japan. Modern-day Japanese people aren't going to buy into that," said Sharon. "That Cabal is living in a fantasy world. The Japanese today are much too savvy to fall for that story."

"Miss Meadows, underlying our modernization efforts is our very strong belief and love of our traditions. Our traditions are what make us unique. The Cabal stands on both sides of the fence. On the one hand, it says Japan is too mired in its traditions. On the other hand, it wants to use the quintessential symbol of our traditions to claim power. Whatever, it does, its effect will be to demoralize our people," Chieko said. "Our feet may be marching in the twenty-first century, but our hearts and heads are in the clouds with our ancestors."

"We'd better find that mirror," said Sharon.

Chapter 28
Boston, Massachusetts

Twenty-Seven walked out of International Terminal E at Logan Airport. His long hair had been cut into a contemporary western style that enhanced his handsome and polished face. His Italian slacks and shirt were tailored perfectly for his tall, slim body. A young man dressed in a dark suit came running up to him and reached for his bags. "My name is Joseph, Sir. This way, please, Sir" he said, leading Twenty-Seven to a black limousine, and opening the back door for him. After Joseph placed the suitcases in the limousine's trunk, he climbed in the front seat with the driver.

Joseph turned to face Twenty-Seven as well as he could. "Sir," he said, "You ordered us to find accommodations for you in Portsmouth, New Hampshire. I was told that you do not want to stay in a hotel. Sir, we rented a small, furnished townhouse for you, central to everything. Internet service has been purchased, and your rental car is in its garage. I believe you will be satisfied. Two men have been assigned to serve you. I am one of them. Robert is waiting at the house. Elliot, our driver, is available to you whenever you wish it. Your documents are in the envelope in the compartment at your side. As you ordered, you will take on a Chinese identity. Your name here in the United States is

Richard Han. You will let me know if there is anything else you require."

Twenty-Seven grunted, put his head back, and slept during the full hour-long car ride to Portsmouth.

Chapter 29
Portsmouth, New Hampshire

The afternoon after his arrival, Han, wiping the distaste from his face, pushed on the grimy doorbell at the Brewster Street rooming house in Portsmouth. Ashley Hartz threw open the door. "What do you want?" she yelled before she said, "Oh, sorry. I thought you were somebody else." Ashley was wearing her white short shorts, but had on a Patriots T-shirt tied in a knot above her navel. Her bare feet were dusty. She stared up at Han, thrust out her chest, and smiled, careful not to open her mouth where her loose tooth had fallen out that morning.

"I'm sorry to have disturbed you. I'm sure you are very busy. I'm looking for a Mr. Russell Hartz," said Han with a broad smile as if he hadn't heard her.

"You and the rest of the world," Ashley murmured, then said, "There ain't no man here."

"I'm so sorry," Han said smoothly. "I must have been given the wrong address. Please excuse me for bothering you. If you would forgive me for saying so," he added with a faint smile, "it is difficult to believe that a young lady like yourself is not married." Han turned to go.

"Hold on, there handsome. Who are you looking for exactly?" Ashley's thumb played with the fake gold ring piercing her navel.

"You looking for my granddaddy? Well, he's long gone. Come on in, anyway. I ain't got nothing to drink but water from the sink. It's cold, though. I've got a jug of it in the icebox. I got some pound cake, too. What's your name? My name is Ashley Marie."

Later that afternoon Han paced the basement of the boarding house. Ashley was bound and gagged and lay on the dusty floor. Han strode over to Ashley and drew his sharp blade across her inner thigh. More blood trickled onto the dusty floor. Ashley had given up trying to scream. She moaned. Her eyes rolled back in her head, and Han slapped her face, "Stay awake. Don't faint," he ordered the young woman. Han sat down on an old wooden chair, and said, "Now Ashley, the next cut I make will be to slice off one of those breasts you're so proud of. Just one. I believe that would be worse for you than two. You'd be... what is the word... yes, lop-sided! You would hate that, wouldn't you? Save yourself the agony and tell me where Russell hid the treasure.... was that a nod? . . . Good. You finally decided I mean to get the information I want no matter how much pain I give you. I'm going to remove the gag across your mouth, but I'm warning you now, if you try to scream, I'll cut your throat. You know I'll do it, don't you. Nod your head, to show me you know I'll cut your throat if you try to scream.... Good. Now I'm removing the gag." He bent over her and with the tips of his fingers and a face that showed his disgust, he removed the wet gag. "Now," he hissed, "tell me where the treasure is. My patience is gone."

"Sister Anne has it," Ashley gasped.

"Who is this Sister Anne?"

"Sister Anne of St. Peter's up the street."

"Are you sure, Ashley? You'd better be sure. If that woman doesn't have it, I'll come back and cut your heart out. Understand?" Ashley nodded and Han pulled the gag back over her mouth. Her face and body were soaking in sweat. Blood mingled with sweat and pooled on the floor. "You're disgusting," he hissed. He wanted to kick her, but he didn't want to get his shoes in the slime. He grabbed the rope and pulled her over to the furnace. Then he looped the ropes around the pipes to prevent her from crawling away. He could see she wasn't going anywhere, but perhaps slipping towards death. But Twenty-Seven was a careful man. He knew the will to live is stronger than pain. He'd come back and finish her, if she wasn't dead already. He checked the knots in the ropes. Then he brushed himself off, climbed out the bulkhead, out into the sunlight.

Chapter 30

Hirobumi Yoshiro closed his cell phone. "Your informant was right," he said to Saito, "Twenty-Seven arrived in Boston yesterday. How many others should we expect?"

"He might not bring others from Japan. He has cells of followers here, in California, and New York. He sent them a message that we're trying to destroy The Twenty-Seven. His American followers might be mobilizing now."

"Can you give us an idea of how many could be mobilizing?" Connie asked.

"I can get an estimate," said Saito. "The Cabal is not just a cult, it is one of our biggest competitors. We keep a very watchful eye on our competitors." Saito opened his cell phone and walked out of Connie's kitchen into the garden.

"You weren't kidding when you said there could be war," Sharon said to Chieko. Inwardly, Sharon was wondering on whose side she would eventually be fighting. In Venice she and Connie had almost come to blows. She knew Connie would be good in a war. She wondered how well Chieko would do. *Why should I kill these Japanese people? I promised Sister Anne I won't kill anymore except in self-defense. And I like Yoshiro. Saito's, well, hot, and Chieko is a gal after my own heart. They're all good guys.*

I could use the money. But I'm thinking the Twenty-Seven are the bad guys. I don't work for bad guys. I promised. 'Good guys, bad guys.' What am I, a teenager?

"I do not wish to fight, but I do not shrink from doing whatever I must," Chieko was saying, "but most important is to find the mirror first, before Twenty-Seven finds it. Once he has it, all is lost.

"If we can find it and take it back to Japan, we will avert the killing. Sharon, Connie, you have no idea of how bad it could be. Not just for us, but for innocent bystanders. The members of the Cabal are fanatics. Connie, you spoke to the Hartz girl and the nun. Did they give any idea of where the mirror is? If I cannot get it immediately, is it at least safely hidden from Twenty-Seven?"

It took Connie only a moment to say, "I honestly don't know, Chieko. Sister Anne is the key. I think she has a good idea where it is, but she is conflicted. We have to talk to her again before Twenty-Seven finds her. We have to persuade Sister Anne to be fully open with us. Chieko, I think you could do that."

Chapter 31

"Good afternoon," Twenty-Seven said to the woman who opened the convent house door after the first ring of the doorbell. "My name is Richard Han. I'm here to see Sister Anne."

"Good afternoon Mr. Han," said the old nun, "my name is Sister Agnes. May I ask: Is Sister Anne expecting you? She said nothing to me about expecting a visitor."

"No, Sister Agnes. Sister Anne is not expecting me, but it is a matter of some urgency that I speak to her."

The nun studied Han for a few moments and said, "Well, like a salesman, you look. You're not here to try to sell something, are you? Sister Anne is not authorized to buy supplies for the convent or school. If you're selling something, you have to see Sister Elbert. But she's not here right now. You'll have to come back." Sister Agnes made a motion to close the door, but Han had wedged his foot against it.

"Sister Agnes, I'm an old friend. I came all the way from Japan to see Sister Anne."

"Young man, I might be old and forgetful, but even I remember that Sister Anne was stationed in Japan before you were born. You can't be an old friend of hers. What business could you have with her? I'll bet you're a salesman. You look like a salesman. Call and make an appointment. I'll tell her you stopped by." She tried to close the door again, but this time Han pushed the door against her hand.

"I must insist," said Twenty-Seven. "I will see her now."

"What's going on here?" The woman's voice came from behind Sister Agnes. "Who are you, young man? And what do you want here?" Sister Anne said, as she stepped in front of the older nun and stared at Han. Then Sister Anne said, "Sister Agnes, I'll take care of this. Thank you." The older nun glared at Han, muttered, "very impolite," then turned and walked away from the door.

Sister Anne stepped past Han and closed the convent door behind her. "Come on, I could use a cool drink," she said. "We'll walk. No, we'll cross down there at the light. The traffic at this time of day coming up from Middle Street is horrendous. Everyone's wanting to get home from work. And they all cut through here. I have no intention of being run over by a speedster. Come on. This way," she ordered. "We'll walk on Islington. The traffic is still heavy there, but everyone knows the cops patrol Islington better, so there won't be any crazies racing home. I suppose you're here about Russell's treasure, too, aren't you? No, wait. Wait 'til we get down to Islington. You can buy me an iced tea at Café Kilim. I'm as thirsty as can be."

"You don't look the least uncomfortable in this heat. A cool customer, aren't you? Why's that car following us? Is that your car? Just tell your driver to pull over and wait for you. It's a terrible waste of fuel. It's important to consider the environment nowadays. It's our responsibility to save the world for the children, don't you think?"

They sat in the shade outside on one of the café's rickety benches. After she took a sip from her tall glass of iced tea, Sister Anne said, "You say your name is Han? That's a Chinese name, but you look Japanese. Tell me about that."

"My father's father was Chinese. But I am Japanese. I am not here to talk about me..."

"I know why you're here. Now you're perspiring. You ought to buy yourself a cold drink, too. The iced tea is good. You can get it with or without sugar. Sugar doesn't look to be your problem. I'm careful about eating or drinking it.

"So, anyway, I know why you're here talking to me, and you're out of luck. You're looking for Russell's treasure. My best guess is that if he really had one, it was buried with him. Sometimes I have doubts that such a treasure ever existed. On the other hand, his obsession could be very persuasive.

"No, Mr. Han. I think if there were a treasure he would have wanted it buried with him. Although Heaven knows, nobody ever paid attention to what he wanted. No human being should have had to live his unfortunate life. Poor Russell. He was a bitter man. And it's no wonder. I pray God has had mercy on his soul, and Russell is happier now than he ever was in life.

"What's that look? You're not a believer. That's all right. Believe or don't believe what you want. About Russell's treasure: Here's what I think. He just said he had a treasure to get attention. I think I knew him better than anyone, and I never saw it. And he was the type who would have showed it to everyone. He liked attention. The truth is, nobody even wanted to know him. Well, there's his granddaughter, Ashley. She knew him, but she didn't want anything to do with him. And he'd never show her anything worth money. She'd steal it," the nun babbled on.

"Here's my thinking on it. First, he said his father stole it out of the Wentworth. I don't believe it. The cops would have been on that man like white on rice—I love that turn of phrase, don't you? The Wentworth had mucho influence in those days. It wouldn't have let a thief off the hook. Second, I didn't know his father. Even I'm not that old. But if he were anything like Russell, that so-called treasure would have been sitting in a pawnshop window in Boston an hour after he'd stolen it. Even if Russell got his hands on it before his father sold it, Russell would have pawned it himself as soon as he could hitch a ride to

Boston. The poor man valued nothing unless he could get money for it. According to Russell, he wasn't to blame. He took after his father in that way. "I regret to say, it's in my genes," he used to say.

"Mr. Han, I don't know how you heard about Russell's so-called treasure, but give it up. Russell Hartz was a pathetic liar. His greatest joy was to get people heated up and running around. Ask the fire department. He was notorious for pulling fire alarms. I'm not saying his treasure didn't exist. It may have, but I never saw it. And I have no idea what it is. Probably a beautiful sea shell. He liked looking for them at the beach. And his personality was such that you didn't know what to believe. Maybe because I never saw it. I just don't believe he had a treasure of any kind." She took a long sip of tea and stared doe-eyed at him.

Han rose from his chair. "I am not walking back to the convent with you," he said. I will just say goodbye for the moment. But you are not fooling anyone, Sister Anne. You know more than you're telling me. I will see you again... soon." Han turned and walked toward Market Square.

Sister Anne took her time finishing her iced tea. *A beautiful, but most unpleasant man. I wonder why God allows that? It isn't God. It's the devil who uses beauty for evil. And I believe what this so-called Mr. Han said. I haven't seen the last of him. Not by a long shot.* Then she shook away a feeling of dread. *Someone walking on my grave—probably Russell.* As she placed the tall glass, still rattling with ice, on the sidewalk, Connie Talent's old Volvo pulled up to the curb. "Hop in," Connie said, "I'll give you a ride back to Saint Pete's."

"Thanks, but I'll walk," Sister Anne said.

Sharon jumped out of the back seat of the Volvo and held the front passenger door open for Sister Anne. "You'll ride, Sister Anne," she said, "we insist." Her voice held a threat. "Here, take my seat if you prefer.

I've got things to do," Sharon ended, walking in the same direction Han had taken.

The nun looked at Connie and said, "She's the most beautiful woman I have ever seen outside of the movies. That hard edge to her voice can be very daunting, though. I suppose that's its purpose. Well, she's not scaring me." Sister Anne rolled her eyes and got into the car. Only then did she notice the other woman in the back seat.

Some minutes later Connie pulled into a wooded area in Newington. She took the time to park her car in a space overlooking the water such that she couldn't be blocked in, and could drive away fast if she had to. Chieko looked puzzled at the way Connie maneuvered the car, and then she understood and smiled. Connie noticed her smile, and said, "My mom's uncle was a spy for the Allies during World War Two. He used to say, "'Always leave an exit route.'"

"Can we get out and walk now?" Sister Anne asked.

"Not yet, Sister," Connie said. "Let's see who's been following us."

"I see only my friends," said Chieko, who pointed with a slight movement of her head at a large silver BMW 760Li that had pulled in and sat just to the left of the entrance to the parking area.

"Who's in the fancy car? You said 'friends'?" the nun asked.

"Yes, those are my friends and protectors," answered Chieko, 'Mr. Saito, and my childhood friend, Hirobumi Yoshiro." She looked around the parking area. "This is a good place, Connie. If the war is going to start, it should be here." She closed her cell phone. "I don't see anyone else in the vicinity who can be hurt or killed. The Twenty-Seven will be here soon. Give me a moment. I'll be right back." Chieko jumped out of the car and ran to the BMW. The doors of that car had already opened. Saito had gone back to the trunk and was unloading weapons. Connie stepped out of Sharon's SUV and went to the back.

"Sister," Connie said, sticking her head back into the vehicle's window. "Looks like there's going to be trouble here in a few minutes. I want you to go over there to that stand of trees. Walk way back and stay behind as many as you can. Then run away when you can. And don't worry about us. We're both very good at this."

"I can't help you with a gun, but I will pray for you."

"That'll be a big help. Now, get going." Connie turned to go.

"Wait," cried Sister Anne. "They want me, don't they? I can't endanger your lives. I'll just surrender to them. I don't want any blood shed for me."

"They want the mirror," Connie answered.

"I believe I may know where it is."

"I know you do, but we'll talk about that later. There's no surrendering to them. Get down."

"Give this to Chieko in case I don't make it." Sister Anne reached into her pocket and pulled out a folded dirty piece of paper. "Russell gave me this a long time ago and asked me to keep it safe. Please give it to Chieko." She handed the paper to Connie. Connie beckoned to Chieko who came running over. Connie passed the paper on to her.

Chieko opened the paper and quickly studied the rough penciled map, then she tore the paper into small bits and let the wind blow them out of her open hand. She peered into the nun's face. "Thank you, Sister. You must help me find this place. Thank you, again. You have done Japan a great service." Chieko's cell phone buzzed and she gazed at it. Then she looked across at Saito who was just pocketing his own phone. "It's starting," said Chieko, who ran off toward the men. "Get behind your car and defend yourselves," she yelled over her back. "We'll take care of the rest."

"Run into the trees. Now!" Connie yelled to Sister Anne. Then she yelled, "Whoa, Nelly!" I expected them to come with a roar," she said of the two black Hummers that were racing swiftly and silently down the long road to the park. "The fun's about to start. I found something interesting in the back. Get moving, Sister Anne," Connie said, pulling a small rocket launcher out of the back of the SUV and pointing it at the front vehicle. In only a few seconds the front of the Hummer exploded, and six men came scrambling out of it. "Damn!" Connie cursed. "I was pointing at the gas tank." She grabbed the rifle she'd tossed in the van.

Yoshiro and Saito were each down on one knee, aiming their assault rifles at the armed men rushing at them. The sixth man from the Hummer had dropped his weapon and had pounced on Chieko. In moments he was laying in the dirt rubbing his broken leg, with Chieko's foot on his neck. She smashed the butt of her rifle against his head and walked away. His five companions were lying dead or writhing on the ground, and the other Hummer had turned and raced away. "My men will attempt to stop them before they get too far," yelled Saito.

Yoshiro had run to look at the wounded and dead men. "None of these could be Twenty-Seven," he said over his shoulder. He took photos of the men on the ground with his cellphone. "I'll send these photos back to Japan and see who these men are," he said. Connie stood and stared at the downed men. "You guys are really good," said Connie to Yoshiro and Saito. "And Chieko! You rock girl!"

Chieko made a very small bow and said, "I had very good teachers."

"You okay?" Connie asked Sister Anne who had rushed back to pray over the dead men.

"All this suffering and death for a bronze plate?" Sister Anne asked.

"This crucifix," Chieko said, pointing to the cross on a chain around the nun's neck, "is only a symbol, but still has great meaning for you. The *Yata no Kagami* is the actual gift of the gods. Not a mere symbol. Yes, it is very precious to us. It is the very soul of Japan."

"Then I must help you to find it and bring it home," said the nun.

"Yes," Chieko answered.

Sister Anne pulled on a metal chain under her shirt. She unclasped it and slid off a worn tin medallion. "Russell said when he was just a little boy he found a dog lying in a ditch near his home. He had heard the

188

dog's yelp when it was hit by a car on the road. It was a bitch and soon after he found her, she had given birth to puppies. The mother and the puppies all died except one. Russell took it home and named it Sparky. He made this rather crude ID for it.

"Russell adored that puppy. He did everything he could to keep the puppy alive. He shared his own meager meals with her and kept her warm in his own bed during the long winters. His mother especially hated Sparky. She said the dog was bound to get pregnant, and there'd be puppies all over their yard. She said she wouldn't spend her money to have it spayed. It's a wonder she or her husband didn't kill the little dog. She chained Sparky out in the front yard, to keep her out of the house. Sparky eventually dug herself a small tunnel to get under the porch. She found shelter there during rain or snow storms. Russell brought Sparky cans of water and fed her scraps from his own plate and from the garbage when his parents weren't looking.

"Such a sad story. Russell said Sparky was the only being he had ever loved; and Sparky was the only being who had ever loved him. There was a good deal wrong about Russell, but one could never accuse him of weakness. He survived his terrible childhood and helped Sparky survive. That took strength.

"Look," she said, showing Sparky's ID to Chieko, "there's Sparky's name that Russell scratched into the tin, and the date he found Sparky, Christmas 1904. He liked to say Sparky was the only Christmas present he ever received. Now on this side," Sister Anne turned the tin medallion over, "is a rough map to where Russell buried Sparky and your treasure."

Chieko stared at the medallion, but said, "I don't understand those scratches. It does not look to me like a map. It is not the same as the map on the piece of paper you gave me."

"The paper showed on what island in the Isles of Shoals he hid the mirror. The medallion shows where the mirror is on the island. I'm sure he intentionally drew two different maps. Russell was very intelligent, but his parents didn't know anything about his intellectual gifts. They treated him like an ignoramus, and he was content to play that role for them.

"When he found your mirror, he knew his father had stolen it, but he didn't know what to do about it. So he just hid it."

"Where?" asked Constance.

"At first, in the only safe place he knew—a large hollow log that was his secret hiding place. Then he moved it to Sparky's tunnel. When Sparky died, he buried it on one of the Isles of Shoals with his dog. His two treasures," answered Sister Anne. She handed the medallion to Chieko. "Here. This belongs to you," she said.

Chapter 32
Newington, New Hampshire

Sister Anne watched Yoshiro and Saito pick up the dead men and throw their bodies into what was left of the Hummer. In a few moments, Yoshiro managed to put the vehicle in neutral. It rolled slowly down the hill, picking up speed, until it reached the ledge and tipped into Great Bay.

Out of the corner of her eye the nun watched the two wounded men hobble away from the parking lot. She took a step toward them. "No, Sister. Let them get help somewhere else," said Chieko. "They're not good to anyone anymore."

Sister Anne took a deep breath, and said, "So much violence and misery. Is it worth it? I feel I owe it to Russell to keep my promise. Russell and I once talked about the concept of sanctuary. I told him if he ever needed help to come to Saint Peter's and find me. I promised to help him. I told him I'd give him sanctuary. I'm such a weakling. How could I have helped him at all? I can't even keep my word to him." Sister Anne's eyes teared up. "I'm sorry. I can't... I promised," she whispered. "I know he's passed away, but I promised never to tell. I've reneged on my promise to him."

Tears had also come to Chieko's eyes. She took hold of the nun's hand. "Sister Anne, I understand commitment and what it means to be authentically what we vowed we would be. My predecessors broke their vows. I will not break mine."

"We are of different religions, but I have also made religious vows. I am a Shinto priestess, and I will soon be the High Priestess. I understand your reluctance, but even so I beg for your assistance.

"Sister, please listen to me. The present High Priestess is very old and is preparing to die. I must find the mirror and hurry home with it before she dies. A High Priestess must always be in residence at the shrine. It is our tradition. I must hurry back. I cannot fail my duty or my country. There is so little time. It is imperative that I find the mirror and bring it to the Ise Jingu. It is my duty.

"The mirror, which we call *Yata no Kagami*, has been in the safekeeping of the Ise Jingu, that is to say, the Ise Shrine, since the seventh century, under the guardianship of the High Priestess. This honored office was traditionally given to a princess of the Imperial family. Since this is not always possible, the office has been given to a girl who is willing and able to endure the training that is deemed necessary to protect the mirror. It is a very great responsibility and requires years of intensive preparation. I have completed this training, and will be the next High Priestess, the *Saio*.

"When I studied in college, I was particularly interested in Kierkegaard's idea of authenticity. Sartre, as I am sure you know, continued this study of authenticity. Although, he... Well, I am completely convinced that to be a true human being one must be true to oneself. My predecessors were not. They were false to themselves and to humanity. The loss of the *Yata no Kagami* is not just a philosophical problem. It is a very crucial loss for our country.

"I am determined to find the mirror. And I am determined the cycle of weakness and non-action will stop. Yoshiro-san and I investigated the records of those who had access to the mirror. We both suspect it was brought to Portsmouth, New Hampshire on the occasion of the Russo-

Japanese Peace Treaty. No, not 'suspect.' We know it to be true. Hirobumi Yoshiro and I have seen the journal of the man who stole it from the shrine.

"It should never have been taken from Ise, but it was," Chieko threw a glance toward Hirobumi, "Now Mr. Yoshiro, Mr. Saito, and I are pledged to return it to its rightful place. Unfortunately, it is not just a matter of finding the mirror. The group calling itself the ETA Cabal is also looking for it. The ETA is a Cabal that is sworn to bring down the Emperor and impose its own rule over Japan. It is a foolish and dangerous goal. A madness. A fantasy that can't come true. The people of Japan would never stand for it. Still the ETA will destroy anything in its path to try to attain its mad objective. Too many innocent people will suffer and die for nothing but the vain ambition of madmen."

Chieko continued, "If the Cabal find it before we do, they will flaunt their possession of it. We must prevent that. The people of Japan must not know the mirror, the very soul of Japan, has been missing for a century. We cannot allow the Cabal to be successful. I trust you. To be truthful, I must trust you. Please help me to find the Sacred Mirror and return it to Ise Jingu."

Sister Anne stared into Chieko's eyes for a few moments as if looking for a confirmation of what she had just been told. Then, she said, "Okay. I can't guarantee it, but I'll bring you to the only place I know it was for many years. Russell said he moved it out to the Isles of Shoals, but we should search here in Newington, in the old homestead area. It's close by.

"And I promise I'll never say a word about this to anyone. But I have one question: if the disappearance of the mirror and your mission to find it is so secret, why is the ETA here?"

"Sister Anne, a woman in the *Saio's* employ was a traitor," Chieko sighed. "The leader of the cult has already killed her. 'Twenty-Seven' is completely ruthless and definitely, how do you say, 'off his rocker'."

"I've lived in your beautiful country. There's no way he's going to assert his will on the Japanese people. They won't stand for it. Japan is one of the most democratic countries in the world today," said Sister Anne.

"He and his followers will hunt down and kill everyone who tries to stop him. I know you are right. In the long run, he can't win. The people will not accept his madness. But he will try and too many will suffer and die."

"Is Twenty-Seven here in the States now?"

"Yes," said Yoshiro. "It seems you had tea with him earlier today."

Sister Anne's eyes widened.

"Our intention is to prevent him from stealing the mirror. If he starts a war with us, we will defend ourselves."

"Shall we go now? It's getting late," said Sister Anne. "I must be back in time for Vespers. We don't have far to go. To what Russell called his log cabin. He said he'd moved his treasure from there. But, when it comes to what Russell had to say, well... Let us just say that it's best to be prudent. If the five of us are going, we should take Connie's larger car."

"No Sister," said Yoshiro. "Mr. Saito and I will follow you in our car."

"Mr. Yoshiro," Connie said, "May I suggest Sister Anne and Chieko go with you. Mr. Saito, may I invite you to join me. We will follow behind as guards."

"I like the way you think," said Saito

Saito's cell phone buzzed. He looked at the screen and said, "Excuse me," before he walked away from the others. When he came back, he said, "We must go. Connie's idea was a good one, but we will lead. And we will not search now. We must go to the safe house." He picked up two rifles and a bag of ammunition. He motioned for Connie to pick up weapons and ammunition, too.

"Do you drive?" Yoshiro asked Sister Anne.

"Yes."

"Good." He turned to Chieko. "Would you choose your weapons, please? I will keep the arsenal back here," he said, jumping into the back seat. "Chieko, you, please, sit up front with Sister Anne. I believe you will be safer there."

In the rear car Connie asked Saito, "How bad is it going to be?"

"Fifteen men in three Hummers."

"Is Twenty-Seven among them?" asked Connie.

"I don't know. Any more rockets for this launcher?" Saito asked her.

"In the back. It looks like it's sealed off, but you can get into it through the back seat. There's a lever on the left there that will unlock the back of the seat. I'm smaller and more limber. I can get back in there easily if you want," Connie offered.

"I believe your eyesight is sharper than mine. Please keep a watch out for the Hummers."

"I'd be happier if I had an automatic weapon," said Connie with a large sigh.

"I very much wish to make you happy," Saito said. "I have no automatic weapon at my disposal at the moment, but there are two more in my car. If my men earn the considerable amount I'm paying them, the first wave of attackers will never arrive to challenge us. In the worst-case scenario, the enemy will at least be delayed and considerably weakened. I will arm you then. Happy now?"

"I sure as hell am," cried Connie. "And I'll be even happier after I take a shower at the safe house."

"I like you. You are keeping cool under so much pressure," Saito said.

"Yeah, I like you, too. But that doesn't mean we're taking a shower together, pal." Saito looked up at her in surprise, then they both laughed.

Chapter 33
Portsmouth, New Hampshire

In his rented townhouse some minutes later, Twenty-Seven threw his handgun on his bed and went directly into his bathroom. He stripped off his clothes and turned on the shower. He stepped in and sighed. He did his best thinking when warm water trickled onto his head and down his lean body. He believed processed soap irritated his skin, so he had packed and used only soap bark from the Quillaja Saponaria tree to rub down his head and body. When he finished scrubbing himself, he stood taking deep, even breaths in the trickling warm water. After he turned off the shower, he stood on the bathmat and shook the excess water away. Then Twenty-Seven gently blotted his hair, face, and body with one of the large soft chamois on the towel rod. Finally, he opened the bathroom door and walked into the cool bedroom.

He felt her presence, before he saw Sharon Meadows leaning against the wall across from the bathroom door. His first impulse was to grab the S & W he had thrown on his bed. But Sharon was pointing it at his midsection.

"You have me at a disadvantage," he said, then added, "I don't enjoy having my body studied by a woman." He tied the large chamois around his hips. "What do you want?" he asked as he knotted the soft leather.

She stared at him for a few moments before she said, "No, the question is: what do *you* want?"

He was staring back at her. Long and hard. Finally, he said, "Your business is not with me. If you leave now, I will not kill you. But if you cross my path again, it will be your last."

"Big words from a guy who has nothing in his hands but a towel. Step away from the doorway," Sharon responded, "or those will be the last words you'll have ever spoken."

"Now why are we standing here threatening each other? It's clear that we should be working together, not acting like enemies." Twenty-Seven's voice had turned into a soft purr. "Look, I'm not moving an inch. I know who you are, Sharon. Let's talk about what we both want," he added.

Chapter 34
Rye, New Hampshire

In the safe house, Saito rapped his teaspoon on the table. "Ladies and Yoshiro-san, according to the information I'm receiving on my cell phone, this is the situation. First, the body of Miss Ashley Hartz was found this afternoon in the basement of the rooming house in which she lived. She suffered deep cuts all over her body. The coroner's guess is that she died from ex-sanguination and shock, but he won't be certain until after the autopsy."

Sister Anne made the sign of the cross, sighed, and grabbed Connie's hand. "The poor kid," was Connie's only remark.

"It was Twenty-Seven," said Yoshiro.

"Yes, I believe so. The girl had a slow and very painful death. It is that sadistic fiend's 'signature,'" answered Saito. "If she knew the whereabouts of the Sacred Mirror, he has it by now."

"Poor Ashley knew nothing about the mirror," said Sister Anne.

"Sister Anne," he said, "you should not return to the convent tonight. It is too dangerous. Please call to tell them you are staying with a sick friend and will return as soon as you can, tomorrow. And please do not argue about this with me. The Cabal knows about you. They would not hesitate to attack the convent. Perhaps other nuns would also fall victim to this madman. You do not want that to happen,

I am sure. Right now the Cabal knows you are not at home in the convent, but with us. The convent is safe.

"My informant tells me that the men in the second Hummer were able to report on everyone they saw in the parking lot in detail. They either named or described each one of us. They were very thorough. The Cabal will be watching the convent to see if you return. This is a safe house for the time being. You ladies will please make yourselves comfortable in the bedrooms.

"As for Yoshiro and I, we will also bed down here in this house for the night. He and I will sleep on the carpeted floor in this room. If you are comfortable with that?" They all nodded their heads. "You ladies will make your own arrangements upstairs, I am sure. Just for our own information, Sister Anne, where are we?"

"We are in Rye, New Hampshire. This is a house my religious order uses for retreats or general meetings. Its isolation on the seacoast is perfect for solitary contemplation. As you saw, the kitchen is not well stocked. According to the newsletter from our Motherhouse, the next occupation is not to be for another month. Groups must bring their own foodstuffs. However, we do not have to be concerned about a gathering of nuns or students walking in on us."

"For now, we are safe. Although, I would prefer it if we could make our way to the sea more easily. These rocky cliffs are pleasant to look at, but there is no easy way to get down to a boat," said Saito. "Well, let us put that problem aside. My information is the Twenty-Seven do not know where we are, and they cannot be sure we are still together. Although they must suspect we are. They are looking feverishly for us, particularly you, Chieko and Sister Anne. They believe we are hiding in Portsmouth."

"You seem to know an awful lot about what the Cabal is doing from moment to moment," Connie said. Her hand had crept to the Glock in her waistband.

"I know all this because one of my men has infiltrated the Cabal," Saito answered. "Having said that, I would not be very surprised to learn a Cabal member has infiltrated my *Yakuza*. These things happen.

"My lieutenant who is in charge of the operation while I am not there, remains alert. He has ordered all my men except for the leaders whose loyalty has been tested and is beyond doubt, to hand over their cell phones until the operation is over. I will have a few men watching this house, Connie. Nonetheless, it is never wise to let down one's guard. I suggest we all sleep with our weapons ready at hand. My men were ordered under no circumstances to enter this house. If a stranger enters, shoot him. Don't waste time asking questions."

"This isn't exactly in the middle of nowhere. Most of the houses along here are year-round homes," said Sister Anne. "And, as I'm sure you noticed, the homes are quite large and pricey. How can your men be watching this house without themselves being noticed? People who live here are used to guarding their homes against house robbers. They all have alarm systems. And the residents keep themselves alert. Somebody would notice your men. The police could be swarming all over us in seconds."

"We are experts at such tactics. We dress and move to blend in with the night. We don't worry about people. Dogs are our worst enemies. They sniff us out, even if they can't see us. We carry tranquilizer darts for that reason."

"Sister Anne," Saito ended, "only God knows how this night will end. I believe it would be prudent to tell all of us where the mirror is. If the worst happens, perhaps one of us will survive, and complete Chieko's mission."

"I'm going to disagree, Mr. Saito," said Connie, "I think she should tell only Chieko, Yoshiro, and you. You are the only three of us intimately involved in this matter. Only you need to know. And Sister, at the risk of seeming melodramatic, I suggest you write it down, show it to them, and then tear the paper to pieces and burn them. Don't forget to scatter the ashes. Better yet flush them down the toilet or the sink disposal. Don't talk.

"The enemy can pick up the slightest sounds and voices, even through walls and from many yards away. So don't talk out loud. Don't even whisper. I know it sounds paranoid, but don't risk it. Also, it doesn't take much at all to reconstruct text from a burnt piece of paper. "

"There is no problem yet," said Saito. "My men will let me know if the enemy has found us."

"Actually, I don't know much of anything. Except one of the places we should look is out in the Isles of Shoals," said Sister Anne, ignoring Connie's exasperated gestures. "I gave Chieko two different maps. She destroyed one that she had memorized. The other is hanging around her neck."

Chapter 35

"The only place Russell ever felt safe was in the forest near his parent's house in Newington. At first he hid everything he valued near the house. They remained in his secret place for years, even after his house was burned to the ground.

"Much later, he said he moved everything and buried them, and Sparky his dog, on an island. Nonetheless, I believe we should first check in Newington," the nun continued. "Not only did Russell lie, but he was forgetful. I used to tell him a successful liar cannot be forgetful. It just doesn't work." She smiled, but her eyes glistened with unshed tears.

Sister Anne stared at the map of the Seacoast area that Connie had pulled up on her cell phone. After a few seconds, she pointed to a place on the map. "I believe the Hartz house was in this vicinity. It burned down when Russell was just a boy, but its stone foundation might still be there. Maybe there is still evidence of charred wood. I believe we could find it."

"Are you saying you believe he buried the mirror in the basement of the house?" asked Chieko.

"No, I don't believe so. I think he hid it where he felt safe."

"Where?" Yoshiro and Chieko asked together.

"In a large hollowed-out log, of all places. A terrible storm ravaged

Maine and New Hampshire in 1899. He was hardly more than a baby, but he said the noise of the wind was so terrifying he never forgot it. Trees, especially large diseased trees, were brought down by the storm. Russell used to play in one of the hollowed-out felled logs. He buried his little treasures like special seashells and stones in the detritus at the closed end of the log. He told me he often crawled inside the log and sometimes, as a child, even napped there, especially when one or the other of his parents was drunk and wanted to use him as a punching bag. He said he would pretend he was an Indian and was very careful about not disturbing the ground near his log. And he camouflaged the opening. They never knew about his hiding place.

"I felt honored that he trusted me enough to tell me about his secret place. He was later sorry that he had told me, even though it had been many decades since he'd sought shelter in his "log cabin". Yes, that's what he called it: his "log cabin." Russell was not at all witty. He was very proud he'd come up with that. And I promised that I would never tell anyone about it. Not ever.... I took an oath on his medallion that I would never tell anyone. But here I am, telling you."

"Sister, we are of different religions, but I feel that Russell would not mind that you are telling us. Especially if good comes out of it. And if the mirror is hidden in the log, then very much good will come of it," said Chieko. "Would a fallen log still be there after one hundred years? In Japan, that would not be the case. Our forests are carefully tended."

"Well, I also told you he said he moved his treasures. The Hartz land went to his cousin, James Jergens. Russell was afraid Jergens would clear the land and build something there. So Russell said he moved his treasures out of his log cabin.

"The only work Russell could find was on the fishing and lobster boats. He got to know the seacoast waters as well as anyone. Eventually, he felt safer out there than here on the mainland. He said he moved his treasures: the bones of his dog and the mirror, out to the Isles of Shoals.... I'm feeling so guilty. I shouldn't be telling you all this. I promised him I would never divulge his secret. I feel I've betrayed him. He'd had enough betrayal in his life."

"I promise you this, Sister Anne: If we find the mirror, I will have a plaque created in Russell's honor and it will be placed in the garden of the Ise Jingu. The plaque will not give any details. It will simply state that Russell Hartz was a great benefactor. Does that make you feel better?"

Sister Anne nodded and said, "I actually think he'd like that." She reached out to touch Chieko's hand that was raised in her pledge to the nun.

"Excuse me for breaking into your tender moment, but I believe it is best to bed down. I would not be surprised if at dawn, we will confront our enemies," Yoshiro said. "The ETA men will want to have a clear view of us. I believe they will wait until daylight. We will want to see them clearly as well. I believe even if they find where we are, they will wait for dawn. They will have strict orders not to harm Chieko and Sister Anne, but to take them prisoners. They must have enough light to distinguish among us before they shoot at us." He drew his cell phone from his pocket and put it to his ear. Then he walked out of earshot of the others. When he returned, Yoshiro folded his cell phone and dropped it back into his pocket. He stood and stared down at his feet for some seconds, then he looked at Connie. "Your Homeland Security is very alert. My friend in our Japanese Secret Service has called me. Your Homeland Security has contacted the JSS. Homeland Security is looking for Tomio Saito and me. When they find us they will deport us immediately. Your Homeland Security did not ask why we are here. They knew the JSS would not answer such a question. Both agencies suspect we are here to create a storm. Chieko, they did not mention your name. However, that does not mean they have not noted your presence.

"Forgive me, Tomio, I spoke for both of us. I told my friend we are not leaving until we have accomplished our mission. You may be sure the JSS will be visiting us. They have a fix on us through my cell phone, or yours, Tomio," he said to Saito. "I don't know which. We can also be sure that if the JSS comes, your Homeland Security people will be close behind," he said to Connie and Sister Anne.

"Under the circumstances, isn't that a good thing?" asked the nun.

"Not until I have the mirror," said Chieko.

Connie didn't say anything. She'd been wondering where Sharon was. As time passed she became more concerned. She couldn't figure out what was more worrisome. Had Sharon been hurt or killed by the ETA, or had she joined forces with them? The one thing Connie was sure about was that Sharon didn't know what loyalty felt like.

Yoshiro noticed Connie was preoccupied, but he turned to Saito, and said, "Saito-San, we all appreciate the service you have done for Japan and for us personally. Words cannot express our supreme gratitude. But it is time for me to take over and relieve you of the responsibility. I'm sure you agree that no one in Japan must know that the most powerful *Yakuza* has been working with the Imperial Guards. That knowledge would not be beneficial to either of us. Please tell your lieutenant that members of the JSS will arrive before dawn. The Service knows nothing of our mission here in the United States. I know if I, an Imperial Guard, ask for their assistance, they will give it. Saito-San, excuse me, but they may not be as cooperative with you. They may not know your men are here in New Hampshire. As you realize, it could complicate the situation greatly if they know a *Yakuza* is involved in this matter. Please disperse your men with our deep gratitude. If I get the opportunity, I will one day thank them publicly. Their service to Japan will not be forgotten. I will leave it up to you if you want to remain here with us, or leave."

Saito didn't hesitate for an instant. "I am staying to guard Chieko until *she* tells me to leave." he said.

"I understand," Yoshiro said.

"Well, Mr. Saito would have known his men when he saw them. How will we know the JSS men from the men of the Cabal?" Connie asked.

"It will not be a problem," said both Yoshiro and Saito.

Saito pulled out his cell phone and spoke rapidly. He didn't walk away for privacy. Connie noticed that Chieko and Yoshiro nodded in approval of whatever Saito was saying into his phone.

Chapter 36

Newington, New Hampshire

"Sister Anne, where are we?" Chieko asked early the next morning.

"I believe we passed the Newington town line just back there." The nun pointed behind her. Then she said, "Here. Stop here. Pull in over there."

"It appears there was once a house here," said Saito after the car had stopped. "One can see a faint outline among the weeds on the ground."

"Yes," said Connie, "Sister, is this where Russell's family's house was?"

"Yes, it burned down decades ago. There used to be traces of the burnt structure all over the ground, but our storms can be quite scourging to the land. If the weather has destroyed most of the remainders of the house, I wonder... Come, let's walk this way," she said, turning away from the clearing and toward a small forest of trees. The nun periodically stopped and examined a felled tree before she trudged on. She turned further into the forest, and they walked for a few hundred feet before she stopped. She stared at the large, felled log half buried under dead leaves. The root end of the tree was barricaded with downed branches and leaves. The branches on the other end still held on to the trunk. "Here. This might be it," Sister Anne said.

Chieko ran ahead and was already clearing leaves and debris from the root end of the log. "Yes, this may be it!" she said. The excitement in her voice made her voice slightly tremble. "Yes, the tree is hollow!" she exclaimed. She grabbed the flashlight from her belt. Before the others could comment, the slim young woman was shimmying into the dirty opening of the log. Sister Anne and the two men rushed over to watch her progress.

Chapter 37

Almost fifteen minutes after Chieko had crawled into the log, they saw her feet as she backed out. She held something so encrusted with dirt; it was difficult to see what it was. The men and Sister Anne were picking leaves, small clumps of dirt, squirming and dead bugs, and worms off Chieko's clothing and hair as she rubbed the object in her hands. Sister Anne said, "Chieko, there's a creek just over that rise. Come on. We'll get you cleaned up in the water."

"I'll hold that for you while you bathe," Saito said, grabbing the object from Chieko's hands. Saito stared at the seashell. "It's nothing but a big seashell," he said and would have thrown it aside, but Chieko grabbed it back.

When they slid down the embankment to the creek, Chieko sighed with pleasure and jumped into the shallow water. Little brown fish darted out of her way. A large brown frog croaked his displeasure at the humans who had invaded his domain. With a delighted laugh, Yoshiro leaned over to grab the frog, but it was gone into the dense foliage before the young man could get hold of it. Chieko stood in the middle of the creek, pouring water over herself with the help of the large clam shell that she'd washed off. "Look," she said. She brought the shell over to the others and turned the inner side toward them. 'R' was crudely scratched in the iridescent nacre. Their smiles turned down into frowns when she said, "That's all there was. Just lots of damp leaves and this."

Saito rubbed at his face and stared into the muddied water of the creek. "Well, Sister Anne," he said, "you were correct about one of Russell's hiding places. Will you please guide us to the other."

Chapter 38
Somewhere in Portsmouth

"Yes, there'll be less of a hassle with your Homeland Security if our war is not waged on the mainland. If we boat to an uninhabited island, they may not be as sanguine as they would if gunfire broke out on the mainland They won't sanction it even out on an uninhabited island, but they may wait to see what exactly is happening," said Yoshiro to Connie. He turned to Saito, "To boat out to the Isles was good thinking. Thank you."

"It was not my idea," Saito answered. "It was my assistant. He is a genius at avoiding confrontations with government forces. He tells me there are uninhabited islands off the coast where it would be best to confront the enemy. He says the Homeland Security would stop us from carrying on even a small war any place in this country. But the agency would be less likely to call out a full-blown military operation against us if we confine ourselves to an uninhabited island far enough out so as not to endanger the mainland or any nearby inhabited island. But he said he wants us to clearly understand: Homeland Security would not endorse anything we do, even if it's defensive. We must proceed unnoticed as best we can. If, or when, they converge on us, they will prevent us from further action. It's best that we get this over with. The faster the better."

"Why don't you tell the JSS exactly why you are here?" Sister Anne asked.

"No," said the Japanese.

"Dear friend," said Chieko, "we cannot risk anyone else knowing our purpose for coming to the United States. It would be too harmful to our people. Please put the idea out of your mind."

"Sister Anne, Miss Constance, you know this area. What is the fastest way to Rye Harbor? Our boat awaits us there," said Saito.

"The men in my family have been fishermen in these waters for generations back," said Sister Anne. "When my father was not fishing, he was out plying the waters, memorizing the currents, and finding the best place to throw his nets or anchor his boat. Even though I wasn't the son he craved, I was often at his side. He knew the Isles of Shoals better than anyone. I learned a lot from him. I haven't been out for quite a few years, but I know the islands that would be most hostile to people. If you have to fight, it should be on Duck Island or Smuttynose. You're less likely to hurt innocents."

"Does Twenty-Seven know where to find us?" asked Yoshiro.

"By now he does," Saito answered with a smirk. "But I don't think that he knows the hunter will soon be the hunted."

"Sister Anne, can you direct us how to get there? I'd like you to leave before the fighting begins." Connie said.

Sister Anne replied with a shake of her head.

"No. You're not leaving, are you. It wouldn't be like you to walk away from anything, even this. Would it, Sister?"

"Constance, now you finally know me," Sister Anne said as the five walked to the car. "Did any of you know that John Paul Jones was from Portsmouth? You can visit his house. We modern Portsmouthians are in the tradition of Jones. We don't shoot 'til we see the whites of their eyes. And we go down with the ship. Well, I personally, don't shoot, period. And I was on the swim team in college, so I don't think I'm going down with the ship, either. But the spirit still lives within me.

"I don't know what help I can be. I don't know if I should take you to where the mirror may be. It will be too easy for the ETA to follow us. I will bring you to what I think the best place is to take a stand, if that helps. I'll do whatever you need. Except I will not use a firearm of any kind to kill, only to wound enough to put someone out of action. You may not think my track record for keeping promises is very good, but I promise all of you I will not be a hindrance. You can trust that promise." When everyone answered her with grave nods, she continued, "I shall be praying hard for all of you."

Chapter 39
Rye Harbor, New Hampshire

When Connie pulled into the parking lot at the edge of the state park, Sister Anne said to Saito, "Your men are like fairy godmothers, Our slightest wish, and pouf! It appears." Her smile drooped, as she added, "But that boat isn't very big, is it?" The old wooden fishing boat tied to the dock was not inviting. Much of the white paint had peeled off, and the blue of the pilothouse was worn away where it hadn't already peeled. The boat was already sitting low in the water. "I don't know about this," said Connie.

Saito answered, "It looks old, but very sea worthy. And it's a smaller target. It will hold us all comfortably. It doesn't appear to be, but I'm sure my men got it right. It is quite heavily armored and armed."

"Old Ironsides," said Sister Anne. Connie smiled. The Japanese looked puzzled.

At that moment, Sharon sped into the lot in her rental car, pulled up beside the nun, and lowered the driver's window. "OK. Connie texted me. I'm here."

Without pause, but waving away some of Sharon's dust-up, Sister Anne continued, "If Twenty-Seven has managed to hire airplanes or helicopters, we don't stand much of a chance if they fire at us from above."

"I believe he still wants to capture you and me," Chieko said. "He does not know if we yet have the mirror. If he thinks we do not yet have it, he will want you to be alive to lead him to it. If he thinks we've found it, he may want to take me prisoner as a means of attaining it. I do not believe he will risk sinking the boat until the mirror is safely in his hands."

"I would never let you fall into that monster's hands," said Saito. "I would kill us both before I would let that happen."

"Thank you," Chieko said, grabbing Saito's arm. "I feel safe with you."

Sister Anne looked bemused but said nothing.

Saito and Yoshiro were first out of the car. They hopped onto the boat and examined it. Connie and Sister Anne helped them stow weapons on the boat. A quick inspection by the nun proved the boat was already fully stocked with firepower.

But Saito's words had again made Sharon think about her situation. She was helping unload the vehicle, but her mind was troubled. *What the hell am I doing here defending the people I contracted to kill? Constance seems to believe these are good people. Well, I guess they are. I promised Sister Anne I wouldn't willfully kill innocent people. Is Twenty-Seven the one who hired me? He didn't admit to it. And I wasn't about to ask him. Well, I don't have the money yet. I...* She noticed Chieko staring at her.

Chieko walked slowly over to her, put her hand lightly on Sharon's shoulder, and stared into her eyes. Chieko turned so that the others couldn't see her face. She whispered, "Sharon listen to your heart. You cannot win. You may get one of us; perhaps, two; but the third will stop you. Or Connie. You know she will not allow it. One of us will stop you forever. If it is money you need, I will provide it. In your heart, you are one of us. Listen to your heart." Chieko gently stroked

Sharon's shoulder, then walked away quickly.

The others had been watching, but turned away. Except Sister Anne. She came to Sharon and put one arm around her shoulders. "Are you all right, dear?" she asked. "Do you need help?"

"Thanks. I'm not sure," Sharon answered, "but I think I just got all the help I need." She slid back into her car, and peeled out of the lot, heading north on Ocean Boulevard.

Sister Anne turned back to the boat. "I do not know which would be the best island for our stand against the Cabal. Summer's over. But it's been warm, so there'll be people about," said the nun. "However, it's a weekday. The usual summer visitors and residents will have gone, but there may be day trippers. We shall have to watch for them or for their boats." Sister Anne looked at each person to ensure they had heard her. "We mustn't allow innocent people to be hurt or killed" she continued. "I believe that Smuttynose might be the best island for us to begin our search. Plus, it is large, uninhabited, and far enough away. It has a terrible, sad history. It was the scene of much violence in the past. Perhaps it's the best place to stand and fight. If there are tourist or fishing boats anchored in the waters, we'll move onto Duck Island. It's the northernmost island, quite large, and rather isolated from the others. The last I heard is that it's a wildlife sanctuary... sanctuary," she smiled, then added, "Let us hope that it is also a human sanctuary."

"Okay," said Connie. "We've got everything from the car onto the boat. Everybody ready to shove off?"

Chieko said, "Ready."

Sister Anne was trying to figure out how to get on board without lifting her skirt too high. Connie stretched out a hand to her. "Thank you, Connie," said the nun. "It is good to be traveling with you."

Connie was stowing the firearms where they'd be safe from the spray, when she happened to stare at the Japanese who had fallen silent. "What's the matter? What's wrong?" Connie asked.

Chieko glanced up at Saito and then at Yoshiro. A moment later, as if they had come to a silent agreement, the three nodded their heads. Chieko said, "Constance, we have not been thinking clearly. I fear we have been swept into the magnificent energy of your country. We momentarily lost sight of our objective. We have not come to wage war on the ETA Cabal. We have come here to find our national treasure and return it to its rightful place.

"When the time comes, we will deal with the Cabal in Japan, not here. Right now, we must make finding the mirror our priority. No one, not the Cabal, not JSS, nor your Homeland Security people, will stop me from doing my duty with the assistance of my two very dear friends." She nodded her head at Yoshiro and Saito. "Sister Anne, you will please guide us to the island where you think the mirror was buried. Russell's maps are firmly etched in my mind, but I do not know the islands. You saw the map. I believe you know exactly where we should search." Chieko looked out toward the water and the islands that dotted the horizon.

"Constance, thank you so very much for your support. I regret endangering your lives, but I shall be forever grateful to you. After Sister Anne has guided us to the island, my memory will take over and we shall find the burial place. Then, it will be time for you to take Sister Anne home and go back to your lives. We will retrieve the mirror and quickly return to Japan. Saito-San has graciously offered us his helicopter that will take us to his airplane so that we may leave as soon as we are able. The ETA will follow us back, and we will confront them in Japan."

Connie thought for a moment before she answered. "I'll be standing by your side until the JSS has you completely under their protection or until you are sitting on Mr. Saito's plane and going home."

"That goes for me, too," said Sister Anne, folding her arms and tucking her hands in her sleeves.

"You haven't seen me in action. I can be very impressive," Connie mimicked polishing her nails on her collar. "We don't know how many of the Cabal's men are out there. You can at least use my help as a look-out while you're searching for the mirror." Connie spoke with confidence, but she was still worried about Sharon, *Where the hell did she go?*

Saito admitted, "It is very unlike the average Japanese man to say so, but your help would be appreciated." Yoshiro agreed and Chieko nodded, although she didn't look happy about it.

"Let's do this," said Connie as she secured the tarp over the weapon stash.

Chapter 40

Homeland Security Command,
Former Pease Air Force Base
Newington, New Hampshire

Colonel Clark Stephens shook hands with Officer Suzuki, and nodded to the four other members of the Japanese Secret Service. Stephens' own men stood silent and unmoving against the walls of the large trailer that had been fitted as an office. "You understand, Sir," said Stephens, "that we can't have people from your country causing mayhem here. You've said you're here to prevent bloodshed. How can Homeland Security be of help? I can muster up any number of men to secure the parties in question and expel them from our country. To be frank, I don't need your cooperation to do it. We might also invite you and your people to board same plane out of here."

"Colonel Stephens, there is a fanatical cult in Japan that desires to overthrow the Japanese government and eradicate the Imperial family. This cult, that calls itself the ETA, has cells all over the world. One in New York and another in Los Angeles. Its largest membership numbers are, of course, in Japan. We have been monitoring the Japanese cells very closely. So far only one member has come to the United States. It is the leader of the cult. He calls himself 'Twenty-Seven'. He is the most dangerous on our watch list. He has mobilized cells here in the United States. They have arrived in New Hampshire from New York and California. They are ruthless. Human life is cheap to them."

"Are they all U.S. citizens? How many will be in Portsmouth? What do they want? Why did Twenty-Seven, himself, come here? He's Japanese, not American, right? What's so important that they're all converging here? Where are they now?" Stephens pelted the JSS officer with questions.

"I do not know the answer to all of your questions," replied Suzuki. We know they are chasing two Japanese men and a woman. Why they are chasing them, we do not know. But the men that are hunted are not helpless. Even with the odds against them, they are capable of fighting their way out of difficulty. However, if The ETA brings many against them..."

"We can't have you Japanese carrying on a war in our country. I'm sure you understand we can't let that happen. We will protect our citizens," said the American.

"I understand and agree completely with you. We are trying to prevent bloodshed. The thrust of our efforts right now is to capture Twenty-Seven. We believe his men will fade away once we have him in our grasp."

"I expect your cooperation in identifying his men who are living in the U.S.. If they are not citizens, they will be deported. Citizens will be dealt with in our own way."

"All our records regarding these men will be turned over to you. We will be glad to see an end to this radical movement."

"Now, as to the people this cult is chasing," said Stephens. "What can you tell us about the woman and two men?"

"Tomio Saito, the older man, is the head of the most powerful gang in Japan. He also has gang members all over the world. He has mobilized a few of his men to act as look-outs only. He has ordered his men not to carry weapons of any kind unless he changes his order. They are to be his eyes on the cults' activities, and will tell him the whereabouts of any of the ETA men at all times. They are ordered not to engage the cult in any manner.

"The younger man is named Hirobumi Yoshiro. He is head of the Ise Imperial Guard—a Samurai descendant—the most important protectors of the Imperial family and our treasures in Japan. Yoshiro has worked with us in the past. He is an intelligent young man and fearless."

"We believe both men have come to the United States to guard the woman, Chieko Shimizu. She will be the High Priestess of a most important shrine in Japan. We know nothing else about her that we can share with you. We do not know why she has come here. Nor do we know why she needs guards. But it's got to have something to do with Japan's Sacred Mirror. It will be Shimizu's job to protect it." The JSS man looked at his phone. "Pardon me, Colonel, the information I have requested is coming in now." He swiped his phone and stared at the screen. "The information is being texted to me. Please be patient."

Colonel Stephens was just checking his watch when Suzuki said, "Three American women have joined forces with the subjects we have been watching. One is a Roman Catholic nun; another is a licensed Private Investigator; and the last is... I'm sorry. She is a question mark. And it is thought she is no longer traveling with the others. We do not know who she is or where she is. We must move. Now," he said to his men. They rose up and sprinted out of the room with their leader.

"Hold on. Where you going?" asked Stephens. "Never mind. This way, gentlemen." He led his own men out of the trailer.

Chapter 41
Isle of Shoals

"Chieko, you destroyed Russell's map to the island. I got a fast look at it, but I'm not completely sure which island we should be heading for," said Sister Anne.

"I remember exactly which island it is. Is there a map on board this boat?"

"No," said Yoshiro, who was at the controls.

"If I draw the map, will you recognize it?" Chieko asked Sister Anne.

"Yes, but how...?"

"Sister, I was blessed with an eidetic memory. Russell's map is etched in my brain. Connie, I believe you have a notebook and pen."

"Yep."

"May I?"

"Of course." The women bent over Chieko as she reproduced the map in Connie's notebook. The men just looked on and smiled proudly.

Sister Anne gazed at the map and then at Chieko. "You're amazing," she said.

"It is a gift. I did not earn it, but I am grateful for it."

Sister Anne was looking out at the water ahead. "Mr. Yoshiro, do you see that red buoy?" He nodded. "Keep to the right of it about thirty degrees. Understand?" He nodded again.

Minutes later, Sister Anne said, "That's Smuttynose. This is really coming together. Now, if you make your way to the seaward side, we'll be out of sight of the mainland and there's a small cove where we can anchor..."

"Sister, it would be too dangerous for us to anchor in a cove" said Chieko. "We don't want to be any place where there is only one way in and out. We don't want to be exposed in open water either...."

Yoshiro was talking on his phone, and put his hand up to stop the discussion about where to anchor the boat. He spoke quickly in Japanese to Chieko and Saito. They both instinctively reached for their weapons. Connie and Sister Anne searched the waters around them as Yoshiro said, "We will be having visitors soon. The cove will have to do if it offers any protection at all. The ETA will probably not want to enter the cove, either. They know the JSS and Homeland Security are following their progress. They will not want to be trapped in the cove. They do not know that Washington has told Homeland Security not to move against the ETA unless they are provoked. And it has ordered the JSS to stand down."

"So we're on our own. Great. Like they say, 'Where are the cops when you need them?' How many boats are the ETA men coming in?" asked Connie.

"Three boats. Fifteen to twenty men."

"Well, I vote we fight them on land," Connie said. "One rocket hitting our boat and we're history."

"She's right," Saito agreed. "Sister Anne, where can we run aground quickly so that we can transport our weapons to the island more easily?"

"Keep to the seaward side where we can run aground. There'll be no fast way to get the boat in deep water again, however."

"Let's hope that will be our only problem," said Connie.

Chapter 42

"Whose phone are they tracking?" Connie asked as they rounded the east end of the island.

"We don't know," Yoshiro answered.

"Well, then I guess you, Tomio, and Chieko will have to break your phones up and scatter the pieces in the water."

"I understand, but no. We need to communicate..."

"You have my phone at your disposal." She turned to Sister Anne with an arched eyebrow.

"Yes, I have one that's not mine. I confiscated it from one of my students who was texting in one of my Catechism classes. I've made an appointment to give it back to her parents, so please be careful of it. Don't break it." They all looked quizzically at Sister Anne who seemed to be forgetting their situation.

"Hirobumi, use the Sister's phone to call your friend in the JSS and tell him what we have done. He will be able to read the phone number when you call. Tell him to use it to contact us until further notice," said Chieko. "Hirobumi and Saito-San, join me in destroying your phones and throwing the pieces in open water before we turn the boat toward Smuttynose. Let us do it now." Her words were a command not a suggestion. "And let us hope the ETA has not yet found Sister Anne's cell phone. I believe it is unlikely."

When Yoshiro closed the cell phone, he was frowning. He said, "Tomio, please take the controls and speed us to the cove. We must seek cover, if it is at all possible. My friend tells me the ETA has hired a helicopter. The JSS has asked Homeland Security to intercept the helicopter, but... well, we just don't know if it will happen or when it will happen."

"We're running low on fuel," Saito warned after tapping the fuel gauge. "Those cans back there are filled with fuel. Fill up the tank, please. Don't throw the empty cans overboard. They could come in handy later. Hang on everybody, I'm going to increase the speed now." The boat roared toward the eastern end of Smuttynose Island. "Sister Anne," yelled Saito over the roar of the engine, "please come up and navigate me toward the cove."

"It's been a long time," she mumbled. "The trees I used to use as waypoints are much taller now. But the boulders should be the same. "There," she said aloud. "See that stand of trees there after the boulder that sticks out over the water and looks like an old man with a big forehead? The cove is just past the trees. We may be in luck. The island is much more overgrown and lush than I remember it, and our Nor'easters have had their effect. If we're really lucky there'll be a lot of downed trees and brush we can use to try to camouflage the boat from the air. It's something to hope for."

"We've got to set up our weapons on top of that boulder. There's enough brush up there to cover us. We should be able to get a clear shot at any boats that cruise into the cove looking for us," Connie said.

"Good idea. There's no time to waste," said Yoshiro. "I'm afraid you ladies will have to help us carry our weapons up there."

"That goes without saying," Connie said, loosening the tarp covering their armory. "One suggestion, though: we shouldn't waste our energy on weapons for which we have no more ammunition."

"That is not a problem," said Chieko. "We are prepared for a long

Marcelline Acosta Jenny

siege. There are enough rockets to sink ten ships. There is a full large box of rounds for the automatics, too. We are, as you Americans say, 'good to go'."

"Gosh, Chieko! I love soldiering with you!" Connie turned to the two men, "You, too," she added.

Chapter 43
Gulf of Maine

Twenty-Seven sat in the cabin of the cruiser. He stared at the water as his men talked softly to one another. His assistant hurried down the steps into the cabin. "Well," said Twenty-Seven.

"Boss," the American said in heavily accented Japanese, "the cell phone signal has disappeared. Our helicopter was intercepted by the United States Air Force and forced down."

"Anything else?"

"Sir, we lost visual contact with their boat, but we know it is somewhere in the area of the Isles of Shoals. It is no longer in open water. It must be anchored off one of the islands. We will find it. We don't need the helicopter."

"Get out!" Twenty-Seven said and stared at the man sitting across from him.

The Sword Master ignored Twenty-Seven and continued to study a map of the islands on the small table. "Why are you looking at me?" he said as he put the map aside. "I advised you to hire someone who knows these islands. And you refused. So here we are twiddling our thumbs."

"I do not want the entire world to know what we are doing here. Do you not understand that?"

"Honorable Twenty-Seven, it would have been just one more. You

227

are good at that. Except for that woman. What happened? Where did she go?"

"The woman named Sharon Meadows made the mistake of not killing me when she had the opportunity. She managed to get away when my incompetent men stormed my apartment. Well, they are no longer incompetent. She killed them all. She did not escape unscathed, though. And I will finish the job. Enough of this. I am fed up with you, too. You can only test my patience so far, before I decide to pitch you in the water, with your entrails attracting the sharks."

"Yes, well it seems I value you, more than you value me. Here is my advice, anyway. It's too bad about the helicopter. Since Japan is a close ally to the United States, I am quite appreciative of U.S. Homeland Security. As your friend and mentor, however, I of course abhor the *gaijin*.

"You have three boats, like this. What you need are speedboats to quickly find and trap the quarry. Then you can simply putter up to the enemy in these monster boats and do what you please. With artillery trained on them on every side, they will have no choice but to surrender."

"Sounds easier than it is," said Twenty-Seven. "They are impressive warriors. With those people at my side I could rule the world. Having them against me is making it difficult to even keep my men in line. Damn the Japanese mind! Some of my people think Chieko Shimizu is under divine protection. I can't even tear such thinking out of my own cell's minds. How can I cleanse all of Japan from such thinking?

"Damn! You see what that bitch has done. She is even undermining my confidence. I will cut out her heart and eat it. I swear on my father's grave, I will." He called to the men waiting on deck. "Find speedboats. As many as you can steal or buy, but no fewer than six. Get out there and find those people. Don't come back until you do."

Chapter 44
Homeland Security Command

Colonel Clark Stephens tapped his pen on the table as he talked on the phone. "Sir, they weren't stupid enough to put up a fight, but that helicopter was filled with interesting weapons.... We've got them cooling their heels in a guarded room here at Pease.... No, Sir, the pilot is known to us. He was hired to fly over the Shoals and look for a boat. I believe him when he said he didn't know who they were and why they brought weapons on board. When he saw the weapons, he refused to fly...until they held a gun to his head. He says he doesn't know what they were up to, why they were looking for a boat, or what they were going to do with the weapons. I believe him. Of course, we're detaining him for further questioning. The passengers won't talk. There's three of them. All Asians. Not one word."

"They say they're just vacationing here. I asked if it wasn't unusual that three men from the Japanese Secret Service are vacationing together in New Hampshire. They just smiled.... Yes, Sir. Very good, Sir." He hung up the phone and gazed at the JSS men sitting across from him. "You're free to go gentlemen. Our government is now talking to your government about your presence here." The three men frowned and looked at each other, but didn't speak before they walked out of the door.

Stephens turned to his lieutenant. "Find that goddamned boat and bring the people on it here to me."

Chapter 45
Smuttynose Island

"The sun's going down," Connie said. "The good news is it's gonna be harder to find us in the dark; the bad news is the mosquitoes will make a feast of us."

"Once it's dark, we can go back to the mainland. There won't be any moon tonight, and it's pretty heavily overcast," said Sister Anne. "We'll break all the running lights and steer the boat toward the shore. The shore will look like it's lit up like a Christmas tree."

"I wish you and Connie to go back, Sister Anne. My friends and I must stay to find the mirror. Sister Anne, please give me Russell's tin medallion on the chain around your neck. My friends and I will use it to find the treasure. If you will, please also leave your cell phone, so we can arrange for transportation away from here and back to Japan. On behalf of all of us, we want to thank you very much for your kindness toward us. You must both please come to Japan so we may thank you properly."

"You haven't yet accomplished what you came here for. I'm not leaving until you do," said Sister Anne.

"Neither am I," Connie said.

"Nor I," said Sharon, startling them as she emerged from the woods. They all stared at her. Connie was first to open her mouth to ask where the heck had she come from. Instead, she asked, "How bad is it?"

staring at Sharon's shirt, crusted in dried blood.

"Just a flesh wound. Didn't even nick a rib—I don't think."

The others clustered around her and welcomed her back. Connie held slightly back from the others. Sharon looked at her and mouthed, "Everything's okay."

Chieko smiled for a moment, but then turned somber again and said, "You have become our dear friends. Yoshiro has been in contact with his friend in the JSS. He was told there are many coming against us. We are on our own. The JSS has been thwarted, and Homeland Security will not recognize us." She looked at each of the women. "We will face the enemy alone. We do not wish your deaths. If we die in our attempt, it is justified. We cannot justify the death of friends."

"I'm going to speak for the three of us," said Sister Anne. "We're not leaving you."

Chieko sighed and studied each of the women's faces again. Then she sighed again but said with a smile, "Well, come along then. We have a bit of a walk across the island, and without light, it could be interesting. We must all carry as many weapons as we can. Even you, Sister Anne."

"Listen, everybody," the nun said, picking up two rifles and a cartridge case. "I haven't changed my mind. I will absolutely not kill another human being. But I have to tell you, that after spending so many hours with you good people, I won't hesitate for a second to wound another human being in the leg or arm." Relaxing her arms, she then muttered to herself, "Oh, I really, really have to go back to the motherhouse for retraining."

"I can barely see the drawing on the medallion in this dark. It is difficult for me to know exactly where we are," said Chieko. "I will need the moonlight to see where we are. A compass would be very nice to have. Yoshiro, you used to be fascinated by astronomy and the night sky. Could you keep us moving northeast?"

"It was a long time ago. And tonight it is very cloudy.... I will do my best."

"I will try to get my bearings. Maybe in that time some of the clouds will move enough for you to see," said Chieko.

"I'm fine with resting for a moment," said Sister Anne.

"Sister, I can relieve you of some of your burden," Saito said, reaching for the weapons the nun carried.

"No, sirree. Thanks. You're very kind. But I refuse to be a liability. I'm fine, really."

Chieko walked a few yards ahead, and leaned against a tree. Her hand was on the butt of her Smith & Wesson. When she saw Sharon walking toward her, her finger moved to the trigger of the small handgun.

Chapter 46

"That's not necessary," Sharon said, holding her empty hands in the air. "What exactly do you think you know about me?" Sharon asked Chieko when she reached the base of the tree Chieko was leaning against.

"Only what your eyes tell me. We have searched the Internet but cannot find you. However, I trust what I see in your eyes," Chieko answered.

"You'll excuse the language, but that's a load of bull... Oh, Sister Anne," Sharon paused as the nun approached.

"Don't mind me," said the nun, "I'm just an inveterate eavesdropper."

"Come join us," said Chieko. "You, too, Connie. Please join us."

"I saw you two talking and was nosy. What's going on?" asked Sister Anne.

"I was about to tell Chieko about me," said Sharon.

"Why? What good would it do?" Connie asked.

"She already knows. I don't know how. But she already knows. As a matter of fact, Connie, she knows more than you do. Should we ask the men to join us?" asked Sharon.

Sister Anne didn't speak. Yoshiro and Saito had already stood up and were walking toward the women.

"I want to tell you everything, because it just doesn't add up. Something's off. I don't know what it is. But something's not what it seems to be."

"Explain," said Chieko.

Sharon took a deep breath, before she said, "I'm a hired gun, a gun for hire, a contract killer. All of those things. That's how I make a living. But, you already know that."

Only Sister Anne expressed her surprise. The others stared quietly into the darkness. "A hired killer? Did you know this, Constance?" asked Sister Anne. Connie nodded. "I thought you were just a security specialist, Sharon," the nun added.

"Yes, Connie knows about my past," Sharon said. "What she doesn't know is that I was hired to come to Portsmouth, New Hampshire, to kill Chieko, Hirobumi, and Tomio." Saito automatically placed his hand on the butt of his gun. In the pale moonlight Sharon noticed the movement, nodded at him, and continued speaking. "What was odd was that I received an email on the same day from Sister Anne asking me to come to Portsmouth to help with what might be a dangerous job. It was too much of a coincidence. I knew it. I felt it. And when I came up and found out the Sister's job had to do with my three potential targets, I was sure there had to be a connection, but I couldn't figure out exactly what it was. I decided then and there I wouldn't act on my contract. I admire Connie. I figured if she thought you guys were okay, then I had to rethink what I was doing up here. Secondly, I don't like being manipulated. And that's what I felt someone was doing. It just smelled real bad." Connie nodded in agreement.

"As you know, things have moved pretty fast. I haven't had that much time to figure it out. Except," she stared at Saito and said, "I decided I wasn't going to fulfill the contract. Besides, I hadn't received a down payment. Connie will vouch for me when I say I don't kill heedlessly. It's not something I enjoy. It's just a job. I'm bad, but I'm not *so* bad that I kill for pleasure.

"After I got to know the lay of the land, so to speak, I decided it must be the guy, Twenty-Seven, who hired me. But the more I think about it, the more I think it doesn't make sense. He does his own killing. He enjoys it. And he's got a slew of people who'd do it for him for nothing. He doesn't need me.

"Chieko, whoever hired me, I don't think he or she is American. And I don't think it's somebody in the ETA. But I do think it's someone in Japan who wants you, Yoshiro, and Saito dead. You three would know better than I who is lumping the three of you together and wants you all dead. I personally don't really need to know. Anyway, I called this morning and broke the contract. But you should know they'll be looking for another contractor. I don't know who or when. But I do know it isn't over or safe just because I'm out of it.

"Well, I'm not completely out of it. You know that old saying about setting a thief to catch a thief? Well, that applies here. I like you guys. And, truth be told, Sister Anne, I like being part of your group. It does get tiresome being the lone wolf. I know what we assassins do. I know what to look for. I'm staying to prevent the next contractor from doing the job." Sharon rested her hands at her sides, hoping she'd convinced this posse of her loyalty.

"How do you get your assignments? Can't you ask whoever it is who contacted you to name the person who's paying?" the nun asked.

"There's honor even among thieves and murderers, Sister Anne. No, if he knows who it is, which is not always the case, my broker won't divulge the name of the client. Not ever."

"Well, you see the problem, don't you?" Yoshiro said. "The contractors will keep on coming until one of them is successful. It is vital to find out who wants us dead."

"How much were you being paid?" asked Saito.

"They offered twenty thousand each. I demanded forty thousand each, and they agreed. But I wouldn't be paid until after the job was done."

"We should be insulted. Surely each of our lives is worth more than forty thousand dollars," Saito said with a smile. Nobody else saw the humor in it.

"There is no standard fee," Sharon said, "if you're trying to extrapolate any clues from the amount. I've already considered that. Generally, it's whatever the broker and contractor agree on."

Neither Chieko nor Hirobumi had made any comments, but frowned and appeared very worried. It seemed as if Chieko were trying to hold back tears. Saito walked over to them. The three conversed in Japanese for some moments. The other women could see that now Chieko was barely holding herself together. Both men had also turned pale. Saito was clenching and unclenching his fists. Hirobumi finally turned toward Sharon and asked, "You were told to go to Portsmouth, New Hampshire to find us?"

"Yes."

"The person knew exactly when we were arriving here?" Chieko asked.

"Yes."

"What documents were you given to identify us? Were photos given to you as well?"

"I received both photos and dossiers on the three of you."

"And where are they?" Asked Saito.

"As you've probably guessed, I destroyed them all."

"Yes, too bad," said Saito.

"You suspect someone?"

"If I were your only target, it would be even more difficult to figure out. I have many, many enemies. And, I admit, for good reason. It amuses me that you consider me a 'good' person. Even my mother would disagree with you, but she nonetheless loves me," Saito mused.

"Sharon, shall you and I go for a walk? You realize that in the present situation I cannot have you standing behind us. You say that you turned down the contract. Should I believe someone in your profession?" Saito asked, glaring at Sharon.

"If your plan is to walk me into the woods and kill me, Saito, you should know that it won't be as easy as you might think."

"No, Sharon. I never underestimate my enemy. My dilemma is that I like you and want to believe you, but my skepticism is more powerful."

"Excuse me for eavesdropping," said Sister Anne, clearing her throat. "But since this is a matter that involves us all, I think we should all have a say."

"Sister Anne, I would have expected everyone but you to gang up on me." Sharon's jaw slackened.

"My dear, your understanding of what is happening here is wrong. Right now what I'm experiencing is pain that you feel so alone. It must be very hard to always feel like you're on the outside looking in."

"I'm used to it, and I'm not into self-pity." Sharon snapped the twig she'd been fingering, and walked off.

Chapter 47

Chieko watched Sharon disappear into the darkness. She murmured in Japanese to Saito and Yoshiro and followed well behind Sharon. Connie stepped forward to stop Chieko but the men held her back.

Sharon didn't walk far away from the group before she decided she'd better not stray too far. Sister Anne would probably come looking for her. No one was more surprised than she when she realized she liked the nun. *Who'da thunk it?* She asked herself. At the faint sound of footfall, Sharon thought: *There she is.*

Sharon turned around just before the dim moonlight backlit the silhouette of a man pulling a knife from his belt. For a split second she worried. *Did he come from the same direction? Are they all being killed? No, I would have heard something.*

"Well, what are you doing out here all alone in the dark?" His accent was heavy and he whispered so softly his words were almost lost in the wind that had picked up from the west.

"I take it you're from the ETA," she answered in a normal voice.

"I'm Twenty-Six. I'm not used to having conversations with my victims. You will lower your voice or my first act will be to cut your throat. Well, never mind. Your friends will soon be dead or dying, and we shall be taking Miss Shimizu back to Japan with us."

"Yeah, I was right. You talk like one of the big shots. You're not taking anyone, anywhere. In fact, you won't be leaving yourself."

"Such arrogance when you are in the inferior position. I find it most surprising. I also find you very beautiful and exciting. Are you not pee-ing yourself in fear? I am almost reluctant to kill you, but, of course, I shall. I don't know your name, and murder is so intimate. What shall I call you while I'm cutting you?"

They both turned quickly to the barely audible sound of feet upon the mossy ground, coming from behind Twenty-Six. Chieko stepped into the small clearing. "You and your men have one fatal flaw," Chieko said. "You underestimate your opponents. Your pitiful followers attacked our encampment, and are now dead and dying. One of them wounded the nun. She was not armed or dangerous. I am very angry about that. Though I killed that man, I am still angry. I am the guardian of tradition. I shall also punish you in the traditional way." She pulled her sword from the scabbard buckled on her wide belt.

Twenty-Six dropped his dagger and drew a pistol from his waistband. "I wish that all the ETA were here to witness the truth of what we've been preaching to them. The old ways can't..." before he could finish his sentence, Sharon shot him in the arm holding the gun. He looked in surprise as the gun dropped out of his hand. At the same time Chieko sliced his body open with one swift movement of her sword. He fell dead to the ground.

Sharon bent over and grabbed the fallen gun. She looked up at Chieko. "Remind me not to do anything to piss you off," she whispered.

"Only seven men attacked our friends," Chieko said. "Others will have heard the gunshot, but..." she stopped and turned toward the sound of someone approaching through the small forest of trees. A moment later, the rest of their party came into the clearing. Sister Anne's arm was in a makeshift sling made from Yoshiro's t-shirt.

Connie wore Yoshiro's shirt. He seemed embarrassed to be wearing only his white undershirt. Saito walked while re-loading his handgun. All three carried more weapons slung on their shoulders. Even Sister Anne held a box of ammunition against her body with her good arm. "There will soon be others," Saito said. "We must find a good defensive position."

"Sister Anne," said Chieko. "I am here on a most serious mission. That is my first concern. You and I must follow Russell's map. We will join up with the others when we are successful." She put her hand up when she saw the nun was going to speak. "No," said Chieko. "There is to be no discussion. I will do my duty, and I beseech you to help me."

Sister Anne said, "Let me look at Russell's amulet for a moment." The two moved into a sliver of moonlight. After the nun had studied it, she said, "We have to make our way to the northwestern side of the island. We'll be ascending a small rise. Chieko and I will leave you at the bottom of the rise.

"There used to be a lookout tower built during World War Two, like the Martello towers in England. It was demolished, but some of the stonework is still in place. Chieko and I will join you there as soon as we find the mirror. You can take a defensive position there," she said directly to the team. "But where are you going?" Sharon had turned away and was walking back toward their boat.

Sharon put her finger against her lips, "shhhhh," and walked away.

Chapter 48

Five men stood listening to Twenty-Seven's soft voice when Sharon walked into the first clearing. The men's hands flew to their weapons.

She pointed her machine gun at them. "I can kill you all, before you can even pull those toy guns out of your belts. Now put those pretty hands up in the air. You, too, Twenty-Seven. If you know what's good for you, you'll stand a few feet away," she purred. "Oh, hell, sorry guys, but I can't have you interfering with my pleasure." She squeezed the trigger and sprayed the men with machine gun fire, as she said, "Twenty-Seven, keep those hands up. I have a special treat in store for you. Oh, stay down, you freak," she said to one man as he struggled to kneel. She shot him in the head and neck. "He won't be getting up again," she said to Twenty-Seven, who was actually smiling at her performance.

"You wouldn't kill me without giving me a sporting chance, would you?" Twenty-Seven asked with an even broader smile.

"Oh, how can you know me so well? So here's the way it's going to be. I've hidden a loaded weapon just like this out there. I'll give you a hint. It's within a hundred feet of this clearing. I'm giving you... oh, let's say three minutes to find it. Then, armed or not, I'm coming after you. You've got three minutes to pray. Starting now." Twenty-Seven turned away and sprinted into the forest. Sharon spent the next few minutes making sure his five men were dead. She knew Twenty-Seven would be watching to see which way she would enter the forest. She decided not to give him a clue. Not yet. She sat on a boulder and waited.

To her surprise, Twenty-Seven stepped out of the forest less than two minutes later. Sharon raised her automatic and pointed it at his chest. He was not carrying a weapon. He stood at the edge of the tree line with his hands in the air. "I've decided not to play your game," he said. "I have a different game to propose to you. If you don't like it, feel free to shoot me." He smiled.

Sharon stared unsmiling at him for several seconds while she zeroed her gun at the middle of his chest. She fingered the trigger of her weapon and said, "I don't need your permission. Talk to me. If I don't like what you're saying, you're a dead man."

Chapter 49

"Sister Anne, do you think it was Russell who carved 'Sparky' on this tree? I am assuming this field is where he buried the dog and the mirror," said Chieko.

"Let me look.... Yes, the dog's name is misspelled" the nun chuckled. "It had to be Russell who carved it."

"That is not a large field, but it will certainly feel very large if we have to dig up every square inch of it. Let us take a closer look." The women walked over to a small field of rough scrub grass. On the far side, the field appeared to have been carefully tended at some point in time. Then Sister Anne uttered an, "Oh, my Goodness!"

"What is it?" asked Chieko. Then suddenly she realized where they were walking. "It's an old cemetery, isn't it? Why is it not being tended? Where are the markers? Oh, they are only rough stones on the earth. Most disrespectful," she said, shaking her head. Sister Anne was surprised to hear Chieko laugh. "What a sly fellow that Russell was. He buried it here, I'll wager. Of course. What better place?"

Sister Anne wasn't smiling. Chieko looked up at her and saw that the nun was deep in thought. She fingered her rosary beads as her eyes roamed over the field. "I wonder...." she said softly as she walked slowly around the perimeter of the field. "Yes, this was the old negro cemetery from ages ago, when people were so ignorant that they only wanted people of their own race buried around them. As if God cared one iota about the color of their skin. And white people wouldn't have tended this cemetery. People can be so foolish…."

"Chieko, we must examine the cemetery very closely and in an organized manner. Look. There are old paths, barely visible now. We should walk each path until we have walked the entire cemetery. I will look to the right and you will look to the left. We are looking for Ada Johnson's name on any of the stones. I know they're very worn and not well cut, and there are so many weeds, but we must take the time and effort to make out the names. Do you understand?" Chieko nodded.

More than halfway through the cemetery, Chieko said, "There. There's a stone. I believe the letters… Yes. They spell 'Johnson.'"

Sister Anne ran over to look. "You're right. There's another one. This must be the Johnson family plot. Now… let us look for… Yes! There it is!" The nun was next to the small gravestone in three large steps.

"The stone says…" Chieko wiped at the grave stone…. "It says 'Ada Johnson' and… I cannot make out the dates."

"I believe we should find sturdy sticks and start digging here around this stone," said Sister Anne.

"Two men can probably dig better in this hard ground," said Tomio Saito. The two women turned. Chieko's face lit in delighted surprise. Yoshiro stood beneath the clearing sky, holding a camp shovel.

"Is Connie with you?" Sister Anne asked.

"Connie went to look for Sharon. When we finish here, we shall all go look for Connie and Sharon if they are not at our agreed rendezvous place," answered Yoshiro.

Chapter 50

"Russell was still a young boy. He was quite small. He probably couldn't have dug too deeply. Of course, it was probably a new grave, so the soil wouldn't have been so hard-packed. I suppose Ada Johnson had just died," said Sister Anne as Yoshiro removed sod and soil with the old shovel.

"I've just hit something. It seems to be a small crate," he yelled, wiping away dirt from the wooden top. "What is the word scratched on it? The letters are... it is difficult to make them out. Sister Anne, can you read them?"

The nun, already crouched over the hole, leaned over Yoshiro's shoulder. "I believe they are: a, n, u, b, i, s. 'Anubis'."

Yoshiro pulled open the flimsy cover. "Huh," he said, tilting his head. "That doesn't look like the remains of a large Egyptian dog...."

Sister Anne looked over his shoulder again. "...but maybe a small *white* dog! Russell said Ada often called his dog 'Anubis' because the dog was the boy's protector—like the Egyptian deity that protected Pharaohs. Ada Johnson must have known a little something about Egypt, and I guess she thought of Sparky as Russell's Anubis," her eyes lit up as she imagined Sparky as a deity.

"Chieko, gentlemen, I think we may have found the guardian of the mirror. Dig out the box. If I'm right, we'll find the mirror underneath."

A few muddy minutes later, the four of them were beaming in the moonlight as Chieko hugged the dirt-covered box and gazed at the sky with a long sigh.

"What's going on?" Asked Connie who had come out of the woods and was running across the field toward them. "Oh," she said, answering the smiles of the others. She stared at Chieko who was both smiling and crying as she hugged a round, deep red, enamel box to her chest. The two men seemed to be close to bursting.

Sharon Meadows next walked out of the woods and stood at the edge of the forest. She watched the others celebrating while her fingers grasped the handle of her machine gun.

Chieko was the first to notice Sharon. She put the enamel box in Hirobumi's hands. "Hold this for me. Keep it safe," she said. "Uncle, raise your gun slowly and hold it on Sharon. If she kills me, make sure you kill her before she turns the gun on you. The mirror must be returned to Ise." She slipped her double-edged dagger from its back holster into the pocket of her jacket and held the handle of the dagger tightly in her right hand. Then she turned and took a measured step toward Sharon.

"Stop, Priestess, and come back," yelled Saito. "You must not take on my job. Hirobumi," he said, quietly, "guard the Priestess with your body." Saito walked toward Sharon as Chieko hesitated. In an instant, Hirobumi had grabbed Chieko and pulled her in back of him. He, too, trained his automatic on Sharon.

"Sharon, point your weapon in the air. I will do the same thing. So will Hirobumi. No one needs to die today," said Saito.

"Listen to him, Sharon. Please," yelled Sister Anne.

"Go back, Tomio. Walk backward," Connie said quietly. A few yards from Sharon, her automatic was raised and pointed into the trees. She spoke slowly, "Sharon, do not look back. You're not alone by the woods. I've got you covered. Come forward slowly. Drop flat on the ground if I say so. Sister Anne," Connie added, "I want you to walk slowly towards the water, just like you're going for a walk.

"Gentlemen, do you see them?" Connie asked quietly.

"Three are on the left behind the big trees," whispered Yoshiro.

"One started climbing up that big oak right there at the edge. He's stopped. He probably figures we'll see him if he climbs much higher," Saito added.

Sharon had reached the group, and murmured, "By my count there are seven further back waiting for the fun to start. Luckily, there's no way they can get behind us. It'd be nice to have some cover though."

A shrill scream filled the salty black air. The nun, habit billowing around her, was jumping crazily. The team immediately recognized the distraction tactic, and fled behind an old stone wall at the far edge of the cemetery. Sister Anne dove behind the rocks after them, then gasped, "Connie...Sharon. Where are they?"

Chapter 51

"By the time we get back there, the fight will be over," Connie whispered. "Where're we going anyway?"

"Stop bitching and asking questions. Just follow me," Sharon hissed. She stopped suddenly, dropped down into some tall sea grass, and pulled Connie down with her. She let go of Connie's arm and pointed with one hand to the left. Her right hand covered Connie's mouth.

Connie peeked out from behind the bushes and saw the boat anchored just yards off shore. An Asian woman carrying a submachine gun stood on the rocky beach. She started to walk toward the grassy mounds, her weapon pointed straight ahead of her. Her eyes searched the dunes. Sharon understood immediately who this was: her replacement.

"Give me your dagger. Move over there where you have that rock to shield you. Then make a small noise. She'll probably shoot first, then come look. Don't worry. She won't make it all the way over there. Keep your eyes open. When the others hear her shots, they'll be racing over here. Have your weapon ready. We'll get 'em in a cross-fire." Sharon mouthed the words silently. Connie nodded, and Sharon moved off in the other direction.

In a few moments, the Asian woman was aiming her automatic

weapon at Connie's hiding place. The woman wore a dark blue jump suit, and her shiny black braids were pinned neatly around her head. Her face dripped with perspiration, even though the weather had turned cool. To Sharon, the woman looked scared as her finger nervously stroked the trigger of her gun. Sharon could see the woman was so intent on looking for Connie, that she probably wouldn't hear Sharon's approach. Still, Sharon kept a watchful eye on the woman as she tread softly toward her. The handle of the dagger was now clutched tightly in Sharon's hand.

Sharon pushed aside her thoughts as she inched toward the woman. *I've never stabbed a woman before,* she was thinking. *In the chest, straight to the heart.* She reached around with one arm to choke the woman. With the other, Sharon plunged the knife deep into the woman's chest. The only sound from the woman was a soft gasp as she dropped her weapon and fell dead to the ground. Sharon grabbed the weapon, slid back into the sea grass, and tumbled into Connie.

After one deep breath she whispered, "Let's get back to the others." Connie agreed.

Chapter 52

Just as Connie and Sharon collapsed with the group still hunkered behind the cemetery wall, a blinding spotlight lit up the rows of headstones.

"Ladies and gentlemen, this is Homeland Security. Please put your weapons on the ground. Do it slowly and carefully," said Colonel Clark Stephens. He and several armed men dressed in camouflage came slowly to the edge of the forest. "We and the JSS have taken care of the terrorists who were following you. The JSS have taken them for questioning. We have boats docked in the next cove. Please follow this officer." One of the camouflaged men stepped into the clearing. "We're all going back to Portsmouth to have a little talk." He stared at Connie and the others, then whispered to the man on his left. "There are two others. A Japanese man and woman. Go find them." Four men immediately ran past the stone wall. He turned to Connie and Sister Anne. "Where did they go?" He asked. His face was set in a grim stare.

"I don't know," Connie answered honestly.

"With any luck they're on their way back to Japan," said Sister Anne. Saito and Sharon remained silent with their arms raised in the air.

"We and our Canadian friends will be watching for your helicopter and plane," Stephens said directly to Saito. "They better be on the ground or heading for international waters," he ended. As he spoke, three Asian men, also wearing camouflage, stepped quietly out of the forest, and stood staring at Stephens. "The JSS," he said. "They proved to be quite helpful once I let them out of my locked office." He gestured to one soldier to come with him and they walked toward the JSS men.

Stephens and Officer Suzuki spoke for a few minutes, then shook hands. The JSS men melted again into the forest as Stephens walked back. "Pick up their weapons," he ordered two of his men, "and let's go." He continued walking. Everyone followed him toward the beach.

"Ladies," said Saito to Sister Anne and Connie, "I regret that you must go through this unpleasantness. Please be assured that we, especially Chieko, will never forget your assistance and kindness." He turned to Sharon and whispered, "Prepare yourself. My men will be here... Ah, here they are!" His voice had returned to full volume. "Colonel Stephens and gentlemen," he made a small bow of his head, "This lady" he indicated Sharon with a nod of his head, "and I would not do well under your scrutiny. We shall leave you now. No heroics please, and do not try to follow us. My men," he indicated by pointing at several men dressed in black and carrying rocket launchers pointed at the HS men, "were ordered not to kill you, but they will not hesitate to render you harmless until we are on our way. And ladies," he said to Sister Anne and Connie, "please do not judge us harshly. It would make no sense at all for Sharon and me to be taken by any law enforcement group." He turned away. "Goodbye all," he said with a wave. Sharon just turned and walked out of the clearing beside Saito.

Chapter 53
Ise Jingu Shrine

"You must conceal a pistol under your robe," Hirobumi Yoshiro insisted.

"I will not allow blood to pollute the Ise Jingu," Chieko replied. "When I have ejected Hideko from the shrine, your men must be ready to take her prisoner. Then you will kindly bring the mirror to me, and I will return it to its rightful place."

"She will not be easily ejected. You must allow me to come and help you. In her heart Hideko is a murderess. She hired Sharon Meadows to kill us. You know that she hates you. You cannot give her..."

"No more words. We have decided it was Hideko who hired the assassin. But we have no proof. We must get her to admit it. You cannot know how much sorrow this gives me."

"Hirobumi, no one knows better than I how much determination Hideko possesses, and how skilled she is in the martial arts. But it is my job to protect the mirror. It is your job to protect the shrine. We shall deal with Hideko later, but my heart aches for her and what must be done."

"As long as Hideko is alive, your life is in danger."

"My life is as nothing compared to the Sacred Mirror. You must not harm Hideko. Her guilt must be proven. And I cannot allow her to be executed. She must be imprisoned. If what you say is true, then as long as Hideko is free, the *Kata no Kagami* is in danger. I can't allow that," answered Chieko although tears were forming in her dark eyes. "All my life, I have loved her as a sister. The thought that she wishes us dead... and the thought of punishing her, greatly saddens me."

"My friend, just keep remembering we have proof that she paid an assassin to kill us. She is not the loving sister you believed she was."

"Yes, I know. Please call your guards. Order them to come outside the gates with you. I do not wish the Imperial Guards to be at all involved in this, even as bystanders. Han's men will stand in their place." Yoshiro took out his cell phone and keyed in a number. After speaking quietly into the phone, he bowed to Chieko and took his place by the shrine's entrance.

As each of the guards marched toward the gate, he was surprised to see Chieko following behind. When the last of them exited the shrine, Chieko strode purposely through the gate. She swiftly crossed the outer courtyard and entered the first building of the outer shrine. Across the inner courtyard she could see Hideko at the entrance to the inner shrine. She stood tall, but looked troubled, "So you have returned," she yelled across to Chieko, "I thought as much. The guards would have abandoned me for no other reason. Hirobumi Yoshiro, also? Has he returned?"

"Take off the holy robe and walk through the outside gate. Do it now. Your jailers await," answered Chieko.

"You abandoned the dying *Saio* and your responsibilities to the shrine. You no longer have the right to give orders here. If you leave now, you will not be harmed." Hideko's voice had become shrill.

"It is you who are in harm's way. I do not wish to hurt you, but I will forcibly eject you, if I must," replied Chieko.

"You could try," answered Hideko, who in a swift move

unsheathed the Samurai sword from its scabbard in her waistband. She walked slowly with her sword held high over her head, and moved toward Chieko.

"It saddens me, but it does not surprise me that you are willing to contaminate this holy place with human blood. Is there nothing left of the good that was once in you? Have you completely surrendered to evil?"

"There is nothing good left in either of us. You abandoned the old woman and left the shrine unguarded. You are not worthy to be the next High Priestess. Only an accident of birth prevented me from being the next *Saio*. Well, I'm taking over now. Leave. Before I kill you and throw your body out."

"Hideko, stop right now." Chieko said, pulling her pistol from her sleeve and pointing it at Hideko's body. "I do not wish to kill you and contaminate this holy place, but I will. You know that I will. Drop your weapon, and I will put away my gun. We will settle our differences in the time honored way." She lifted her pistol up to point it in the air.

"You know that I cannot win a hand-to-hand contest against you."

"You cannot win against this pistol, either. Hideko, it's over. Accept your defeat, and begin the process of atonement."

"You know that I cannot do that, either." Hideko was within striking distance of Chieko and raised her sword high over her head.

Chieko could see the tears running down Hideko's face but also the grim determination in the set of her jaw. Her stance and sword were in strike position. Chieko quickly lowered her gun from pointing into the air and shot Hideko in the forehead. Hideko's eyes opened wide with surprise before they closed and she slumped to the ground. Chieko tried to hold back her sobs as she looked down at Hideko's body.

"Take the body off temple grounds. Then bring fresh tatami mats, wash cloths, cleaning fluids, and water from the sacred well. Quickly!" she ordered Hideko's shocked servants who had rushed into the courtyard and were now staring down at Hideko's lifeless body. The servants bowed to Chieko and ran to pick up the body.

Hirobumi burst into the courtyard from the doorway in which he had been standing and watching the two women. He used his sleeve to wipe at the tears running down Chieko's face. "If you hadn't shot her, I would have. It had to be done. I could not allow her to kill you," he said. "Now, I will help you to purify the shrine," he continued as the servants began splashing buckets of clear water onto the paving stones to wash away the blood.

Chapter 54

"My friends," said Chieko, "Thank you for traveling the great distance to bring closure to our 'treasure hunt'. If they knew, all of Japan would be paying tribute to you. As the new *Saio*, I offer you my deepest gratitude. I must also say that our time together was a most adventurous way to spend my days before being forever cloistered. I have ·so many memories that I will be happy to revisit. You are all my heroes.

"Please, I wish the Sacred Mirror to remember the dear faces of our heroes." She held up the *Yata No Kagami* and walked up to each of them, one by one, holding the mirror to their faces. "I will always remember you in my heart," the *Saio* said, "and hope that you will remember me." She pressed her hand lightly against each of their chests, and added, "Now it is time for you to leave. The *Yata no Kagami* needs peace. The shrine needs its solitude and quiet. Thank you my dearest friends. Yoshiro-san, your alcove has been refurbished for you. Are you as happy as I to be home?" Gazing at his smiling face, she said "Yes, I can see that you are."

Out on the street Saito bowed to each of the women as they exited the shrine. They returned his bow before he stepped into his limousine.

"I guess Connie and I are taking the first plane home. Is that right, Connie?" Sister Anne asked, turning to the private eye.

"Yep. Can't wait to be back in the good ol' U. S. of A. And especially can't wait to hunker down and sleep in my own comfy bed. Sharon, do you want to come back with us and spend a few days unwinding?"

"Thanks for the invite," said Sharon, shaking her blond hair loose from its ponytail, "but I've got a date." She grinned, and slid after Saito into the long black limo.

After her husband passed away in 2008, Marcelline Jenny decided to retire from teaching and move to New Hampshire. Jenny has a B.S. from Rutgers in Mathematics, an M.A. from Seton Hall and ABD from Columbia in Asian Studies, and a D Litt in History from Drew University (earned at age 70). She taught in the Asian Studies departments of Seton Hall and Montclair State Universities for  many years, but upon her retirement decided to concentrate on what she'd been wanting to do for years: write fiction.

She has written short stories and several thrillers, including another in the Constant Talant series. *The Shinto Treasure* is the first novel that Jenny has agreed to print.

www.ingramcontent.com/pod-product-compliance
Lightning Source LLC
Chambersburg PA
CBHW050405260626
47156CB00003B/882